Nancy Drew

Read all the titles in the Nancy Drew Mystery series

Carolyn Keene

The Secret of the Forgotten City

The Strange Message in the Parchment

MULBERRY EDITIONS

This edition published exclusively for Mulberry Editions
by HarperCollins Children's Books 1992

A division of HarperCollins Publishers Ltd,
77–85 Fulham Palace Road, Hammersmith,
London W6 8JB

Printed in England by Clays Ltd, St Ives plc

Contents

The Secret of the Forgotten City

First published in a single volume in hardback in 1979 by
William Collins Sons & Co Ltd.
First published in paperback in Armada

·1·

Fleetfoot Joe

"Au! Au! Au!" cried Ned Nickerson, as he eased himself out of his car and hurried towards the open front door of the Drew home.

Nancy, who was waiting for him, leaped to his side. "Ned, what happened? You're hurt!"

The tall dark-haired athlete burst into laughter and kissed her. "No hurts at all. I didn't say '*Ouch, ouch, ouch!*' I said, 'Au! Au! Au!' "

"What does that mean?" asked the attractive strawberry blonde, as she led him indoors. "Please stop talking in riddles."

The couple sat down on the living-room couch. "Well?" Nancy prompted.

"Au refers to a treasure buried deep underground," Ned replied. "Want to help find it?"

"Of course," Nancy said, excited at the thought of a mystery. "Where is it and what is it?"

Ned grinned. "I'll give you a hint. Think of some chemistry symbols."

At once Nancy guessed the answer. "How stupid of me not to have thought of gold. *Au* is the symbol for it. Tell me where and what this treasure is."

"Not until everyone gets here," Ned replied.

"Everyone? Who is everyone?" Nancy asked.

Ned's eyes twinkled. "First there were two. Then there were four. Now we number six."

"You're being exasperating," Nancy said. "Shall I guess again?"

When he nodded, she mentioned her closest friends, Bess Marvin and George Fayne, who were cousins. The three girls lived in River Heights and had been friends for years. Then she named two boys who were fraternity brothers of Ned's at Emerson College.

"Right," Ned replied. "Your Dad, who, by the way, is enthusiastic about your recovering this gold, invited them here to dinner tonight. Your kind housekeeper, Hannah Gruen, knows the secret and is preparing my favourite dish."

"Which is—hot-pepper salad," Nancy teased. "But tell me, why all the secrecy? It's not my birthday!"

Ned answered with a grin. "We wanted to see if we could keep our plan a secret from the world's most famous girl detective."

Nancy blushed, but before she had a chance to answer, she and Ned heard shouting out in the street.

Ned leaped to a front window. Nancy, glancing out of a side window, saw a man dashing down the long Drew driveway towards the rear of the property.

A woman's large handbag swung from one hand!

"Quick, Ned!" Nancy shouted. "Follow me!"

As the couple dashed through the kitchen, she called to the startled housekeeper, "Hannah, run out the front door. I think a woman on the sidewalk has just been robbed!"

Nancy and Ned rushed from the kitchen door in time to observe the thief pausing at the thick hedge that separated the Drews' yard from the property at the rear. Seeing the couple, he pushed his way through the bushes, since they were too high for him to vault.

"Nancy, run to the side street," Ned suggested. "If that man tries to escape that way, yell and I'll come running."

As Ned finished speaking, he was halfway through the hedge. Nancy ran back of the garage to the side street. She looked up and down the pavement, then into the yard. Suddenly the thief dashed out from behind a neighbour's house towards a car whose motor was running. A man sat at the wheel.

"Stop!" Nancy cried out. When the suspect kept going, she ordered, "Drop that handbag!"

The stranger did neither, but just as he reached the car, Ned leaped towards him. The man tossed the bag at Nancy with a vicious thrust and jumped into the car. It roared off. Ned had missed him, and Nancy had had to move aside to avoid being hit by the car.

Her mind, however, had recorded a good image of the suspected thief. He was five feet ten, rather large-boned, had tanned, tightly-drawn skin, black eyes, and shiny black hair.

"Part Indian," Nancy told herself, as she picked up the handbag and was joined by Ned.

"Too bad that fellow got away," he commented. "I memorized the licence number." He repeated it to Nancy. "The man should be easy to trace."

Nancy and Ned walked to the front lawn to find out what Hannah had learned. An odd picture met their eyes. A short, stout Indian woman, about fifty years old, sat on the ground with her legs crossed under her. She was staring into space, oblivious of Hannah Gruen, who was trying to comfort her.

The Indian kept murmuring, "Nancy Drew, Nancy Drew!"

As the girl appeared, holding the handbag, she said kindly, "Here is your bag, and I am Nancy Drew."

The woman looked up, took her property, and without speaking opened the bag. An expression of dismay crossed her face and she uttered an involuntary "Oh!"

"Is something missing?" Nancy asked.

"Records. My ancestors' records."

Then the woman thought of something. She unzipped a pocket in the lining of the bag and drew out a thin stone slab about five by seven inches, on which several crude figures and symbols had been chiselled.

"These are petroglyphs and very old," the woman explained. "There were six other tablets in the bag. I planned to bring only this one, but I didn't want to leave the others unguarded in my house, so I brought them."

Hannah Gruen spoke. "I think we should all go into the house and talk."

"And call the police," Nancy added. "I'll do that immediately. Oh, by the way, what is your name and address?" she asked the Indian.

"Mrs Wabash. My home is in Nevada, but I am staying at the River View Motel across town. I walked over here."

As Mrs Wabash rose, with Ned helping her, Nancy hurried into the house to phone police headquarters. By the time she had given all the pertinent facts to the sergeant on duty, the other three walked inside. Everyone sat down in the living-room except Hannah, who went to get cool drinks and pieces of nut-covered sponge cake to serve to the guests.

Mrs Wabash apologized profusely for all the trouble she had caused, and thanked Nancy and Ned sincerely for recovering her handbag and at least one of the stone tablets.

"I'm sure the thief will be caught soon," Nancy assured her. "Anyway, what could he do with the records?"

The Indian woman sipped the drink Hannah had served. "I'm not sure," she said. "I have studied ancient stones with petroglyphs—that's picture-carving on stone—and made a sort of dictionary of their meanings. The only copy I had was in my handbag."

There was a pause, then Nancy said, "It's a shame the pages were taken. Had you translated the history of your family or of any tribe?"

"It is still a puzzle as to what the history is, but I've done the best I could," Mrs Wabash replied. "Many symbols could have two or more interpretations. For instance, the mark of a hand with twisting, turning lines emerging from it could have indicated a journey's end; or it could be the artist's signature. I have heard you are clever at codes and thought maybe you could solve this mystery."

As the Indian finished speaking, the phone began to ring. When Nancy answered it, a man's deep voice said, "Is Mrs Wabash still there? Yes? Tell her I have her stone tablets and papers and won't give 'em up. As for you, Miss Drew, don't try to help her. You're quick, but you're no match for Fleetfoot Joe. My spying on Mrs Wabash has paid off. Now the Great Flying Bird is carrying me away." The man hung up.

Nancy stood lost in thought for a few moments, then

returned to the living room. "Mrs Wabash," she said, trying to keep her voice calm, "do you know a Fleetfoot Joe?"

"I've heard of him out in Nevada. He's only part Indian. A bad man. He steals things, then sells them to tourists as old artifacts he claims to have found himself."

Suddenly Nancy jumped from her chair, excused herself, and hurried to the telephone, repeating the words, " 'The Great Flying Bird'. Surely that's an aeroplane. But is it privately or commercially owned?"

She dialled the number of the River Heights Airport, got the information desk, and asked whether a plane had just left for New York.

"Yes," was the answer.

"Did anyone make a reservation for someplace in Nevada?"

Nancy waited while the assistant checked. The answer was no, and the woman could not recall from Nancy's description any passenger who resembled the suspected robber.

The young detective now asked, "Did a private plane take off?"

She was transferred to another office. There she learned that a privately owned plane had left ten minutes earlier. Its destination was St Louis.

"The owner is named Robert Wapley," the speaker concluded.

"Thank you," said Nancy.

Before leaving the phone she called her friend Police Chief McGinnis and gave him a word-for-word account of what had happened since her previous report. He was astounded and said he would get in touch with security officers at the St Louis airports, public and private.

Then he added, "Great work, Nancy! We'll have this Fleetfoot Joe in custody in no time!"

Once more Nancy returned to the living-room. Everyone was standing, and Mrs Wabash was saying goodbye.

"Mrs Wabash," said Nancy quickly, "what was your real purpose in coming to see me?"

"It's no use now," the Indian woman replied. "All the papers and most of the plaques I planned to show you are gone. I have no clues to offer."

"Clues to what?" Nancy asked.

Mrs Wabash looked at the girl with tears in her eyes. "Clues to a lost treasure in the Forgotten City."

·2·

Safari Plans

EVERYONE in the Drew living room leaned forward in his chair, eagerly awaiting more of Mrs Wabash's story.

"There are many, many pictures cut into the stolen tablets," she said, "but the main theme seems to tell when and where a treasure of gold was hidden. As you know, the ancient Indians in the United States did not use gold to any extent. Probably one reason was that it was too difficult to work with, and their tools were crude.

"It is a great mystery as to the exact nature of this treasure, but from what I can judge, the tablets depict several golden sheets. How big they are, one cannot tell. And when they were made and where they came from is also a mystery."

Just then someone pounded on the front door, and the bell rang loudly. Puzzled, Nancy went to open the door.

"Hi, Nancy! Surprise!" cried four voices together.

Nancy beamed. Bess Marvin, George Fayne, and their dates were standing there, grinning.

"The surprise is great," Nancy replied. "Come in. I have a surprise of my own to show you."

16

George, a girl who enjoyed her boyish name, walked in first. She was slender and athletic looking and wore her hair short. Bess in contrast was blonde with longer hair. She was slightly plump and pretty.

Burt Eddleton, George's date, was brown-haired and of stocky build. One could surmise at a glance that he was a football player. Dave Evans, Bess's friend, had dark hair and eyes, and though he too was a football player, he had a much slighter build than Burt.

The young people walked into the living room and were introduced to Mrs Wabash. "I am very glad to meet you," she replied. Smiling, she added, "I am Nancy's surprise."

Ned laughed. "Well kids, the joke is on us. We thought we were going to keep a secret from Nancy Drew, and I find she's way ahead of us. She has a wonderful lead."

"What is it?" George asked eagerly.

Nancy requested Mrs Wabash to repeat the part of her story she had already told, and then to continue with the rest of it.

"You probably wonder how I happened to come to see Nancy Drew. A friend of mine who sometimes lectures at the University of Nevada, Professor Donald Maguire, has been trying to help me decipher the petroglyphs. The tablets came into my possession a few months ago. We concluded that the pictures indicate that several golden sheets were hidden, probably in the desert."

Dave spoke. "Mrs Wabash, have you any idea how old the gold sheets are?"

The woman shook her head. "I am hoping that when they are found, they will contain symbols that will tell us their age and where the gold came from."

The whole story intrigued Nancy, who wanted to start out at once to hunt for the precious treasure. Each new case fascinated her from the time she first was asked to solve *The Secret of Shadow Ranch* through many adventures up to the most recent one, *Mystery of the Glowing Eye*.

Mrs Wabash went on, "Don Maguire heard at the University of Nevada that Nancy was going on a dig out in the desert."

"I was what?" Nancy interrupted.

The other young people laughed and Ned said, "That was really the surprise we had for you. Some Emerson students and their friends are joining a group from the University of Nevada and going into the desert to search for a forgotten city, or at least some of the artifacts the ancient people may have left."

Nancy's eyes sparkled. "How wonderful!" she exclaimed. "You all did manage to keep the secret, and even though I accidentally came upon what may be a clue, you did surprise me. I think this is exciting. When do we leave?"

Ned replied, "We consulted your dad and he said you may go any time, but you will probably want to finish a little job he has given you. He thinks it will take two or three days."

Mrs Wabash said, "Professor Don Maguire told me that Nancy is the finest amateur detective in the country, and that is the reason why I came all the way to River Heights to see her."

She informed Nancy's friends about the theft of her dictionary and her precious stone tablets and concluded by saying, "I don't know whether I have an enemy or the thief merely wanted to get hold of the tablets. With them he could try solving the mystery himself and find the gold.

"In any case, I have decided to leave this one tablet with you, Nancy. See what you can figure out, and if you can possibly trace the others, it will make me very happy."

"Thank you," said Nancy. "I'll make a drawing of this plaque and keep the original in a safe place. When I come out to Nevada, I'll return it to you."

Before saying goodbye the Indian told the young people that a young woman in Nevada named Miss Antler might be of great help to them. "Try to locate her when you get out there."

·Dave offered to drive Mrs Wabash back to the motel and she accepted. Nancy's thoughts returned to the tablet, which she picked up to study.

Suddenly the young sleuth wondered if her eyes were deceiving her. A small figure in the lower left-hand corner was glowing. It looked like a scorpion, its head raised high.

"Look, everybody!" Nancy cried out.

As her friends crowded round the tablet, the figure faded. Though Nancy tried hard to explain what she had seen, the others thought the girl detective was joking.

"Nancy Drew, you're imagining things," Bess said. "I don't see a thing there. All those funny little pictures are on the other parts of this tablet."

No more was said, but Nancy wondered about the strange occurrence. The scorpion did not light up again, but through her magnifying glass, Nancy could see the arachnid plainly. She continued to study the scorpion. Had some trick of the sunlight coming into the room suddenly made it glint? She tried holding the tablet in the exact position she had held it before. Nothing happened.

"What is the thing you saw?" Bess asked.

Nancy shrugged and said she would get a book on wild animal life in the south-western United States. Presently she came to the conclusion that what she had thought was an arachnid was a chuckwalla, a sixteen-inch iguanid lizard, which was harmless, although it looked menacing. She reported this to her friends.

"Here's something amazing about it," Nancy said. "The chuckwalla can wedge itself into a crevice and then inflate its body. This makes it almost impossible for an enemy to drag the creature out. By the way, it says here that at one time the chuckwalla was used as food by the Indians."

"Maybe," George said, "there was a group who called themselves the Chuckwalla Tribe."

Afterwards, Nancy begged her friends to tell her more about the trip they had planned. Ned explained that it would be a caravan.

"There'll be trucks, cars, Land Rovers, and even a whole kitchen on a truck chassis."

George grinned and looked at Bess. "That's the place for you, cousin. You can cook all the goodies you want."

"Okay," Bess retorted. "I'll fix you. I'll make a tasty dish just for you and fill it with red peppers!"

The others laughed, and Burt remarked, "I guess that will hold you for a while, George."

At that moment the young people heard a car turn into the driveway. Mr Drew was arriving home. In a few minutes the tall, good-looking lawyer entered the living-room and greeted Nancy and her friends.

When he heard how Nancy had received advance information about the treasure hunt, he laughed. But his smile turned to a frown a little later, when he was told about Fleetfoot Joe and his attack on Mrs Wabash.

"I'm sorry to hear this," he said. "Nancy, of course you've notified the police."

"Yes, Dad. They promised to call if there were any leads on the thief, but I haven't heard from them."

Ten minutes later Hannah Gruen came into the living-room and announced dinner. Everyone went into the dining-room, where the housekeeper had set a lovely table.

Nancy gave the motherly housekeeper a hug. "Now I know why you wouldn't let me in the kitchen," she said. "How attractively you've arranged the flowers! And what a delicious-looking salad!"

This was to be the first course. After everyone was seated, Mr Drew said grace, then the meal started.

The group was about halfway through dinner when Togo began to bark frantically. He raced from the kitchen through the dining-room and into the living-room. Here he jumped on to a chair and gave a series of short, quick barks. Then he ran to the front door and barked again insistently. Nancy left her chair and followed him.

"What's the matter, Togo?" she asked. "Do you hear another dog outside, or is somebody at the door?"

The bell had not rung, but Nancy opened the door and let Togo out. Seeing no one, she was puzzled and ran after Togo.

Suddenly a man's voice cried out from the darkness,

"Don't follow me! And call off your dog, or I'll shoot him!"

·3·

Vanished Guests

WHISTLING loudly and clearly, Nancy hoped Togo would hear her and come back. She called his name, clapped her hands, and whistled some more. The little terrier did not return.

.Suddenly she heard a shot. Nancy's heart sank. Had the dreadful man carried out his threat?

"Oh, it just can't be true!" she told herself. Again she called loudly, "Togo! Togo! Where are you?"

By this time Nancy's friends and Mr Drew had rushed outdoors. They could not see Nancy but could hear her, and set off in the direction from which the sounds came. Finally they reached her.

"What happened? What's up?" Ned asked.

Quickly Nancy explained and there were murmurs of anger and sympathy. Ned and George had brought torches, and now everyone searched for footprints. Apparently the fugitive had been standing in mud, and it was easy to follow the indentations left by his shoes. Right beside them were Togo's tiny prints. The group hurried on. Finally all the impressions ended at a main road.

Mr Drew said, "The man must have entered a car here."

Bess's eyes were filled with tears. "Do you think he took Togo with him?"

The lawyer said he had no idea, but there was one thing of which he was sure: up to this point the dog had not been shot.

"Let's hope," said Bess, "that the man didn't take Togo away and kill him somewhere else."

It was a doleful group that walked back to the Drew home. Hannah had prepared a delicious apple-snow pudding with raspberry sauce. Everyone ate it, though there was little conversation.

When everybody had finished, Nancy said she wanted to examine the man's footprints. From a casual first glance at them, she was sure they would match those that had been left before by Fleetfoot.

Mr Drew said, "After you do that, I think we'd better call the police, especially if the footprints do match those in our yard."

All the young people went outdoors, some to follow Nancy and the others to look at the prints at the rear of the Drew home.

"There are good impressions near the hedge," Nancy told the group, as she beamed her torch on the latest series. She was convinced they belonged to the same man, Fleetfoot Joe.

"I'll call headquarters," Nancy said, "and ask if there's any report on Fleetfoot."

When she reached the phone, Nancy changed her mind and called Chief McGinnis at home instead of headquarters. He was astounded at the latest bit of news and angry about the dog's disappearance and possible death.

"We have no leads yet on Fleetfoot," he told Nancy,

"but my men are working on it. Up to now we assumed he had skipped town, but evidently he's still around. What do you think he wants?"

"I believe," Nancy replied, "he's looking for the one tablet he did not take from Mrs Wabash's bag. We have it here."

During Nancy's telephone conversation, her friends scoured the neighbourhood in all directions. It was possible that Togo had been shot just before the man got into the car and was trying to make his way home. After a twenty-minute search they returned to the house and reported failure.

Bess put an arm round Nancy. "This is dreadful, but don't give up hope. You know Togo is a very smart little dog. Let's hope that somehow he gets away from Fleet-foot."

Nancy smiled and gave Bess a hug. "Thanks. You're sweet to be so concerned."

The girl detective felt that with Fleetfoot still in the area, Mrs Wabash might be in danger. She decided to alert the woman to the possibility. She dialled the motel where Mrs Wabash was staying and was shocked at the reply she received from the operator there.

"Mrs Wabash checked out and left no forwarding address."

Nancy was surprised that the Indian woman would leave without telling her, but perhaps she had received some message from home and had decided to go back at once. Nancy tried to learn from the desk clerk and the porter whether or not Mrs Wabash had made a plane reservation.

"No, she didn't," was the reply.

She had scarcely put down the receiver, when Nancy

heard aggressive barking at the front door. She literally leaped across the hall and flung the front door open. Her little terrier jumped into his mistress's arms.

"Oh, you're safe! You weren't shot after all!" she cried out, hugging her pet.

His response was to lick her cheeks, then jump out of her arms and race towards the kitchen.

Hannah greeted him with a joyful, "Togo! You're back! And you want something to eat. Well, I certainly think you deserve it."

Everyone had followed the little dog into the kitchen and George remarked, "If Togo could only talk!"

Suddenly Nancy leaned down and looked at the dog's collar. "Here's a note!" she told the others. Quickly she opened it, read the message, then re-read it aloud:

> Leave stone with pictures by old oak tree at entrance of abandoned mine in Ironton after sunset tomorrow.

"So Fleetfoot was here to get the plaque!" Nancy exclaimed.

Hannah beamed at Togo. "And this little fellow scared him away."

Nancy asked her father what he thought they should do about the note. He felt that it should not be ignored and suggested they contact Chief McGinnis. Once more Nancy dialled the officer's home and spoke to him.

Upon hearing the message, he chuckled. "You work fast on your mysteries, Nancy Drew," he commented. "Let me see, now. I guess the best thing would be to play along with this fellow. Suppose you find a stone about the same size as the tablet and wrap it up in a package. I'll send an officer in plain-clothes for it tomorrow afternoon."

At once Nancy told him that Ned, Burt, and Dave were at the house. "Couldn't they leave the package?" she asked.

Once more the man chuckled. "Well you've made pretty good detectives of them, I admit," the chief said. "All right, you do it that way and let me know what happens."

After hanging up, Nancy had a sudden idea and she said to her friends, "If we give the thief an unmarked stone, he'll know right away we didn't carry out his wishes, and will probably return to do us more harm. Why don't we try to please him and yet frustrate him?"

George wanted to know how Nancy intended to do this.

The young detective smiled. "Evidently the series of tablets tell an important story, and perhaps even give directions to the treasure. One wrong link in the chain of pictures might spoil the whole thing."

Mr Drew, who was in the background, listening, grinned. "An excellent idea, Nancy," he said. "What do you have in mind? Carving some petroglyphs?"

Nancy replied, "Exactly." She turned to the boys. "Tomorrow morning, would you mind hunting for a stone that looks like the one here?"

The boys agreed and took a good look at the tablet. Nancy found a short ruler and measured the length, width, and thickness of the stone.

Bess remarked, "This old tablet is quite reddish. Is there anything that colour around here?"

Mr Drew answered the question. "Over in the next county the earth and the stones are quite red. I suggest you go there."

"Good idea," Nancy said.

In a short while the boys left with Bess and George to return to their homes for the night. Nancy and Ned stayed up for another hour while she made a careful drawing of the tablet that belonged to Mrs Wabash. Then she began designing a new set of petroglyphs to put on the stone the boys would bring.

When the drawings were finished, Ned laughed. "That's misleading all right," he said. "You've turned a sheep into a goat, rain into sunshine, and a long line turning to the right directly to the left."

Both young people began to yawn. Nancy picked up all her work and headed for the stairs. "I'll finish this tomorrow."

Ned kissed her goodnight and said, "See you in the morning."

"Goodnight, Ned. Sweet dreams."

Soon after breakfast the following day, Ned set off to pick up Burt and Dave. In a short time George and Bess arrived at the Drew home.

Up in her room Nancy showed them the drawings she had made for the new tablet.

"It's so much like the other and yet so different," Bess remarked.

"The whole thing, I hope," said Nancy, "will portray a misleading story to be put on the stone the boys will bring."

Bess looked at the work, then asked, "Would you mind explaining to me what all this means? It's worse than a jigsaw puzzle."

Nancy smiled. "Part of this is guesswork, of course, but here's my interpretation of the original story."

·4·

The Wiretapper

BESS and George sat on the floor in Nancy's bedroom
and waited for the young detective to tell her story. She
held up the drawing and pointed.

"You see this big man here? I believe he was the
leader of a group represented on this plaque. You'll
notice he has something on his head that could be a
fancy headdress. I understand that in ancient times the
leader always covered his head to indicate this rank."

Bess interrupted to ask, "And this string of smaller
people, who are they?"

Nancy's guess was that they might be his family or
his servants.

George remarked that some of the human figures
wore skirts. "Did women wear skirts thousands of years
ago?"

"Apparently," Nancy replied. "I read some place
that the skirt was really like a working outfit. It may
have had pockets or loops through which cooking uten-
sils could be slipped."

Bess began to giggle. "Imagine carrying a stone fork
and spoon around with you for cooking!"

George added, "To stir up venison stew, flavoured
with some bitter tree roots. Probably better for you,

Bess, than that sweet, gooey gravy you make out of chicken-leg stock and honey."

Nancy laughed, then said, "Venison is delicious if you have good strong teeth!"

She now continued with her guess about the meaning of the petroglyphs on Mrs Wabash's tablet. "Whether it was the weather or the long trek or some other reason, I believe a great many members of the tribe became ill or died. This is indicated by the figures in the line who are lying on the ground.

"Then, too, some of them may have been attacked by wild beasts or poisonous scorpions or vicious birds. Here are pictures of all three. This is a bucking ram. Over there is a huge raven. And down here is a rock scorpion."

George asked, "Are there any poisonous scorpions?"

"According to this animal book, yes," Nancy replied. "They have slender tails and are yellow in colour. It says here that the poison causes pain over one's entire body."

"Ugh!" said Bess. Then she asked, "How does a scorpion sting anyone?"

Again Nancy referred to the book and read, "The sting is located at the end of the tail. It consists of a very sharp, curved tip attached to a bulbous organ. This organ contains glands that secrete poison. It's like a poison reservoir."

Bess looked alarmed. "And we're going to find scorpions out at our camp-site in Nevada?"

"Sure thing," George replied. "If you get bitten, it'll be a long walk for you back to town to a doctor. And of course the rest of us will be too busy to drive you there."

"You're horrid," said Bess, tossing her head. "Just

the same, I don't want a scorpion to bite me!"

Nancy interrupted George's kidding to say that the article explained what could be done for a scorpion sting.

"First you tie a tourniquet near the puncture between the sting and the victim's heart. Then put an ice pack over the sting. Even better than that, fill a vessel with half-ice and half-water, and have the person completely submerge the stung area."

"Please, no more," Bess begged.

Nancy changed the subject and went on with her story about the tablet. "See this symbol that looks like a rake? Mrs Wabash said it is supposed to indicate rain, probably heavy rain."

"I see it," said Bess. "Maybe these poor people were lost in a flood."

"That's possible," Nancy agreed. "At one time there must have been plenty of rain because this whole area was very lush and in places quite swampy."

George was sceptical of this. "How can they tell that?" she asked.

Nancy said mainly through the trees. "In the Valley of Fire in the desert outside of Las Vegas, there are pieces of petrified trees. They had to be submerged in water with chemicals in it for a long, long time before they became petrified.

"Also, by reading the rings on tree trunks, as you know, one can count the age of a tree because each ring represents a year. If the rings are wide that means there was plenty of water. If they're very narrow, there's been a drought.

"Apparently in the place where we're going to camp, the vegetation went from very green and watery, probably millions of years ago, to less and less rainfall. The result was that by ten thousand BC, streams slowly began to dry up. Finally the area became a desert."

George asked, "What are these lines for?" She pointed. "They look like steps with no sides or support."

Nancy nodded. "I think it represents a stone stairway chiselled out of the rock by the people who lived at a certain spot. George, do you know what this means? The steps might even lead down to that buried golden treasure!"

George grinned. "Don't get carried away, Nancy."

Bess interrupted. "Here come the boys."

The three girls raced downstairs, and each asked, "Did you find anything?"

Burt took a slab of rock out of his pocket. It was a perfect specimen for Nancy to use for a substitute stone.

"That's great!" she exclaimed. "You boys are going to be wonderful at the dig in the Nevada desert."

"Hope you're right," Ned replied.

He took a package tied in cloth from a bag he was carrying.

"Here are some up-to-date chipping tools for you to use, Nancy. But, really, it isn't fair. You should chip as the ancient Indians did, with a sharp stone."

Nancy laughed. "I'm afraid I was born too late for that! Anyway, it would take too long, and we must hurry."

Before beginning her work, she studied the series of pictures she had drawn. Some of the figures were like the original but several had been changed. Among these were the stone steps. She had substituted pointed spikes joined by lines.

Nancy heard the phone ring. In a couple of minutes Hannah Gruen came to tell her that Mrs Wabash was calling.

"Good!" the girl sleuth exclaimed as she left the room.

Mrs Wabash said she had been threatened while staying at the motel and had been in touch with the police. They in turn had advised her to move out inconspicuously and to leave no forwarding address.

"I thought of returning home immediately," the Indian woman said, "but I wanted to see you again and talk over several things. I have taken a room in a private home. It's very secluded."

The thought rushed through Nancy's head that her own home might be bugged, and she had better find out.

Quickly she wrote on a pad, "Surround the house in case of a wiretapper."

She waved the note towards the group in the living-room, and Ned came to her at once. He read the words quickly and gave orders to different friends to leave the house by the various exits. He would go out the front door.

The group hurried away in all directions, and in less than a minute the house had been surrounded. Ned spotted a teenage boy hidden behind thick bushes in front of the Drews' brick home. He was holding a listening device against the house. Earphones were attached to the gadget.

"Come and get him!" Ned yelled to his friends.

Like lightning, he accosted the boy and took the instrument away from him. The youth glared at Ned.

"Just who do you think you are?" he asked.

"Never mind who I am. Who are you, and what are you doing here?"

The boy sneered. "I don't have to tell you anything. Let go of me. I've got my rights!"

By this time Bess and Dave had run round the corner of the house and had come up to the boy. He stared at them malevolently.

"Who is he?" Dave asked.

"He won't tell me," Ned replied, "but maybe he'll tell you."

"I'll tell nobody anything," the youth answered. "I got my rights. You have your nerve, grabbing hold of me."

Ned's eyes blazed at the insolent youth. "I want to know why you think you have the right to be here with a listening device. Who put you up to that?"

The boy refused to answer.

In the meantime Mrs Wabash was saying to Nancy, "My name while I'm staying here is Mrs Mary Morton, and I'm from New York City."

Nancy giggled. "Is Mrs Morton coming over here?"

The Indian woman said she would not dare do so for fear of being seen and attacked again. "Could you and Ned possibly come to my place this evening?"

"Of course."

As soon as Nancy finished her conversation with the Indian woman, she hurried out the front door.

When Ned saw her, he said, "Here's your wiretapper."

Nancy looked at the boy, whom she had never seen before, and asked him who he was. The youth refused to answer this or any other questions.

"We'll take him down to police headquarters," Ned

offered. "Unfortunately this wiretapping device is not a
recorder, so we have no way of knowing how much of
your conversation was heard."

Nancy heaved a great sigh. She was suddenly worried that the youth had heard about Mrs Wabash's new
name and the substitution of the stone tablet!

·5·

The Fake Tablet

As Nancy and her friends walked towards the front door, she said, "Instead of you boys taking this young man to the police, I'd rather hold him and ask the police to come here."

· The others looked surprised, and the youth became angry. He shouted, "You can't keep me here! I got my rights!"

Ned spoke up. "You do not have the right to bug a person's home unless you have permission from the proper judiciary."

The boy broke away from the front door but Ned, who was next to him, grabbed the youth and yanked him back. Glaring, the boy said no more, and they all walked into the living-room and sat down. Nancy's friends looked to her for an explanation of why she wanted to hold the suspect.

"We have no legal right to search this boy," she replied, "but the police do. It's just possible he has a tape recorder hidden on him. If so, an officer can play it back. I'd like to hear what's been recorded."

She went to phone Chief McGinnis. Within a few minutes, he arrived with one of his men. They advised the prisoner of his rights and started to search him. He objected violently and began to fight. But he was soon subdued.

"Good guessing, Nancy," the chief said. "Here's a tape recorder in a pocket of his jacket."

The gadget was very small but efficient. The tape began with directions to Mozey from some man to spy on the Drew home. He was also to make a recording of any conversation he could pick up on the bugging device. Mozey had been told to bring it back to the boss.

"Who is the boss?" the chief asked him.

Silence.

The tape continued with conversations inside the Drew's house. Nancy held her breath for fear it would continue with Mrs Wabash's conversation. But it ended soon after the telephone had rung and Nancy had answered the call. The young detective was relieved that it had not revealed the Indian woman's assumed name and temporary address.

Ned said to the chief, "Nancy quickly scribbled a note instructing us to surround the house and hunt for a wiretapper."

The two officers smiled. The chief patted Nancy on the back and said, "Good work again." He turned to the teenage boy. "Come along, Mozey," he ordered.

The two officers left with their prisoner, taking the tape with them to use as evidence against him.

"I feel positively weak." Bess sighed. "What a day!"

Nancy smiled. "You can rest while I start chipping the stone the boys brought."

She went upstairs to get her ski goggles so that none of the fine pieces of stone would fly into her eyes. The other young people watched her work and were amazed at the precision she achieved.

First she took some hard white chalk and carefully drew the outlines of the petroglyphs on the new tablet. Since the pictures on the stone were very small, Nancy worked slowly and carefully. Presently she had finished a deer. A few minutes later she completed a shining sun instead of the rake symbol for rain.

"Anybody else want to try this?" she asked.

The only one who said yes was Dave. He was studying archaeology at Emerson College and could draw very well.

He exchanged seats with Nancy and picked up the tools. Dave used the tiny hammer and the little chisel meticulously, and a few minutes later displayed the figure of a sheep.

"They're perfect imitations," Ned observed. "Foxy Fleetfoot is sure going to be fooled."

Dave made one more figure, which looked like a cross. Then Nancy went back to work.

There was an interruption. A phone call came from Chief McGinnis. He said that Mozey's fingerprints had been found in their files.

"His home is in Gadsby, not far from River Heights. The police there said he had a record of petty theft, car stealing, and participation in gang war.

"He's on parole, which, of course, he has broken," the officer added. "We'll hold him here. By the way, he still refuses to give the name of his boss."

"I have a suggestion," Nancy said. "Will you ask him if he was supposed to do an errand after sunset today for his boss." She held the phone for a full five minutes before the chief returned.

"I'm afraid my report is not much help," he said.

"Mozey still refuses to tell the name of the man for whom he's working. But when I asked him your question, he did look scared. I have a feeling he's afraid of the boss, whoever he is, and that if he says anything, he'll be punished by him."

Chief McGinnis promised to call Nancy if there were any new developments in the case.

"And good luck on your project tonight," he added, chuckling.

Nancy returned to chipping, which she finished hours later.

"Now comes the tricky part," she announced to her friends.

Bess giggled. "I'd say the whole thing is pretty tricky. What's this little thing down in the corner?"

"You remember the tiny lizard that I thought lighted up at one point?" Nancy answered.

"Oh, you think that's some kind of an identification mark?" Bess queried.

Nancy nodded. "That's why I didn't change it from the original. If it's on the other tablets, the 'boss' would notice at once that it was missing or changed."

"I see," said Bess. "Is the stone ready to be delivered now?"

"Oh no," Nancy replied. "Next comes the ageing process."

Bess looked puzzled. "But you have to deliver it this evening. That doesn't leave much time for ageing."

Nancy laughed. She called to Ned, who had just finished watching the final scene of an exciting western movie.

"Yes?" he said, reaching her side.

Nancy asked if he would mind doing an errand. "I'm

not sure where you can find gypsum, but try the timber yard first. I want a little bit of it."

Ned grinned. "I won't return until I have it."

The others asked what they could do to help.

Nancy's eyes twinkled. "Want a real dirty job?" she asked.

"No thanks," Bess replied promptly. "I have on one of my best suits, and I don't want to ruin it."

George gave her cousin a side-long disapproving glance and said to Nancy, "How dirty is the job and what is it?"

Nancy told her she needed some lamp-black. "Since we don't have any paraffin or oil lamps here, we'll have to use something else. I suggest black soot from inside the fireplace chimney."

Burt stepped forward. "That sounds more like a man's job," he said. "How much do you need?"

"Oh, three or four tablespoonfuls. Ask Hannah for an old dish and the scraper."

Burt went off to get the articles, then returned, took off his sweater, and rolled his shirtsleeves up to the shoulder.

At that moment Hannah Gruen appeared in the doorway with a large cover-all apron. "Put this on," she told the young man. Burt burst out laughing but obeyed.

At once George said, "Nancy, where's your camera? This picture is too good to miss."

"Up in my room," Nancy replied. George rushed off to get it.

Bess came forward. "Nancy, I don't want to stand around doing nothing. Isn't there some clean job you can give me?"

"Yes. Take some of this chalk out to the kitchen and crush it to a fine powder with a rolling pin."

By the time the chalk and the lamp-black were ready, Ned returned with some finely-powdered gypsum. The young people trooped into the kitchen. Nancy was carrying the tablet with her. Now she spread a newspaper on the kitchen table and mixed the three powders together. When they were well mixed, she added lukewarm water, about a quarter of a teaspoonful at a time.

George heaved a sigh. "Nancy, your patience is beyond me. Let's get this job over with."

Nancy smiled but said nothing. When she had what she thought was the right consistency of paste, she smeared it over the top of the tablet, temporarily obliterating the petroglyphs.

"This has to harden," she explained. "Then I'll turn the tablet over and do the other side. In the meantime, how about a little music? Bess, do you feel like playing the piano?"

"Sure."

The young people gathered in the living-room. Nancy opened her guitar case and asked who would like to play. The others insisted that she and Dave take turns.

For the next half hour they sang old songs and new. Dave amused them with an original verse.

> "We're off, we're off
> To the Forgotten City.
> If we don't find the treasure,
> It'll be a p-i-t-y!"

"I'll say it will be," George echoed.

Presently, Nancy left the group to return to the kitchen. She felt the paste on the tablet and decided it was hard enough to turn the rock over and "antique" the underside. This took only a few minutes. Soon she was back with the group, but kept one eye on her watch.

Exactly half an hour later, Nancy returned to the kitchen. This time the others followed and watched as she wiped off the paste. She saved it in case the stone needed another layer.

"I guess it's done," she said. "Now for the polishing job."

She put a little wax on a cloth, went over the stone carefully until it matched the original. None of the "ageing process" rubbed off!

"That was a great job," Ned said to her.

The original and the new tablets were compared, and it was agreed that anyone except an expert on artifacts would be fooled by the substitution.

The boys could hardly wait for the sun to set. As soon as it did, they left. Ned carried the new tablet, wrapped in brown paper. They rode part of the way to the old mine, then walked the rest of the distance from the highway.

Ned was holding the package so it was prominently displayed. After a while he said, "I guess this is the right oak. Wow, it's a whopper!"

He laid the tablet on the ground beside it; then the boys started walking back to the main road.

In the meantime, Nancy, Bess, and George had followed in Nancy's convertible. When they reached the old road that led into the mine, Nancy started up the overgrown dirt path. She stopped the car, and they waited. There was a slight rise in the road, so the girls got out and walked ahead in order to see better.

"There's not a sound," Bess whispered.

Presently they spotted their friends coming from the old oak and starting along the road. Suddenly, and without any warning, a gang of boys, who apparently had been hiding behind trees, jumped the three Emerson boys and viciously started to beat them up!

·6·

The Dangerous Hole

THOUGH taken off guard, the three football players from Emerson fought well against the attacking gang. Ned heaved one of them to the ground in a football tackle. Burt held two of them and cracked their heads together. Dave got one young gangster round the waist and pitched him off in a somersault.

Bess was screaming, "Stop! Stop!"

The hoodlums paid no attention, and the girls could see that the ratio of ten fighters to three was overwhelming.

"I'm going in there to help!" George declared, and she started forward.

Both Bess and Nancy held her back.

George struggled to get away. "I want to try some judo on a couple of those fellows!"

"Don't!" Bess shrieked. "They'll—they'll make mincemeat of you!"

Nancy said quickly, "Let me try something else first. I have a police whistle with me. It may scare them!"

She pulled the whistle from her pocket and blew a shrill blast on it. The effect was instantaneous. The attacking gang, apparently thinking the police had arrived, scattered in all directions.

Ned, Burt, and Dave looked startled. The blast on the whistle had been so unexpected and authoritative, that they too had stopped fighting. The girls now hurried towards them.

"Who blew that whistle?" Burt asked.

The three girls burst into laughter, and Nancy admitted that she had. "It's the first time I ever tried to play a policeman, but I must say it worked."

"Yes," Bess added. "I never saw people run away so fast in my life."

The three boys laughed, and Dave declared, "From now on I'm going to carry a police whistle in my pocket, too."

Nancy grinned. "This isn't an authentic police whistle," she said. "You can buy one like this in any toy store, but if you blow hard enough on it you can really make a loud noise."

"I'll say," Ned agreed.

Suddenly the stillness was broken by a shout from the woods. The young people were afraid that the gang, realizing they had been tricked, were coming back to fight again. Nancy and her friends stood silently for a few moments, but no one showed up.

"Who was that?" Bess asked.

There was another shout, and then a voice called out, "You won this time, but watch out. We're friends of the guy you put in jail. We'll get you yet!"

After that there was silence. The group remained where they were for nearly a minute.

Finally Ned said he wanted to see whether the package was still at the old oak tree.

"Yes it is," he called out. "Right where I laid it."

George spoke up. "So the gang was not really after

the package. They followed us only to punish you boys for having their friend arrested."

The young people returned to the two cars. Nancy and Ned climbed into her convertible. Ned took the wheel and they set off for the Drew home. The rest of the group rode directly behind.

By this time, nightfall had come and the moon was shining brightly. Presently Nancy detected a moving shadow among the trees. She asked Ned to stop and signal the other car to halt.

"Look over there!" she said, pointing out of the window.

A tall lanky boy was warily walking in the direction of the old mine. The next second he disappeared.

Nancy and her friends got out of the cars and watched for a few minutes, but did not see the youth again. They could still see the old oak tree. No one was near it.

Finally Nancy spoke. "I believe something happened to that boy. He must have fallen and knocked himself out, or perhaps he slipped into an old mine hole."

Thoroughly alarmed, the young people went towards the spot where the boy had disappeared, holding their torches.

"Watch out for a trap!" Ned warned.

The searchers walked carefully, surveying every inch of the ground before they walked over it.

"Listen!" Nancy said suddenly. "I think I heard a cry for help."

Her friends stopped short and waited for another call. There was no doubt about it when another feeble plea came.

"Help! Help!"

The group swung their torches round but could see no one. Nancy walked forward.

"I'd say that cry came from down below. Let's look for a hole."

The group crept forward, and presently George said, "I see it!" She played her light on the spot.

A tangled mass of vines had apparently covered the opening. Now they were broken. Torches were beamed down into the hole. It was deep.

"Help! Get me out of here!" a frantic voice cried.

"We'll try," Nancy shouted.

She examined the hole and found a rickety wooden ladder on one side. The girl detective beamed her strong light straight down into the hole and could see the lanky young man lying on the ground.

"Climb up the ladder," Nancy told him. "I'll guide you with the light."

"I—I can't do it. My arm's broken. It's no use."

"Then I'll come down and help you," Nancy offered.

Ned stepped forward. "Don't you think I'd better go?"

Nancy shook her head. "That ladder looks mighty rickety and I'm a few pounds lighter than you."

"A good many!" he corrected. "All right, but be careful."

Nancy had no trouble descending the ladder until she came to the third rung from the bottom. Then, without warning, it splintered and threw her off balance. She landed in a heap beside the stricken boy.

From above Bess cried out, "Oh goodness! Nancy, are you hurt?"

"No. I'm all right," Nancy shouted, as she scrambled to her feet. Then she leaned over the boy. "Tell me what happened to you. Didn't you know about this place?"

"No, and I didn't see the hole in the dark," he replied. "But how am I going to get out of here?"

"Can you stand?" Nancy asked, wondering if the boy had any further injuries.

With her assistance he got up. "I guess I'm all right except for this arm." It hung limp at his side.

"I'm so sorry," Nancy said. She then asked him to try climbing the ladder by using one hand for support. "I'll help boost you up," she offered.

With the old wooden ladder now groaning and cracking, she managed to help him until those above could grab his uninjured arm and the back of his jacket and pull him to safety. Nancy scrambled up the few remaining steps.

Ned began to question the boy, who said his name was Jim Gorgo.

"We'll take you to a hospital," he offered. "Have you any choice about which one?"

"No," Jim replied. "But I guess the River Heights General would be the best."

He was helped into the rear seat. "You're regular folks," he commented. "And I'm mighty lucky you happened to come along."

Nancy spoke to him kindly. "Jim, you're a very good sport. I know that you're in pain, but please explain why you were in that particular spot in the woods."

The boy took so long to answer that she and Ned thought he was being evasive.

Finally he said, "I might as well tell you the truth. A man sent me for a package that was supposed to be left at the old oak tree. I thought I'd take a short-cut, but now I'm sorry I did."

Ned asked him, "Are you a member of the gang who tried to beat us up?"

"What gang?" Jim replied quickly. "I don't know anything about any gang. I came here on my own. The man who wanted the package said he'd pay me well for getting it. I wasn't supposed to tell anybody, but you folks have been so good to me, it's the least I can do."

Jim suggested that maybe one of the boys would like to go back and get the package and deliver it himself.

"I guess the man wouldn't care as long as he got the package."

Nancy and Ned exchanged glances. She asked Jim, "What's the man's name?"

"I don't know."

"Oh come," said Ned, "you must. Otherwise, how would you know where to deliver the package?"

Again Jim took a long time before answering. Then he said, "Honest, I'm telling the truth. I don't know the man's real name. He told me to call him Fleetfoot."

Fleetfoot!

Nancy was so delighted she could hardly keep from showing it, but she calmly asked, "Maybe one of us could make the delivery. Where would we find this man?"

Jim answered, "You know where the Waterfall Motel is?"

"Yes," Nancy replied.

"Well, I don't think Fleetfoot's staying at the motel," Jim said, "but he told me to meet him in the garden there."

"That sounds easy," Ned said. "As soon as we leave

you, we'll decide what to do."

In a few minutes the group reached the hospital. Ned drove up at once to the emergency entrance and went for a nurse, who came outside with a wheelchair. Jim climbed into it. Again he thanked the young people for rescuing him; then the nurse opened the door and pushed the new patient inside.

At this moment the other two couples drove up. "That boy is lucky," Dave remarked. "If we hadn't happened to go out there, he might have died of starvation in that pit."

The thought sobered the others, and there was little conversation as Ned turned Nancy's car and they all went back to the site of the old oak tree. The package was still there. Dave got out of the other car and brought it to Nancy.

"Thanks," she said. "Now which of you boys is going to the Waterfall Motel to deliver this?"

Dave said, "Suppose I do the errand alone. Fleetfoot has never seen me and won't suspect my motives are anything but good."

The two cars stopped some distance from the motel. As Dave started off with the package, Nancy whispered to him, "Don't try to capture Fleetfoot. I want him to get the fake tablet!"

·7·

Petroglyphs

DAVE walked slowly among the trees in the garden of the Waterfall Motel. It was large and well kept, with meandering walkways among various flower beds. Light filtered through from motel windows and doors.

"It's just dark enough," the Emerson student thought, "so it will be easy for me not to be detected as a substitute messenger."

Clutching the package under one arm, he sauntered along, watching the various paths but keeping out of sight.

"I hope I'm not too late," he told himself. "If Fleetfoot expected Jim Gorgo some time ago, he may have left."

At this moment, Dave saw two men coming along a walk near where he was standing. One was about five feet ahead of the other. Dave wondered whether or not they were together.

"Probably the one behind is a bodyguard for the man in front," he told himself.

Dave decided not to announce himself but to wait for some sign from the men. To his disappointment there was none.

They walked on for some distance. Then they stopped abruptly, turned, and, taking the same positions, retraced their steps towards the spot where Dave was hiding. Now he was sure they had come for the stone tablet. Was one of them Fleetfoot?

When the man in the lead reached Dave, the boy called out, "Pardon me, sir, but are you waiting for a package?"

"Yes, I am. Have you got it?"

Instead of replying, Dave asked, "What's your name? I can't deliver it to the wrong person. It's too valuable."

The stranger became surly. "Never mind what my name is, but if yours is Jim Gorgo and you have the package, hand it over."

Before the men had arrived, Dave had laid the wrapped stone petroglyph on the ground with a special purpose in mind. As he leaned over to get it, he pulled a miniature camera from his pocket. It could take pictures in the dark, without a flashbulb.

The whole episode lasted about two seconds. A picture was snapped as the package was being handed over.

Apparently the two men were unaware of what had happened. One of them quickly grabbed the stone tablet, and the two hurried up the walk.

Dave did not follow. Instead, he set the little camera in motion to develop the picture. When it was ready, he tore the paper out and walked towards a light. He had photographed the faces of the two men, and they were clear enough to be identified. Excited, he returned to Nancy's house.

"How did you make out?" she asked.

Dave wore a big grin. He pulled the photograph from

his pocket. "Here are the men who came after the package," he announced.

Nancy stared at the two faces, then said, "Neither of these men is Fleetfoot, but that was a great piece of detective work, Dave."

"What will you do with the photograph?" he asked. Nancy said she would take it to police headquarters at once and find out if these men were among wanted persons. "Let's go!"

"It's my turn again," Dave spoke up. "They may want to see my camera."

Ned grinned and made no protest. Nancy and Dave set off for police headquarters. Chief McGinnis was not on duty, but the sergeant at the desk knew Nancy and the story about Fleetfoot.

He looked at the photograph, then sent for a book containing pictures of wanted persons. After a long search he announced that they had no record of the two men.

"They must be Fleetfoot's pals," Nancy suggested.

The sergeant nodded. He offered to have duplicate pictures made for Dave and Nancy. He would keep the original.

While a young policeman was developing the extra prints, the sergeant asked to see Dave's camera.

"We don't have one as fine as this in our department," he said. "Where did you get it?"

Dave said it had been a gift from his uncle, who had partially invented the camera. It was not on the market yet.

Presently the young policeman returned with the pictures and handed them to Nancy and Dave. The sergeant said he would discuss the case with Chief

McGinnis, and some men would be alerted to watch for the two suspects.

Nancy and Dave went back to the Drew home, but the group soon decided to separate and return to the girls' individual homes.

"Breakfast at eight," Nancy sang out, as the others were leaving.

The following morning a phone call came from Chief McGinnis. He reported to Nancy that his men had had no luck in tracing the two suspects who had taken the package the night before.

"I'm afraid," the officer said, "that Fleetfoot and his friends had too much of a head start. They probably left town right after the pick-up."

As Nancy finished the conversation, the front doorbell rang. The postman was there with a special-delivery letter for Ned. Nancy signed for it, then took the letter to him.

"This is what I've been waiting for," he said. "Our tickets! I asked the travel agent to send them here."

Ned opened the envelope quickly and pulled out plane tickets for the whole group. He explained that they would fly from River Heights to Chicago, then to Las Vegas, Nevada.

"We'll stay there with one of the boys from the University. He's going on the dig with us."

"When do we leave?" Nancy asked.

"Tomorrow morning."

There was a loud squeal from Bess. "Why didn't somebody tell me? I must go right home and pack. I haven't even decided what to take."

Ned reminded her that all she had to put in her suitcase were her clothes. Everything else was to be ready for them in Las Vegas.

"I burn so easily," said Bess, "that I'd better take plenty of suntan lotion and a big hat."

George asked, "Nancy, are you going to carry the precious stone tablet with you or return it to Mrs Wabash?"

"I'll call Mrs Wabash—I mean Mrs Mary Morton, and do as she wishes."

Nancy phoned the woman and asked her what she wanted done with the tablet. At once Mrs Wabash requested that Nancy keep it.

"You have a lot of people with you, so there is less chance of it's being stolen from you than from me. I'll be travelling alone."

"Are you going back home soon?" Nancy queried.

"Yes."

The girl detective now asked if it would be possible for the Indian woman to come to the Drew home and decipher the symbols on the tablet. "Do you recall what was on the other tablets?"

"Vaguely," she said.

Mrs Wabash agreed to disguise herself a bit and take a taxi to Nancy's home. When she arrived, Nancy brought out the tablet. Mrs Wabash began to explain some of the symbols.

"This wavering line means a stream. Over here, near the deer, is a cloud."

Nancy asked, "These two men with crude spears—what do they mean?"

"I believe," Mrs Wabash replied, "that it indicates a fight between the men. By the way, notice that their crude spears are launched from atlatls. These were heavy pieces of notched wood. By putting the foot of the spear into this, a man could launch his weapon much farther than he could with his hands."

There was silence for a few moments, then the Indian continued, "I think perhaps the two men who are fighting represent two tribes. They probably had had a war, but there is nothing here to indicate for certain who won the battle."

"Maybe that's on another tablet," Nancy suggested.

"Possibly," Mrs Wabash agreed. "The tablets had no marks on them to indicate the order in which they were to be read. I was working on that just before they were stolen from me."

The conversation was interrupted by the telephone, and Nancy left to answer it.

Chief McGinnis was calling. "I have a little news for you," he said. "I don't know how useful it is, though. Two of my patrolmen spotted the men in Dave's picture. But they declared they had already delivered the package and were innocent of any wrongdoing. They would reveal nothing about Fleetfoot, nor would they identify the man to whom they had given the package as being the thief we're looking for.

"Of course, we had to let them go," McGinnis continued, "but they'll be kept under surveillance. If anything else comes in, I'll let you know."

Nancy thanked him, then went back to hear more of Mrs Wabash's story. She confessed to having thought the chuckwalla lighted up but probably was wrong.

Bess had been studying one of the human figures. She giggled. "This creature doesn't seem to be wearing any clothes but has a very fancy headdress."

The Indian woman said she had translated this to mean that the two figures, which she thought were male and female, could indicate a battle between the chief and his leaders and the common people.

"I believe the common people won," Mrs Wabash said, "because of the elaborate headdress, which no doubt was taken from the chief and put on the head of the rebel leader."

George remarked, "That's a fascinating theory. It will be fun to prove it someday."

As they all stared at the other figures, Nancy, who had been using her magnifying glass, suddenly exclaimed, "Look at this!"

·8·

Say It in Code

IN the lower right-hand corner of the plaque, Nancy had detected an almost obliterated oblong mark.

"It has very faint petroglyphs on it," she announced.

First Mrs Wabash, then Nancy's friends, looked at it through the magnifying glass.

Finally Bess said, "What do you think the marks represent, Nancy? It doesn't look like much to me."

Nancy waited for Mrs Wabash to answer but when she did not speak, the young detective said, "Could this carving depict one of the golden tablets?"

Ned remarked that if it were, this was an amazing deduction. Nancy, now thoroughly intrigued, went for an even stronger magnifying glass, which her father kept in a desk drawer. She trained it on the faint petroglyph.

"This looks like a man gathering something from a stream. I think this hairline mark indicates a stream. Maybe he has found gold nuggets and will make a plate from them!"

She handed the magnifying glass to the owner of the tablet. "What do you think, Mrs Wabash?"

The Indian woman gazed at the symbol a long time. "I believe you're right, Nancy," she said, smiling.

She added that Nancy had made a valuable contribution to the mystery. "I would even guess that the
long-forgotten city ran along the banks of this stream.
The golden plates perhaps were made from nuggets
found there, and the plates are hidden in that area."

Bess sighed. "Do you think we can ever find that city
and the sheets of gold?"

"I'll wager," said Burt, "that if anybody can find
them Nancy Drew can."

The young sleuth grinned. "It's a big order, but I
hope you're right."

Mrs Wabash rose to leave. She said she would meet
the young people in Las Vegas.

"I'll memorize your address there, so if anybody
takes my purse again, it won't reveal where you are."

Nancy thanked her for thinking of this. "Now my
friends and I will memorize your address and phone
number."

They all repeated it several times, then said goodbye
to the Indian woman. Soon afterwards the three couples separated to attend to their packing.

Early the next morning they gathered again at Nancy's house, and Mr Drew said he would drive them all
to the airport. Hannah Gruen said goodbye to them all,
her eyes moist with affection. She pleaded with Nancy
to be careful of Fleetfoot and of poisonous serpents or
reptiles like the gila monster.

"I'll do my best to avoid them," Nancy agreed.

She hugged the housekeeper affectionately and hurried to the car.

On the way to the airport Nancy said to the others,
"Don't you think it would be a good idea if we had a
signalling system in code?"

"Great," Ned agreed. "You mean hand signals?"

"No, that is too obvious," Nancy replied. "How about three or four sentences? The third word in each sentence will be a message to the rest of us."

"Give us an example," Dave suggested.

The girl detective thought for a few moments, then said, "I always suspect bargains. Sometimes I'm standing near a sales counter. And inspect nearby merchandise."

For a couple of seconds her listeners looked blank, but Mr Drew said, "I get it. The message is, 'Suspect standing nearby.' "

"Pretty cool," Burt commented. "Anybody else smart enough to think of one?"

At first nobody answered, but finally George grinned and said:

> *Please, Santa, look in my empty sock.*
> *Fill it up real high.*
> *A hole's in the toe, but never mind.*
> *The Christmas tree won't sigh.*

The others burst into laughter. Dave thought it was a bit corny, but George's message was good. It said, "Look up in tree."

By this time, Mr Drew had reached the airport, and farewells were exchanged. When the travellers arrived at O'Hare Airport in Chicago, they learned that the plane to Las Vegas would be late.

"We have a long wait," Bess complained. "I'm going for a tall chocolate float."

The three boys said they would rather take a walk. Nancy and George went with Bess to the concourse for a cool drink. On the way back to the gate at which they would board the plane, Nancy bought a newspaper.

She had soon scanned the first page and turned over to the next one. Suddenly she exclaimed, "Oh!"

"Bad news?" George asked.

"I don't know," Nancy replied. She pointed to a headline which read:

RUMOUR OF GOLD IN NEVADA DESERT
RUSH TO SPOT EXPECTED

"Is it where we're going?" Bess asked. "And do they mean the gold——"

George grabbed her cousin's arm before she had a chance to give away their secret to anyone who might be snooping.

"Here's a map of the area," Nancy said, pointing it out in the paper.

The three girls studied it carefully and finally Nancy said, "Apparently it's in the opposite direction from the one we'll take out of Las Vegas."

Bess sighed with relief. "Thank goodness. We've had enough trouble with strangers already."

In a few minutes the boys rejoined the girls and Nancy showed them the newspaper story.

Ned whistled. "I hope none of the gold seekers come our way. That would spoil everything."

As the group walked towards the boarding area, Nancy said suddenly, "What number are we? It's like being in a maze. We'd better watch carefully for our sign."

For a couple of seconds her friends said nothing. To an outsider Nancy's conversation would seem perfectly rational. To her friends, using the third word in each sentence, she was saying, "Are being watch."

One by one, members of Nancy's group found an excuse to turn round completely to see who was watching them. All agreed upon a casually dressed young man. He seemed to be walking round aimlessly, but he always stayed close enough to hear as much of the young people's conversation as possible. When he realized that they had detected his purpose, the man hurried away.

"One thing I'm sure of," said Nancy, "is that he is not going on our plane. But he may want to make certain we're aboard so that he can telephone the news to someone in Las Vegas."

The trip to the South-west was uneventful. On their arrival the young people went into the city in two taxis. They exclaimed over the garish downtown area.

"There must be billions of electric lights on the electric signs of these hotels, restaurants, and clubs," remarked Bess, who was riding with Nancy.

It was a busy city, with taxis and private cars going up and down the streets in a steady stream. In a little while their cabs reached the residential area, which was very attractive and much quieter. The cabs pulled up in front of Neil Anderson's home. It was spacious and had a beautiful flower garden.

Neil and his parents were charming people who made the visitors feel at home at once. A girl who was about fourteen years old came into the room and was introduced as Debbie, Neil's younger sister.

"I'll take you to your rooms," she offered.

On the way through the split-level house, they passed the dining-room. In it was a very long table set up as if for a banquet.

Debbie saw the looks of surprise on the visitors' faces. "Big party here tonight," she explained. "The rest of the Emerson group is in town and all the people going on the dig are coming here to dinner."

"That's great," said Nancy. "Now we'll be able to meet everyone. Debbie, I just can't wait to see our caravan."

"It's pretty super," the girl said. "I wish I could go on the dig, but they tell me I'm not old enough. I guess because I have so many little accidents, they think I don't know how to be careful. I might ruin something precious that's dug up." She giggled.

"We'll take lots of pictures," Bess said kindly. "We'll see that you get some."

Since the dinner hour was only thirty minutes away, the young people quickly bathed and changed their clothes.

By the time they appeared, the other diggers had arrived. There were introductions, a lot of conversation, and a great deal of laughter.

Nancy was thrilled. What fun it was to join this jolly group and to try solving the mystery of the Forgotten City!

After dinner, the young people gathered in the garden. A graduate student from the University of Nevada, named Archie Arnow, immediately walked over to Nancy's side to speak to her. At first she answered his questions lightly, but eventually she realized that he was trying to get information from her.

"I'll pretend not to notice this," she thought, giving him vague answers.

Several times Nancy tried moving away from him so she might talk to other people. He followed her very closely, and before she could say anything to her new friends, he would ask her another question.

"What a pest he is!" she told herself.

Nancy spotted Neil Anderson at one side of the garden. She made a sudden move, wedged her way through a group, and managed to get to Neil before Archie was aware of what had happened. Quickly Nancy asked Neil what kind of a person Archie was.

"Oh, he's an archaeological whiz," Neil replied, "but he's not well liked. He's very opinionated and secretive. Be careful, Nancy, or he may try to solve your mysteries for you."

Nancy smiled. "Thanks for the tip."

She said Archie had been following her around and asking questions. "I don't know how much he has heard about what we're going to hunt for out on the desert, so I thought it best not to tell him anything I knew."

"You were wise, Nancy," Neil said, "and you'd better warn your friends."

Nancy alerted each one in her group.

George made a wry face. "I didn't like Archie from the moment I met him. I wondered how you could be so patient, talking to him as long as you did."

Nancy chuckled. "I couldn't get away, but he didn't learn anything from me."

The following morning Nancy telephoned her home in River Heights. Hannah Gruen answered and told her that the police had phoned.

"They reported that Fleetfoot Joe had definitely left town," she said. "McGinnis had phoned the Las Vegas police to be on the alert. So far he has heard nothing and suggested that if you should call, I should tell you to phone the police out there for information."

Nancy did so at once but was told there was no news of the elusive thief.

As she left the phone, Nancy saw Ned coming towards her. She relayed her latest clue.

"Keep your eyes open," he urged her.

Ned now told Nancy that he and the other boys would be busy the following day, helping to get the caravan ready.

"Is there anything we can do?" Nancy asked.

Ned shook his head. "Why don't you girls go off and do some sightseeing in town?"

"I'd rather go out in the desert and visit the Lost City Museum."

George and Bess were intrigued by this idea and immediately agreed to go with her. Nancy rented a car the next day and the three set off. The place was about fifty miles from Las Vegas and was situated in a desolate spot.

The museum was an attractive oblong tan stucco building. In front was a beautiful Palo-Verde tree, which was unusual because everything about it was green—bark, stems, and leaves.

The girls were welcomed by a friendly man who said he was the curator. He offered to show them through the museum and explained that everything in it had come from the surrounding area.

"Are you girls interested in archaeology?" he asked.

"Yes we are," Nancy replied. "In fact, we're part of the group of diggers who are coming out to the desert tomorrow to work for a little while."

The curator smiled and said he was glad to hear it. "Where are you going to be located?" he asked.

"Above the Forgotten City," Nancy answered.

"Which one?" the man queried. "You know the Indian villages were strung along the Muddy River for some thirty miles. Of couse, now they're all buried. In fact, you wouldn't believe it but four civilizations are buried in this territory."

"Four?" Bess asked in astonishment.

"That's right," he said. "Their civilizations were built one on top of another. The top one was settled by people we here at the museum call the pit dwellers. This is because they built their dwellings or houses partially underground. Come outside and I'll show you some that have been restored."

He led the girls towards beehive-shaped clay huts. They were reddish-tan in colour. The visitors peered inside the first one. In the centre of the floor were the remains of a fire.

"You see there's a hole in the roof," the curator explained. "The smoke went up through there."

"How do you get in?" Bess asked. "There's a doorway but no steps. Did the Indians jump down? I know from studies that they were rarely tall people."

"They managed somehow," the man replied. "But most of them entered through the roof. They climbed up a ladder to get there. Why don't you step down inside? I think you can make it."

Bess grabbed the sides of the doorway and put one foot down on to the floor. The next moment she skidded, turned her ankle, and went down in a heap.

"Oh, oh!" she cried out, pain creasing her face.

·9·

The Weird Valley

INSTANTLY the curator jumped down through the opening and assisted Bess to her feet.

"I'm very sorry," he said. "I should have stepped in first and helped you."

By this time Nancy and George had come through the doorway.

"I see what happened," Nancy said. "Here's a little round stone. Bess, you must have skidded on it."

She knelt down to look at Bess's ankle, hoping it was not sprained.

"Let's see if you can stand on it," George suggested.

Bess found that she could but said it hurt to do so.

The curator spoke up. "My wife, daughter, and I live in the house connected to the museum. My daughter has had nurse's training. Let's see what she can do to help you."

Bess put an arm round Nancy and George's shoulders and hobbled on one foot back into the museum, then out on to a porch. Here it was shady and cool in contrast to the heat outside.

The curator went to get his daughter, who was very pleasant. In a short time she had bandaged Bess's ankle tightly and the girl declared it felt much better.

"Bess, I suggest," the young woman said, "that you leave the bandage on until you can ask a doctor just what the trouble is. My personal opinion is that it's only a sprain." The others were relieved to hear this.

Nancy and George felt that Bess should remain on the porch while they looked through the museum.

"Okay," she agreed willingly.

The fascinating collection of relics in the museum included many different kinds of objects. There were arrowheads, stone spears, petroglyph tablets, bits of turquoise jewellery, pottery bowls, and scraps of baskets made from grasses.

"These baskets are probably the oldest things that have been found," the curator said. "The Basket Makers belonged to the first civilization that was here."

Nancy said, "Then some of the archaeologists have dug that deep?"

"It's hard to say," the man replied. "This basket might have been carried to this area in a stream, and picked up by someone from a later civilization. It's very fragile. That's why we have it behind glass."

The girls spent a lot of time looking at each article.

Finally the man called to them. "I want you to see something special over here."

They hurried to his side. He was standing beside a large case containing a complete human skeleton and many artifacts.

"This was a thirty-two-year-old woman," the curator stated.

George remarked that the position of the skeleton seemed like a strange one in which to bury a person.

"It was the custom," the man told her. "The Indians buried their dead in the pre-natal position."

He told the girls that the cause of the woman's death was a mystery. He looked at his visitors with a twinkle in his eye. "Perhaps you'd like to guess what it was?"

Nancy studied the objects in the case. Finally her eyes settled on a small stone plaque on which two sets of marks, one under the other, had been painted.

She said, "These lines are so jagged, they remind me of lightning. Is it possible that this woman was struck by lightning and killed?"

"That's a reasonable guess," the man replied.

George asked, "Do you have bad storms around here? I thought it rarely rained in the desert and that's why it's so hot and dry."

The curator said she was partly right. "However, we do have thunderstorms and when we do, they're really frightening, let me tell you." He grinned. "When you're camping out in the desert, and one of those storms is coming up, you have to batten down good and stay under cover. The wind can be fierce, and sandy dirt and uprooted weeds blow all over the place."

George asked if this was what was called tumble-weed, and did it actually roll across the desert?

"Some of it, yes," was the answer.

The man excused himself, telling the girls to continue looking around. In a few minutes he returned with his wife. She was a smiling, motherly type of woman.

"We'd like to have you three girls stay to lunch," she said.

"Thank you," Nancy replied. "I'll accept for all of us."

She and George followed the woman out to the porch, where Bess and her "nurse" were sitting at a table. The others seated themselves. The curator said grace and Nancy was much impressed with his giving thanks for the works of the Deity, including the wonders of the desert.

Afterwards he described the foods that might be found in the arid territory. "There are many uses for the cacti, even candy, and of course there are wild animals that can be shot and cooked."

Bess remarked, "You have such a pretty garden. Where do you get water for it and for yourselves?"

"From an artesian well."

Nancy was intrigued to hear this. So there was water, deep under the surface. Maybe at some time this had been part of the Muddy River!

When there was a lull in the conversation, Nancy asked the curator if he knew Mrs Wabash.

"Oh yes," he answered. "A very fine woman." He laughed and looked directly at Nancy. "She has a fantastic secret. Why don't you ask her about it sometime?"

Nancy and George were afraid Bess might say something, but this time she kept quiet.

"I'll do that," Nancy said, deciding to ask the woman how much the curator knew.

He inquired, "Where are you going from here?"

Nancy said the girls planned to visit the Valley of Fire.

"Yes, do that. It is a fantastic place—one of nature's great wonders. After you go to the Visitor's Centre there, ride on ahead for a little way and see the Mouse's Tank."

Bess giggled. "What a funny name! What is the Mouse's Tank?"

The curator chuckled. "It was the hide-out of a famous bandit."

"With this bad ankle, that leaves me out," Bess remarked.

"I'm afraid so," the curator's wife said. "You must climb to get there."

The girls learned that at one time the area had been very wild, but now there was a good road leading to it, and a picnic spot had been built below the Mouse's Tank.

When the group finished eating, the visitors thanked their host and hostess and their daughter, then drove off.

The three sightseers reached the first part of the Valley of Fire, where they looked around in awe, for they had never seen such an amazing sight. Enormous sandstone rocks were piled up, helter-skelter, to the height of a big hill.

Presently Bess cried out, "Look at that rock formation! It's the perfect image of an elephant!"

They drove on a short distance, then George asked Nancy to stop. "See that strange formation up there! I want to get a picture of it."

The rocks looked like three huge, perfectly formed birds' claws, attached to part of a foot.

"This is like a wild animal jungle turned to stone!" Bess exclaimed.

"It's too bad we don't have time to get out and walk among these rocks," Nancy commented.

George returned to the car and a few minutes later asked Nancy to stop again. She pointed to a huge, rocky mound surrounded by green ground cover.

"That rock looks just like a sleeping cow," she said.

"You can almost imagine that it's going to get up soon and start grazing."

Nancy had been silent for some time. Bess asked what she was thinking.

The girl detective smiled. "I was just trying to figure out this place. Perhaps once upon a time the area was fertile and huge beasts roamed around.

"One could almost imagine that there was a sudden volcanic eruption that tossed out rocks and a type of sandstone lava. The great beasts and birds were taken unaware and had no chance to escape. They died from the gas coming from the volcano."

George looked at the girl detective. "Do you also believe the poor things turned to stone like a petrified tree?"

"Who knows?" Nancy countered. "The beasts might have been covered with lava that hardened. I suppose you'd have to crack the rocks open to see if there were any bones inside. Of course lava is so hot that it might have disintegrated the beasts' whole body but left an outer coating."

Bess sighed. "There are times, Nancy," she said, "when your theories are way beyond me. I'm afraid this is one of them. Where do we go now?"

"To the Mouse's Tank."

The spot was deserted. The restaurant-and-gift shop at the base of the rock was closed, and there were no cars around. Nancy parked and she and George got out.

"I'll stay here," Bess said. "My ankle doesn't hurt, but I'd better not do any climbing."

Nancy and George left her and walked forward. They were sorry no one was around to give them directions, but they finally found their way up to the entrance of the bandit's cave and walked in.

"This sure is spooky," George remarked. "What a place for a hunted man to hide! I wonder how deep the cave is."

Nancy reminded her that since they had not brought torches and it was late in the afternoon, they had better not walk very far inside.

The words were barely out of her mouth, when the girls heard a faint scream. Both of them tensed.

Had it been Bess who screamed? Had she been attacked, or was she trying to warn the girls about something or somebody?

·10·

Call for Miss Antler

"WE'D better run!" Nancy exclaimed.

She led the way towards the entrance of the Mouse's Tank, with George only one step behind her.

At the opening, they pulled up short. Almost in front of them stood a man.

"Fleetfoot!" Nancy cried out.

He looked up, startled. Both girls dived for him but the thief was agile. He turned quickly and hurried down the rocks to the road with little trouble.

Nancy and George scrambled after him as fast as they dared. Apparently he was used to climbing up to this cave and knew how to get down safely and quickly. Now Fleetfoot began to run and soon he far outdistanced the girls.

When they reached the ground, Nancy said, "Let's chase him in the car!"

She and George jumped in, and Nancy started the motor instantly. She swung the car round and sped off.

"Who is he?" Bess asked. Learning that he was Fleetfoot, she said, "Oh, be careful, Nancy. You know he's dangerous."

The man leaped along the road like a deer. When he realized that Nancy was catching up with him, he veered off and scrambled up the side of a huge rock.

"Let the old mountain goat go!" Bess cried out.

Reaching the top of the rock, Fleetfoot hurried down the other side and disappeared from view.

"Oh, heavens!" George exclaimed, using one of her pet expressions. "Why did we have to lose him when we were so close?"

Nancy accepted the matter more philosophically. First she thanked Bess for warning George and her of Fleetfoot's approach.

"But I'm sorry we lost him just the same," Bess said.

Nancy went on, "We've proved two things, and both are important."

"Like what?" Bess asked.

"One is that Fleetfoot definitely is in this area. The other is that no doubt he's using the Mouse's Tank as a hideaway."

Bess nodded. "So now all we have to do is notify the police and they'll know where to hunt for him. Then we won't have any more to worry about."

George was sure it would not be so easy. "We can look for a lot more trouble from that thief," she predicted.

Bess added, "I suppose there's no use wishing, but I hope Fleetfoot doesn't find out where our camp is."

"I'll bet he knows already," George said. "He probably watches everything that's going on in this desert."

"And steals what he can," Bess added.

Nancy had not spoken for some minutes. She kept looking right and left across the uninhabited landscape. There was not a house or other building in sight.

Finally Bess said, "Nancy, you look concerned. Why?"

Nancy said she had been watching her falling fuel gauge.

"It's almost on the empty mark," she said. "I hope that even when it's marked empty, there's a little fuel left in the tank."

She drove for another ten minutes, then slowly the engine sputtered to a halt. The car rolled for another hundred feet under its own momentum and stopped.

"Oh, don't tell me!" Bess said. "It's a long way back to town—miles and miles. I couldn't possibly walk."

George said, "I don't relish a hike of twenty-five miles myself."

Nancy suggested that if they could get to the main road, there surely would be help.

"Bess, suppose you sit behind the wheel and steer. George and I will push the car."

They tried this, but after doing so for a mile, Nancy and George were exhausted. Bess pleaded with them to rest.

"You won't have to ask me twice," George replied with a groan.

She flopped down on the ground at the side of the road and stretched out. Nancy, too, lay down. The two girls closed their eyes against the sunlight and soon were ready to fall asleep.

Suddenly Bess awakened them with a loud scream and cried out, "Nancy! There's a hairy scorpion on you!"

Nancy jumped up instantly, flinging off the creature. It crawled away.

"I guess it's safer in the car," George said. "Nancy, let's get back inside and rest in a safe place."

Another ten minutes went by. Then the girls heard

the sound of a motor. Nancy and George got out. A car was coming up the road. They waved frantically and it stopped. A young man sat at the wheel.

"You having trouble?" he asked, leaning out of his window.

"We sure are," George responded. "We're out of fuel. We don't have one drop."

The young man grinned. "I can siphon off enough to get you to the first filling station," he said. "I can't give you any more than that. I'm going deeper into the desert and don't dare run short."

Nancy thanked him for the help and said, "You're a life saver. Two of us tried pushing the car for a mile and that was enough. Our friend in the car has a sprained ankle."

"That's what I call hard luck," the young man said.

He had already hopped from his car and was now opening the boot. In a few moments he took out a narrow piece of hose and measured the distance between Nancy's fuel tank and his own. The hose did not quite reach, so he drove his car closer, then measured again.

"It's long enough now," he said. "Well, here goes." He grinned. "Open your tank and we'll get started with this life-saving job."

Nancy unscrewed the cap and he did the same on his car. Then he inserted the hose into his petrol tank and squeezed the air out of the hose with his fingers. He put the open end into Nancy's tank and the fluid began to flow.

He called to Bess to watch the fuel gauge. When it reached a little above the empty mark, he removed the hose.

The young man refused to take any money, saying, "This is my good deed for the day." He wished the girls luck and drove off.

The rest of their journey was quick. Nancy stopped at a filling station, then went directly to the Anderson home.

The boys were there and Ned said, "The Andersons are taking us to a hotel to dinner. I'm sure you'll want to shower and change to something suitable. See you later."

The girls scooted off to their rooms. Twenty minutes later they reappeared, refreshed and ready for the dinner party.

The group was going to the hotel in several cars. Nancy and her friends set off first in the one she had rented. When they reached the lavish hostelry, the young people waited in the large lobby for the others to arrive.

"This place is ostentatiously furnished," George said. "I like things simpler."

"It's too noisy to suit me," Bess commented. "This town never goes to bed, I hear."

In a few minutes Nancy and her friends noticed that telephone operators were paging various guests and announcing telephone calls for them.

Bess giggled. "How would you like to have that name?" she asked, repeating the call for Miss Shirley Rainbow.

A few moments later there was a call for Mr Bill Verythin. The next few were simple names like Smith and Jones.

Presently the operator called out, "Miss Rosemary Bluebird! Call for Rosemary Bluebird!"

Nancy and her friends were laughing by this time.

"I'm sure," said Ned, "that these are names of people who are here incognito; perhaps famous persons like movie stars."

The others agreed and continued to listen eagerly for the next one. Suddenly Nancy, Bess, and George were electrified to hear a familiar name called out.

"Phone call for Miss Antler! Important call for Miss Antler. Will Miss Antler please answer the phone nearest her?"

The girls looked at one another and Nancy said, "Miss Antler? Antler? That was the name of the person Mrs Wabash told us to try to find while we're here!"

Ned asked, "Do you suppose she has something to do with the desert secret?"

"I think so," Nancy replied. "Mrs Wabash said she would be very helpful to us. Let's hunt for her!"

The hotel was large and there were so many telephones that it was hard to know where to start.

"This is going to be a real job," George commented.

Nancy suggested that the group separate and scatter to various places in the lobby.

"If you see a young woman at a phone, try to find out if she's Miss Antler."

The six young sleuths hurried away to begin their search.

·11·

New Clues

MEN were making calls from most of the telephones in
the lobby, but there were a few women. Bess and
George had no luck with the women they approached.
Burt and Dave, too, were unsuccessful.

Ned went up to a young woman who was evidently
waiting for a long-distance call and was holding the
receiver.

"Pardon me," said Ned, "but are you Miss Antler?"

The young woman began to laugh. "No—*dear*. I'm
Miss *Lamb*kin. Ba-a! Ba-a! What can I do for you?"

Ned ignored the crude humour. "Do you happen to
know Miss Antler?" he asked.

Again the young woman giggled. "Come now, is that
her real name?"

Ned decided not to tell her. "Who knows?" he said,
walking away. At that moment the young woman's call
came through, and she began to talk with someone.

A little later Ned joined the rest of the group, which
had already gathered. Nancy had found Miss Antler,
and now she introduced her to the others. She was a
young Indian woman, very pretty and charming.

"I'm so glad you found me," she said in a musical
voice. "Mrs Wabash wrote to tell me that you were

81

coming, but unfortunately she did not say when.

"I'm a graduate student of geology and surveying. This is how I became interested in the desert area. It was through some experimental work I've done here that I met Mrs Wabash. Unfortunately, I left no forwarding address, so she couldn't get in touch with me again."

Nancy smiled. "That was a lucky telephone call. To be truthful, we have heard so many amusing names paged here, we decided all of them were probably people who were travelling incognito. We even wondered if you might be."

"No," the young Indian woman responded, her black eyes twinkling. "It's really my name but I am teased a good deal about it."

Ned spoke up. "Mrs Wabash said you could help us in our search in the desert."

Miss Antler said she believed she could. "I was helping Mrs Wabash translate the petroglyphs on those ancient tablets. Now we can finish the work."

"Didn't you know," Nancy asked, "that all but one tablet were stolen?"

"No. How dreadful!"

Nancy told her the whole story, including the few clues that she had.

"My friends and I hope the police will pick up Fleetfoot."

"I hope so, too," the young Indian woman said. "In the meantime, in my work I have collected stories and legends from the older Indians who live in this area. I think there are some good clues in them as to where some rewarding digging might take place."

"That sounds wonderful," Nancy told her.

"Terrific!" George exclaimed. "Could you draw us a map?"

Miss Antler smiled. "I was hoping that maybe you would invite me to go on the dig with you."

Nancy was excited by this idea. "Could you? We'd love to have you come."

"I'd love to accept," Miss Antler replied. "Since we'll be working closely, I want you to call me by my first name. It's Wanna."

"What a pretty name!" Bess remarked.

"I think so, too," Wanna said. "When are you going to start your trip?"

"We're planning to leave tomorrow morning," Nancy told her. "Could you be ready by that time?"

"Oh yes," Wanna said. "I'll bring some special tools and surveying instruments with me." She smiled broadly. "I'm really excited about this. Will you be in touch with Mrs Wabash?"

Nancy said she planned to telephone her that evening and hoped the woman would have returned from her trip.

"I know she'll be pleased that we found you," Nancy said. She gave Wanna the Andersons' home address; then the Indian student said goodbye. "I'll see you all in the morning."

Bess saw the rest of their group arriving and soon they were all together. A big table had been reserved for them, and in a short time they were eating and watching an amusing stage show.

After they returned to the Anderson residence, Nancy called Mrs Wabash.

"I've just come home," the woman said. "Before leaving River Heights I spoke with the police. They had heard nothing about the stolen tablets."

Nancy surprised the woman by telling her she had seen Fleetfoot at the Mouse's Tank and among the rocks in the Valley of Fire.

"We reported the incident to the Nevada Police, and they are hunting for Fleetfoot and the tablets he has."

"That's good," Mrs Wabash said. "When do you leave for your trip to the desert?"

When she heard that it was early the following morning, Mrs Wabash said, "Then I won't see you for some time. I'll be eager to know whether you find anything of interest."

Nancy told her about meeting Wanna Antler, and said the young Indian woman would go on the desert dig with her group.

"I'm glad," Mrs Wabash said, then added, "Good night, Nancy. Have a restful sleep and a wonderfully successful dig."

After hanging up, Nancy had a hunch. Could Fleetfoot have hidden the tablets somewhere in the Valley of Fire?

"Or was he just about to hide them at the Mouse's Tank when Bess screamed?" the young detective asked herself.

She decided that at the first opportunity she and her friends would go to investigate the place. Nancy thought about it long after getting into bed, but finally dropped off to sleep. In the morning she was awakened by George.

"Get up, sleepyhead," her friend said. "You'd better hurry, or the caravan will leave without you!"

The girls were downstairs in a little while. Mrs Anderson had breakfast ready for the group, then they went outside to assemble. It had been decided that Nancy would keep the rented car, since she wanted to make some other trips in connection with her sleuthing.

By eight o'clock, the caravan was ready to leave. Despite all that the girls had heard, they were still amazed at the size of the vehicles assembled, and the equipment in them. One truck carried tents for the whole group. Another was literally a kitchen on wheels, with a smiling chef in charge. There was a large refrigerated car with so much food in it that Bess's eyes bulged.

George teased her. "Watch that waistline, cousin. But then, if you work hard enough, maybe you won't put on any more pounds."

Bess made a face but said nothing. She had a continuous battle with the problem of gaining weight. Furthermore, there was no advice that helped, and each time she began to diet, her friends teased her.

One truck carried all sorts of digging tools, shovels, and spades. On a rig in one vehicle was a drill with electric motors to run it.

Wanna had joined the group and now said to Nancy, "I don't think they'll be using that drill much. Archaeological and geological digging is mostly a matter of hand labour. I've brought some special sieves for our group. Also some drawing pads, pencils, and crayons. Everything has to be very precise and accurately reported."

Nancy took Wanna around to introduce her to Professor Donald Maguire, who was in charge of the dig, and to the students from Emerson College and the University of Nevada. Some of the latter knew her through her geological papers and lectures.

"Glad to have you aboard," said Archie. "I have a theory I want to discuss with you."

Ned winked at Nancy. If this should happen, Wanna had his sympathy!

The professor and the students, together with Wanna and the three girls from River Heights, climbed into various private cars and trucks. The journey into the desert had begun. Wanna was now seated in the car with the professor, leading the way to the spot where she thought they should make camp and work.

The trucks rattled along the road, then turned off and clattered over the parched sands far from the roadway. Nancy's group was intrigued by the beautiful, stately yucca plants with their clusters of white flowers.

"They're as tall as I am!" Bess said as their car passed a group of three plants in full bloom.

In a little while they came to a small rock formation from which cacti were growing. On one of them was a huge, beautiful pink flower.

"Oh I must get a picture of that," said Dave. "Ned, please stop a moment."

Dave jumped from the car and took two shots of the plants with his special camera. A few seconds after getting back into the car, the pictures had been developed and he showed them to the others.

"They're gorgeous," Nancy said. "You'll send these to your uncle? I'd say his camera is perfection, day or night."

During the brief stop, a couple of other cars got ahead of Ned. As a result, they were almost the last to arrive at the site where apparently Wanna had suggested they camp. They could hear loud talking and angry shouts at the head of the line.

"I wonder what's the matter?" Nancy said. "Let's go find out!"

Bess was still being careful of her ankle and said she would not join the others. The rest hurried forward.

"What's up?" Ned asked one of the other Emerson boys.

His classmate pointed ahead to a group of angry, gesticulating men. "They can't speak English, but they're saying that we can't camp here!"

·12·

A Deadly Necklace

IT was evident from the strangers' language that they were speaking Spanish, but it was so garbled that it was hard to understand.

Nancy and Ned walked closer to listen. The group of swarthy men were waving their arms wildly, indicating that the newcomers were to leave at once.

When no compromise seemed to be near, Nancy walked up to Professor Maguire. "I've travelled in Mexico a good bit," she said, "and picked up some of the dialects. Perhaps I can translate what these men are saying."

"Thank you," he said. "I'll be glad of any help. This is a bad situation."

Nancy spoke to the men in the vernacular of the Spanish-speaking province from which she thought they had come. At once they quietened down and listened.

The young detective asked them several questions, then turned to the professor. "They have heard about the gold rush and their directions led them here."

"Oh, is that it?" he said. "Well, tell them that it's many miles from here, probably a hundred in that direction." He pointed.

Nancy told the Mexican group that it was unfortunate they had come so far out of their way. She pointed in the direction they should take. "I hope you can get rides part of the way," she said.

The leader of the group had a long black moustache twisted at the ends. He wore a sombrero. The man looked at Nancy, puzzled. She knew what was going through his mind. How could a young girl living in the United States speak his language and also know where the gold rush was, since it was so far away?

She gave him a big smile. "I am so sorry you made this journey for nothing, and I wish you lots of luck in your search for gold."

"We will go," he said finally.

There were murmurs from his companions, but they obeyed their leader. The men picked up all their belongings and started the long trek across the desert.

Now work on setting up camp for the diggers, who hoped to locate the Forgotten City, began. A job had been assigned to each of them, and they worked with precision. Two hours later the place was ready for occupancy. Professor Maguire consulted his chart and called out the names of tent mates. There would be six in each shelter. Wanna was assigned to the tent where Nancy, Bess, and George would be, along with two lovely girls who were studying at the University of Nevada.

The tent in which Ned, Burt, and Dave were to sleep was not far away. The boys were with three other Emerson students.

By the time camp was set up, it was very warm outside and the group was glad to take shelter under the tents. When Nancy and George arrived at theirs, they waited for Bess, but she did not come. The Nevada girls were concerned.

"One can get a sunstroke out in this desert," said Betty Carr.

"I'll bet I can tell you where she is," George said.

"Where?"

"In the kitchen. It's already past meal-time and if there's one thing that bothers Bess it's going too long without lunch."

The Nevada girls laughed. Doris Dunham said, "I hope you're right about where she is but if you don't find her there, come and tell us. We'll help you hunt for her."

The kitchen was some distance away, but Nancy and George trudged there hopefully. Actually both girls were worried about Bess. With her bad ankle, how could she have walked so far, even if she was starving?

Finally Nancy and George reached the kitchen and went in. There was a great deal of activity and a meal was almost ready. Bess was not there. Nancy asked the chef if he had seen her, but the answer was, "No."

Now George was sorry she had been facetious about her cousin. "The poor girl may have turned over on her ankle again and may be lying somewhere out there in the sand and dirt, literally burning up!"

Nancy said nothing. She had heard a car coming. Wondering if Bess could be aboard, she walked over to where it was parked. To her astonishment, and George's, the driver hopped out. Archie! He went round to the other side, opened the door, and assisted Bess to the ground.

"Where have you two been?" George asked at once.

Bess giggled. "Playing Cowboys and Indians. Only

we weren't on horses. We were in Archie's car."

"That's right," the boy said. "We decided to see if those Mexicans really left and didn't plan to double back."

"And they hadn't?" Nancy asked.

Archie said pompously, "Well, with me following them, they didn't dare."

Nancy was disgusted. Bess thanked him for the ride, saying she had had a lot of fun. Then she joined the other girls, who assisted her back to their tent.

"I thought you couldn't stand Archie," George chided her cousin.

"Oh, he's harmless and he can be fun. But I must admit it was a bumpy ride across this desert. Those Mexicans were actually running. Can you imagine that in this heat?"

"No," Nancy and George answered together.

In a short time lunch was brought round to each tent. They were told that the evening meal would be served outdoors, and the whole group was to gather near the kitchen.

When they assembled at dinner-time, Nancy asked Wanna if she would tell some of the stories and legends she had heard from the older Indians.

"Glad to," she replied.

After dinner she began. "You know, until recently the Indians had no written language outside of their pictographs and petroglyphs. So a great many of the stories were handed down just through the telling of them.

"When the tribes went to war, mixed marriages usually occurred. The young people and their children adopted the customs of both tribes. So at times one finds a combination of cultures."

Nancy said, "Then the Basket Makers could have joined other peoples, who wove more intricate patterns on their products." Wanna said this was true.

"What were baskets made of besides grass?" Ned asked.

"Yucca and apocynum fibres. Later the people made sandals to protect their feet from rocks, heat, and the thorny cacti."

Wanna paused for a drink of water, then asked, "Do you know the story of the Great Drought?"

"No," Bess replied. "Only the story of the Great Flood."

The Indian girl smiled. "That was only forty days and forty nights of rain. The drought here lasted for several years. The Indians who settled nearby were farmers who grew thousands of bushels of corn each year. However, one year's supply would have to feed a whole community for perhaps three years. Without rain and with streams drying up, there was no crop, year after year."

"You mean there was no fresh food for the people?" Bess asked.

"That's right. Besides the loss of corn for eating, piñon nuts and berries dried up or didn't develop. The wild animals, too, were affected and went to look for fertile lands."

"What happened to the people?" George queried.

"Some died, I'm sure," Wanna replied. "But apparently most of them took their belongings and trudged off to find a new settlement along some stream." Wanna smiled. "Well, I guess you've heard enough legends about the ancient Indians."

"Oh, no!" Nancy exclaimed. "Please tell us some more."

"There's time for only one before siesta," the Indian girl said. "Thousands of years ago the people here declared that a white man had come down out of the sky, riding in a giant gourd. He was some kind of a god and promised to return again. So far he hasn't come, but——" Wanna grinned. "Maybe the modern aeroplane that travels here has taken the place of the flying gourd."

Ned chuckled. "The first flying machine!"

When Wanna concluded her story, everyone went to the tents to read or write. Nancy asked for another legend about the ancient Indians.

Wanna thought a moment, then said that turquoise beads seemed to have been part of the dress of Indians from the earliest times.

"I have a necklace that was given to me by a very old Indian woman."

Wanna opened her suitcase and pulled out a box, which contained an exquisite necklace made of turquoise and gold beads.

"I have had these beads carbon-dated," she said, "and they're probably five thousand years old."

George whistled. "Five thousand years old!"

"That's right," Wanna continued. "This necklace was given to me by an old Indian woman whose son fell into a deep, dry well. When they finally learned about the accident and pulled him out, he had died of starvation. But while he was still alive, he apparently found the beads and put them into a pocket.

"The old woman had made the necklace herself from the beads and I argued with her for wanting to part with anything so precious. However, she insisted that I take the necklace and wear it and keep it with me always."

All this time Nancy had been thinking and finally said, "It's possible that the well was at a level where the first Indians lived; in other words, the earliest of the four civilizations."

"It's an excellent guess," Wanna replied, smiling.

A wild idea popped into Nancy's mind. "Why don't we find the well, enlarge it, and go down there ourselves?"

The young Indian woman shook her head. "I'm sorry, but now no one knows where it is. A freak storm filled it up, and all efforts to clear it out have failed, according to my elderly friend. Now it is totally overgrown with vines and weeds."

Wanna went on to say, "I've had some wild ideas about that well myself. I believe the water came from a stream with a vein of gold alongside it. But the well was abandoned years ago, perhaps because of the boy's accident."

The Indian girl said that while she could not show the girls the actual well, she did want them to see something else.

"I believe I know where an underground stream supplies a small spring that is above ground.

"I think the underground stream runs through a mountain, but at one time no mountain was there. Over the centuries sand and dirt have blown across the area and formed a high covering over the stream."

Nancy was eager to see the place. "Maybe we can find clues to the treasure in the Forgotten City!" she said.

All this time, Wanna had been dangling the necklace in her hand. Now she laid it down on top of her suitcase. George, who was seated near her, reached across and idly picked it up. She decided to try on the necklace and was about to clasp it around her neck, when Wanna snatched it away.

"I wasn't going to hurt it," George said.

"It's not that," Wanna said more-or-less in a stage whisper. "You don't understand. No white woman must ever wear this! She will become violently ill!"

·13·

Tell-tale Wallet

QUICKLY George laid the turquoise-and-gold beaded necklace back on Wanna's suitcase.

She said, however, "I'm not the least bit superstitious. I'm sure nothing would happen to me if I wore the necklace, but tell me, why do you think so?"

The young Indian woman looked steadfastly at the girl. "I'm not superstitious either and I hated to believe the story. But twice I've let friends of mine wear it with nearly disastrous results."

Nancy spoke up. "What happened to them?"

Wanna told the girls that one of the friends had been in a bad car accident while wearing the necklace.

"The other one developed some strange blood disease, which several doctors could not diagnose even though they were specialists."

"Did your friend die?" Bess asked.

Wanna shook her head. "Fortunately, no, but she almost did. Since that time I've had more respect for the warning given me by the old woman who gave me the necklace. She said no one but an Indian should wear it."

George remarked that this was like having a curse on the necklace. "Such beliefs belong to witchcraft and things like that. Sensible people don't believe in all those signs and omens Man thinks up."

At that moment Archie stuck his head into the tent. "What you-all doing?" he asked.

"Come in," Wanna invited. She told the young man the story about the necklace.

"But," said George, "I can't believe it."

Archie looked at her almost pathetically. "My dear girl," he said, "as you get older you will learn that there are many unexplainable things in this world.

"Much of it has to do with objects that for one reason or another should not be touched by certain humans. In this case it happens to be white people, and that reminds me of Egypt. Have you ever heard of all the white people who became ill after they had dug into King Tut's tomb?"

Bess said no. The others remained silent.

Archie went on. "It seemed as if the boy king's tomb was never to be opened. But archaeologists thought otherwise and went in there. They brought out all sorts of objects that had been laid with the body. After a while every one of those white men became ill.

"Doctors were puzzled and came to the conclusion that germs can linger underground for thousands of years. I agree with Wanna that none of us white people should touch this necklace."

His listeners said nothing. Archie Arnow, having decided he had made his point, marched off pompously. Now the girls burst into laughter.

"Okay, Professor Archie," said George, "what are you going to do when we dig down among the Indian relics here? Are you going to tell us not to touch them?"

Wanna now laughed too. "You win," she said, "but

just to be safe, suppose I put this questionable necklace away where nobody can touch it." She hid the ancient jewellery in her suitcase, locked it, and kept the key.

The next morning Nancy took Ned aside. "Let's ask permission to visit the Valley of Fire. I can't wait to search for the missing tablets out there. I have a strong hunch they're hidden among the rocks."

Ned was eager to go and said he would find Professor Maguire and ask his permission. It was quickly granted, and the couple started off in Nancy's rented car.

When they reached the fantastic conglomeration of red rocks, they drove as close as possible to one section, then started to climb. The couple followed a trail but stopped every few minutes to exclaim over rock formations. It became a game between the two to see who could find the most unusual shapes.

"Here's one that looks like a rock cactus," Ned remarked. "And sitting on top of it is a big bumble-bee."

Nancy laughed. "You really have to use your imagination on that one."

A few minutes later, however, Ned grinned at one she pointed out.

"So you think that looks like a castle among the rocks with a moat round it." he chuckled. "If I stand up there alongside it, may I be the knight in shining armour?"

Nancy laughed and the two went on. They had carefully examined every crevice and hole to see if one of the valuable old tablets could have been hidden in it. They found none and went on, trudging up and down over the uneven paths.

After a while the couple sat down to rest. Ned leaned

back and in doing so his hand came in contact with a paper. Turning, he gently pulled it out of a hole.

"It's a comic book!" he exclaimed. "Why would anyone stuff this in here?"

Nancy answered, "No one is supposed to litter this spot, so what better place than this to hide something?"

She had been smiling. Now she became serious, got up, and peered into the hole herself. Nancy had learned not to put her bare hands into such places in case there were poisonous insects or reptiles of any kind resting within. She beamed her torch inside but could see nothing alive. A small object was lying at the back of the hole, however.

"I see something," she said, reaching in. Nancy pulled out a somewhat dilapidated wallet. In it was a small amount of money and two diamond rings! As she replaced them, Nancy turned the wallet over. On it were two initials: F. J. "Fleetfoot Joe!" she exclaimed. "What a find!"

Ned said he was sure the rings had been stolen. Fleetfoot had hidden the wallet here until he thought it would be safe to bring it out and sell the jewels.

Nancy agreed. For a few seconds she sat, lost in thought. Finally she said, "If this is one of Fleetfoot's hiding places, maybe one or more of the tablets is buried around here."

The two began a careful search. They scraped away loose sandstone and cleaned out crevices and indentations.

Suddenly Nancy cried out, "I think I've found one!"

The flat object, wrapped in a cellophane bag, had been wedged between two rocks.

Ned hurried to Nancy's side, and together they pul-

led the object from its cover. There was no question
that this was another one of the tablets. Nancy took her
magnifying glass from a pocket in her jeans and
examined the plaque.

"Here is the identifying mark in the lower left-hand
corner," she said. "The familiar chuckwalla symbol."

She handed Ned the magnifying glass. He was
intrigued with the petroglyphs on the tablet but could
not decipher them. He did, however, spot the same tiny
oblong symbol in the lower right-hand corner that they
had come to believe indicated the golden tablets.

As Nancy put the ancient plaque under her sweater
and was about to hunt for another matching one, Ned
suddenly said in a loud voice, "Run, because you
should be in the shade. Desert sunburns are deadly.
Any person being caught here is a target. Be on watch
for sunstroke."

For an instant Nancy was puzzled, since she was not
particularly hot and was wearing a big hat. Then,
suddenly, as she repeated the words in her mind, she
realized that this was a coded message to her.

It was saying, "You are being watch."

Without question she hurried along after him until
he stopped. He whispered, "A man suddenly appeared
up above us. I'm sure he was Fleetfoot!"

Nancy was aghast. Now that he knew she had the
tablet, the thief might attack both her and Ned! Then
what?

"We mustn't let him harm us," she told Ned, fearing
he might throw a large rock down on them. "And we
ought to take this tablet back to camp as fast as we
can."

There was a further whispered conversation. Ned felt

that they should not return to the car the same way they had come.

"But we have to get back to it in order to escape," Nancy reminded him.

Ned thought he had the rocky area pretty well figured out. "I believe there's a shortcut we can take. It may be rough, but I think we'd better try it."

The two scrambled off the path, over a series of jagged rocks, and came to another trail. They hurried along this in what they thought was the right direction.

Finally Nancy said, "I have a strange feeling we're going in the wrong direction."

"Then let's turn round," Ned suggested.

The two hurried on. The trail ended. They looked far below them but could see no sign of the car. Furthermore, they could not see Fleetfoot or anyone else.

"Ned," said Nancy, "don't you think we'd better keep going down? Eventually we'll come to the desert floor, and then maybe we can figure out how to get to the car."

"All right," he agreed.

The couple went on, first down, then up, then down again. At last they sat down to rest. They could see nothing around them but jagged red rocks.

Not a word was said for several minutes, but finally Ned spoke. "Nancy, I'm afraid we're hopelessly lost."

·14·

Hidden River

AFTER Ned announced that he and Nancy were lost in the Valley of Fire, the two stood up and looked around. They were silent for several minutes: each was trying to figure out which way would lead them out of this maze. Then they began to walk.

Finally, Nancy said, "I wonder if Fleetfoot is still around. He seemed to be familiar with this place and probably wouldn't get lost."

"But if he tried to follow us to get back the stone tablet you're carrying," Ned said, frowning, "he may not care how far we go. In the end he'll outwit us."

The two walked on. Long shadows began to creep across the landscape. The stranded couple did not want to spend the night in the Valley of Fire.

Nancy had just rounded another corner between two huge rock formations when she cried out, "The car! I see it!"

Ned looked too. The car was almost directly below them but far, far down. Both he and Nancy wondered how much they would have to slip and slide down the steep incline to reach it.

The two held hands, dug their heels into the sandy rock, and slowly went down in a zigzag course. They knew this had been the way Indians ascended and descended steep slopes.

"You all right?" Ned asked, as Nancy's right foot suddenly skidded under her.

He kept her from falling and she declared that the slip had meant nothing. At last, to their relief, they were able to jump down the last few feet to the desert floor.

"Thank goodness!" Ned murmured.

They hurried forward to the car. Nancy wanted to look at the tablet again but thought it might not be wise. Fleetfoot could be spying on the couple, even with binoculars.

"Let's get back to camp as soon as possible," Nancy suggested as Ned took the wheel.

"If you don't mind the bumps I can go over this flat desert as fast as you want. What do you say? One hundred or one hundred and fifty miles an hour?"

Nancy laughed and this broke the tension. They stopped worrying about Fleetfoot and realized how lucky they had been to find the tablet.

"Only five more to go," Nancy said.

Ned groaned. "Only five?"

Barely three minutes had gone by when he and Nancy saw the bobbing lights of a car coming towards them.

"Oh I hope it's not that thief!" Nancy said, worried.

The other car began to blow its horn incessantly. Was this a signal for Nancy and Ned to stop?

"Don't stop!" Nancy begged.

Ned was debating whether or not he should shoot past the other car when his own headlights picked up the licence plate of the oncoming car.

"It's one of the camp cars!" he said.

Nancy was sure it was a rescue party and knew the rescuers must be Bess, George, Burt, and Dave.

"Am I glad to see you're safe!" Bess exclaimed, as the vehicles pulled up side-by-side. "You had us worried sick!"

"Sorry," Nancy said. "We got lost!"

The three couples sat and talked from the windows of their cars.

"Did you have any luck?" George asked.

"I'll say," Ned replied. "Nancy found one of the missing plaques."

"Honestly?" George burst out. "Heavens! You're really getting ahead of that thief Fleetfoot, Nancy."

"But wait until you hear the rest of the story," Ned said. He quickly brought the other four up to date on what had happened in the Valley of Fire.

"Some adventure!" Burt remarked. "Well, we'll follow you back to camp."

The person most delighted over Nancy's find was Wanna. She looked at the tablet, trying to decide what the petroglyphs meant.

Presently she said excitedly, "I believe these pictures prove my theory that there is an underground river with gold nuggets on its shores."

Nancy said she could hardly wait to start a search for the stream.

Dinner that evening had been delayed because of the camp's worry over Nancy and Ned. But now everyone gathered for the outdoor get-together.

Each camper was given a large metal frying pan with wooden handles, and the delicious hot meal was put into this.

Afterwards there was singing and guitar playing.

Archie was in the front row, making wise-cracks and telling some corny jokes. Nancy's group had to admit, nevertheless, that the young man had a very good singing voice.

"He ought to stick to singing," Burt remarked, "and not try to tell jokes."

When the concert was over, Bess said to Nancy, "I'm terribly worried about your having the tablet. Suppose Fleetfoot or one of his buddies comes in here and takes it!"

Ned overheard her. He answered the question. "Don't worry. Several of the boys brought good watch-dogs along. They'll take care of any prowlers." Bess felt better.

Her thought made Nancy decide to produce a faithful drawing of the petroglyphs on the plaque she had found. Then she asked George to walk with her to the kitchen unit.

"There's always someone on duty there, and I think they'll let me hide this tablet behind some of the food, where it won't be noticed."

The chef, who was just tidying up, was glad to have his place used for the hidden treasure. "Don't you worry about a thing, Nancy," he said. "I'll be like a watchdog around here."

It seemed to be no more than a few minutes between the time the girls said goodnight to one another and the time the alarm went off at five in the morning. Nancy, George, Wanna, and the two Nevada girls yawned but got out of bed. Bess merely turned over.

"Bess Marvin," said George, "you'll have to get up. We have work ahead of us."

Bess grunted. "Why do I have to get up so early?"

George told her that if she did not, she would be left alone all day. Did she want that? The thought made Bess climb out of bed instantly.

Professor Maguire, the students from the University of Nevada, and all the Emerson boys except Ned, Burt, and Dave, had already chosen a site at which to start digging. Wanna had received permission to take Nancy's group to another location. Bess and Dave borrowed a small sports model and would follow the others.

Nancy's car was crowded, with five people and all their working equipment. "I sure hope we don't get a flat tyre!" Ned said.

Wanna directed the young man straight across the desert, which was only reasonably smooth for driving. The bumps set them all laughing, and made the journey seem shorter.

"We stop here," the young Indian student said a little later. "We'll walk down this hill to a water hole, which the Indians say is a spring bubbling up."

When they reached the spot, Wanna pointed out what appeared to be no more than a pool of water that came out of the mountain and ran back into it on the other side.

Wanna saw the looks of disappointment on the faces of her friends. "You expected more, I know," she said, smiling. "I believe that at one time this was a tributary of the Muddy River. By the way, now it's called the Moapa River after the small tribe of Indians that live nearby.

"I haven't quite figured out just what happened. Perhaps there was a great landslide, and the only spot where the water bubbled to the surface was right here.

But that wouldn't have been enough for maybe a thousand people. So they moved out."

Nancy asked, "Do you think the Indians needed water badly and might have tried to tunnel into the river so it wouldn't stop running?"

"It's a fascinating idea, Nancy," Wanna replied. "Maybe someday we can find out. One thing I do know is that the well where the poor young man lost his life is very close."

"Let's not stand around talking any longer," Ned suggested. "Come on, fellows, we'll bring the tools down from the car and see if we can unearth this stream with the hidden gold plates."

As work started a few minutes later, Nancy reminded the others that they were not to dig fast and furiously.

"Remember," she said, "we are to take a shovelful at a time and put it through a sieve."

There was complete silence for a while. Bess sat down to work with a sieve, since her ankle ached a little, while Dave carried shovelfuls of earth for her to sift.

An hour went by. Each one in the group hoped to find some ancient treasure, but so far nothing had turned up.

Nancy walked over to Bess and dropped to the ground beside her. "Would you rather go back to the car and rest?" she asked.

"No, no," Bess replied, "but what I think I will do is lie back and relax for a while."

Nancy stayed there and took up one shovelful after another of the soil. No interesting items showed up. She kept digging deeper. In a little while the young sleuth reached a very wet place. Was this part of an underground river?

She called to Wanna, who came over. The geologist immediately became excited.

"Nancy, I think you've figured out the direction of the underground stream. Apparently it wasn't straight."

As she was speaking, Nancy dug up another shovelful of sandy dirt. She put it into the sieve and began to shake the contents.

"Oh, I've come across something!" she exclaimed.

Nancy picked up a small round object and cleaned it off as best she could in the muddy water.

"It's a turquoise bead!" she cried out. "Exactly like those in your necklace, Wanna!"

Before Wanna could pick up the gem, Bess screamed. "Nancy, throw that bead away! Throw it away! That's bad luck!"

·15·

Gold!

AT Bess's frantic request, Nancy laid the turquoise bead on the ground. Now she looked towards Wanna and asked her if she believed the lovely little light-blue gem would harm her.

The young Indian geologist smiled. "No, I think not. Keep it."

As Nancy slipped the turquoise into her pocket, Bess set her lips primly. She said nothing but Nancy knew she was worried.

"Please don't panic, Bess," she said. "At the first sign of my becoming ill or acting strangely, you take the turquoise away from me."

"I don't want it!" Bess said firmly.

The others laughed and finally Bess's dimpled cheeks broke into a grin. "You win," she said.

The little group of young archaeologists continued to work industriously for some time before anything else was found.

George sighed. "This is becoming monotonous. If I could only find a piece of a bowl or an arrowhead or something, it would be more exciting."

Wanna looked at her. "Archaeologists must develop an unbelievable amount of patience. They sometimes work for weeks before making a discovery."

There was silence again for some time. Suddenly it was broken by Bess, who gave a loud squeal of delight. "Here's a real treasure!" she exclaimed.

Her shovel had brought up a small clay doll, which had broken into several pieces.

"You're lucky," Dave remarked. "If you like I'll help you put it together."

"Thanks a million," Bess told him.

The two carefully worked on the doll as if it were a jigsaw puzzle. Finally they figured out exactly how to put it together. Only one small piece was missing.

"Suppose you hunt for that little piece," said Dave, 'while I go for the cement. It's up in the car."

While he scrambled up the hill, Bess took a sieve and carefully put the remaining dirt from the shovel into it. The missing piece was not there.

"Too bad," Wanna remarked. Then she smiled. 'Maybe it will make the clay doll look more authentic."

Dave returned in a little while with a tube of plastic cement and half an hour later the ancient doll had been repaired.

Nancy had been looking on. Now she said, "Since the doll was not buried very deep, it probably belongs to the fourth, or top, layer of civilization here—the people who lived in pit houses."

Wanna nodded. "I'm sure you're right. Bess, you may have the honour of presenting it to the museum. The curator and the state will certainly be thrilled."

Bess would have liked to keep her interesting souvenir, but she knew this was against the rules. She must turn it in.

Meanwhile the other searchers had been concentrating on digging straight down, with the hope of eventually finding the underground river. By now the hole was fairly deep.

Nancy looked at her watch. "Time for a mid-morning snack," she called out.

Everyone was glad to stop work in the terrific heat. At that moment Ned and Burt, suspended on ropes, were down in the hole, working.

"It's much cooler down here," Ned called up. "How about sending something down?"

"No," Nancy said. "Our instructions were to stop work at a certain time. We must eat and rest a while."

Reluctantly the two boys pulled themselves up. Everyone sat down while Nancy passed around the food the chef had packed for them.

George served the cold drinks. As she walked round, she began chanting:

> Time to rest and eat
> In 102 degrees,
> Oh where is there a place
> Where I can slowly freeze?

The others laughed, and Burt suggested that the next archaeological dig she went on had better be at the North Pole.

All of them found that it was getting hotter, and they wondered how long they could stand it. While they were discussing this, the group suddenly became aware of a low roaring sound.

"What is that?" Bess asked quickly. It was evident she was nervous.

The sound grew louder. Then, before anyone had a chance to run, a geyser of water gushed from the hole where the boys had been digging! The force of the water soaked the young people and knocked some of them down. The others scattered.

The water continued to gush from the hole. Everyone was wet but uninjured.

As suddenly as it had shot up, the stream subsided. Not another drop came from the big hole.

"Thank goodness Nancy made us come topside," Ned remarked to Burt.

"Yes, we'd have shot into the air like a couple of rubber clowns," Burt replied.

"That geyser was the strangest thing I ever saw," George commented. "Wanna, what's the explanation for such a phenomenon?"

The geologist said there could be several explanations, but the one she favoured was that the geyser had come from the underground river. Something had given it great impetus. The stream must have found an opening, and the force behind it had sent the water shooting into the air.

"Now that force is gone," she said. "It's my guess the river is continuing to run along peacefully."

Nancy wondered if such a geyser had ever erupted down at the water-hole. Perhaps this was how it had been formed in the first place. Everyone in the group continued to talk for some time about the strange phenomenon.

Then George remarked, "You know I was singing about giving me a place to freeze. That geyser was like ice water, but it sure felt good."

In the heat not only their clothes but also the terrain

dried up in a very short time indeed.

"I'd like to go down to the bottom of that hole and investigate," Ned said.

There was a short discussion about this. Some thought it was too dangerous. There might be a cave-in, or another geyser might shoot up.

Ned laughed. "Let's take a vote! Everybody in favour of my going, put up a hand!"

Bess and Dave did not raise theirs, but they were the only ones who were opposed. Ned was tied securely, and the other boys held the rope to help him descend slowly. George grabbed the end of it to lend extra strength if necessary.

Ned reported that while the sides of the hole were muddy and it grew narrower, he could see the bottom with his powerful torch.

"It looks like water down there all right," he said.

For several minutes there was no report, and the two holding the rope began to wonder if everything was all right.

Finally Burt called down, "You okay?"

There was a muffled answer of "Yes, I'm okay. This is some hole."

Less than a minute later, there was a tug on the rope, and slowly Dave and George pulled Ned to the surface. He was a sight, and the others began to laugh. Ned was covered from head to foot with mud.

He ignored the laughter and said, "He who laughs last laughs best. This time I have the last laugh. Look here!"

Ned held up a gold nugget.

Now everyone became excited. Ned said he was sure that he had reached the underground river. "Digging along its banks may reveal an ancient Indian village—the Forgotten City."

Nancy's eyes were shining with excitement as she added, "And eventually the golden sheets!"

Wanna was happy too. But she was less demonstrative.

"We mustn't allow ourselves to be disappointed if we're wrong," she said, "even though I want to believe this fairy tale as much as you do."

Nancy advised that the group keep the whole matter a secret. "I'm afraid if the story leaks out, we'll be overrun with gold seekers!"

The others agreed.

Bess giggled. "Cross my heart!"

At this point the group became aware of a motor. They were surprised and looked up. Coming down the slope was a beach buggy.

"That must be Archie," said Ned. "He brought one of those along. Well, I'd better get down to that waterhole and clean up a bit so he won't ask too many questions."

Ned scooted off, and a few minutes later Archie arrived. He stopped a short distance beyond the hole and jumped out.

"Well, I must congratulate you all," he said pompously. "This looks like a lot of work. How did you get so much done in a short time?"

George spoke up. "Oh, haven't you heard about the wizards of Emerson and River Heights?"

"Now what kind of an answer is that?" Archie demanded. "I'm part of this expedition. I have a right to know what's going on. Did you find anything?"

Bess dimpled and squinted her eyes at him. In a

childish voice she asked, "Would little Archie like a baby doll to play with?"

The young man was furious. "I don't deserve such sarcasm," he said pettishly. "By the way, where's Ned?"

Burt answered. "Oh, he has gone to the Roman baths."

This remark was too much for Archie. "I'm leaving," he said.

In his anger he put his beach buggy into reverse gear and shot backwards. The car backed into the hole!

·16·

A Skeleton Dance

FORTUNATELY the beach buggy was too wide to fall into the hole. The rear end had gone down but it hit the wall beyond, and the vehicle now hung over the rim.

After Archie's first look of fright and surprise, he shouted, "Get me out of here!"

"With pleasure," said George, walking up and offering him her hand.

He ignored it and got out of the vehicle himself, then surveyed the buggy bitterly.

Finally he said in a more conciliatory voice, "Come on, fellows. Give me a hand. See if we can push this thing over the edge."

Nancy suggested that they tie several ropes to the front bumper. "Some of us can pull, the others push."

"Okay," Archie agreed, then stood still, doing nothing.

The others tied the ropes, then Burt suggested that Archie go to the rear and push as hard as he could with him.

"Wanna and the girls can pull the buggy from the front."

This strategy worked, and in a few minutes the beach buggy was safe again.

Archie climbed in and started the motor. "It works!" he said. "Thanks a lot, kids. See you at camp."

The others were glad he was leaving but to be sure he would not be alone should his vehicle get stuck, Burt offered to go back with him.

Ned returned from his clean-up job. Since it was time to go back for lunch and siesta period, the diggers gathered up their tools and other paraphernalia. They carried them up to the car.

When they reached camp, Wanna suggested that she and the girls go on to the museum and hand over the clay doll. Ned and Dave said they would see them later.

When the Indian geologist and the girls reached the Lost City Museum, the curator greeted them with a big smile. "I can tell from your outfits that you have been working. Any luck?"

Proudly, Bess opened a case in which she had been carrying the clay doll she had found and mended with Dave's help.

The man blinked. "You found this?" he asked.

"Yes, I did," Bess answered. "There were several pieces. We couldn't find the one that belonged in here." She pointed out the hole in one of the doll's arms.

"It was probably crushed underfoot," the curator stated. "But it hardly shows."

He accepted the doll with thanks, saying the state of Nevada would be very happy to receive this.

"Incidentally," he said, "you did a great job of mending this. Very professional looking. It is perfect."

Bess beamed happily, then she said, "We made a great discovery. I don't know whether Nancy wants to tell about it or not. We're trying to keep it a secret."

"Yes, we are," Nancy told him. She laughed. "But I

think it's safe to tell you about it. We just don't want a lot of gold seekers coming to the place where we're working. One of the boys actually found a gold nugget way down underground."

"What!"

"That's right," Wanna spoke up. "As you know I have some pet theories concerning the desert. The students seem to be proving that my ideas are correct."

"That's wonderful!" the curator said. "Do you want to divulge any more?"

Nancy told him about the morning's adventures and the finding of the turquoise bead.

"But the greatest thing of all was the geyser." As the man's eyes opened wider and wider in astonishment, she went on to describe it.

"This is amazing," he said. "Why, you know, we might even be able to make this valley fertile again!"

At the remark George grinned. "And bring back American elephants and camels and maybe even giant sloths."

"Oh stop!" Bess begged.

The others laughed and Wanna said, "All joking aside, if we could have a river running through this desert, it wouldn't take long before it became a good place to live."

She and the girls said goodbye to the curator and drove back to camp. The cool quarters and hearty lunch were a welcome change for Nancy and her friends.

Afterwards the other group of diggers displayed some of their finds. They had uncovered many arrowheads, some stone mallets, and a highly polished cylindrical stone about two inches thick.

Professor Maguire said, "I believe this was a rolling pin, which the squaws used to crush corn into flour."

"What a weapon to use on an enemy!" George remarked.

Nancy picked up the stone. "Um, heavy," she said, putting it down quickly. Then she tried rolling it. "In ancient times it seems to me people always did things the hard way."

"They had to use what was at hand," the professor told her.

At four o'clock that afternoon Nancy and her friends were ready to start out again. They could hardly wait to continue their work. Everyone hoped there would be no more visitors. Archie, meanwhile, had told the whole camp about the opening where Nancy's group was digging.

It was decided that the first thing she and her friends would do would be to enlarge the hole near the lower end. The diggers would take turns going down on the ropes, two at a time. For a while they turned up only pieces of broken pottery and stone axes.

"This must have been a well-populated area at one time," Ned remarked to Nancy, who was his partner.

The young sleuth did not reply, for at that moment a trowel she was using hit something solid. Hoping it was a valuable piece and not just a rock, Nancy carefully worked around it. She turned her torch full upon the spot.

Then she exclaimed, "Ned, this is a bone of some sort!"

"Are you sure?" he asked as he moved himself to a position alongside her. The two worked in silence and as quickly as they dared. In a little while an elbow began to protrude from the sand, soil, and rock formation.

Ned whistled. "A human bone! What a find!"

Nancy's heart was thumping. She had never been more excited in her life.

"I wonder how much of this skeleton is here and how we're ever going to get it out."

Ned admitted that they would need help. Apparently the skeleton, if it was all there, lay beside the hole.

Up to now, the small amount of dirt they had dug had fallen down into the stream below and had been partially carried away by the water. For further digging they probably would have to remove a good bit of earth. Should it be dropped down?

Nancy suggested that they try to trace any bones they could locate without digging. This worked for a few minutes.

Nancy uncovered a hand, which had fallen from the wrist. Ned got up as far as the skeleton's shoulder and found that at the joint it was loose from the upper arm.

"I guess there are several pieces," Ned remarked. "We'd better get buckets and more help."

Nancy agreed. She and Ned pulled themselves to the surface and told the others what they had found.

"We'd like to see if we can find the whole skeleton," she added.

Bess said she could not believe such a fantastic find. "It's utterly magnificent!" she exclaimed.

Ned said he would suggest that they take an extra rope down, to which the buckets could be tied. The dirt he and Nancy took out from around the bones would be put into the buckets rather than dropped below. The buckets could be hauled up and the earth dumped

Burt said, "You don't know how deep into the side of the mountain you may have to go. Why don't we take turns digging?"

"That's a good idea," Nancy agreed. "It's hard hanging in that rope-sling and reaching in to dig out the dirt around the skeleton. The earth is packed solid."

Wanna offered to be one of the first to go down. She was eager to see how far above the water the skeleton lay. This might tell her which civilization it might have belonged to. She and Burt were the next two down.

The others took the buckets of dirt as they came up, and carefully spread the contents on the ground. While waiting for each bucket, they carefully examined the sandy soil for more relics.

None were found, but Burt called out that he was coming topside and bringing part of the skeleton with him. He appeared with an arm, though it was in three pieces.

The next time Dave went down and Wanna came up. George took a turn. They had found the left leg, which was also in pieces.

The work continued for a couple of hours until finally a complete skeleton had been unearthed. It proved to be that of a man. Wanna said she believed he was young and she judged from an indentation in the skull that he had been killed by a spear.

"Ugh!" said Bess, who secretly was glad that her ankle would not permit her to go down into the hole.

She liked the artifacts, but abhorred the idea of finding the skeleton of someone who had lived long, long ago.

"Let's wire this man together," Burt suggested. "I'd like to take him back to camp in one piece. Later the curator can do a better job."

Dave ran up to the car to find the proper drilling tools and the wire. When he returned, everyone in the group started putting the prehistoric skeleton together. When it was complete, Burt held it up.

"He was very short," Bess remarked.

Wanna said, "Most of the Indians in this area were short."

Burt began to jiggle the skeleton and make him dance. The others laughed.

Dave said, "I have an idea. Tonight the whole camp is to have a meeting around a campfire. How about our putting on a spook show?"

He outlined his plan.

"We'll all stay in the background. Then just as the meeting finishes, we'll make queer sounds. Burt, wrapped in a blanket, will come in, holding the skeleton and making it dance."

When Burt agreed, Dave whispered something to him and the other boy nodded and smiled.

Later, at the right moment, Nancy's group made low, moaning, crying sounds. Everyone round the fire looked startled. Then Burt stepped forward, intoning weirdly. He made the skeleton dance, then said in a deep voice: "I am from another civilization. Do not disturb my sleep!"

The whole audience burst into laughter.

At that moment Nancy suddenly felt a strong arm around her waist and a big hand was clapped over her mouth. Before she could resist, the girl detective felt herself being dragged away!

·17·

A Capture

FLAILING her arms and struggling to free herself, Nancy tried hard to loosen the grip of her abductor. Presently she realized that he was powerful and she could not fight him physically. She would have to outwit him.

. "I must do something and do it quick!" she decided.

An idea that had worked before came to Nancy. In a few seconds she went absolutely limp, as if she had fainted. In surprise her captor nearly dropped the young sleuth and relaxed his hold on her.

The ruse had worked! Instantly Nancy was free, and she started to run back towards the rest of her group.

"Help! Help!" she yelled.

Her captor, realizing he had been outwitted, began to run. Several of the boys raced after him. One lanky youth from Emerson College, who was a star track man, soon caught up with the fleeing abductor. He brought him down with a resounding thud.

Within seconds the other boys reached them and pulled the suspect back to camp. Nancy and her friends crowded around.

"Fleetfoot!" cried Nancy.

The man looked at her with hatred in his eyes, but he would not give up so easily.

"You can't hold me!" he roared. "I haven't done anything!"

Nancy gazed at him scornfully. "What do you call abduction? It's a federal offence. I think we had better call the police."

Fleetfoot now took another tack. With a forced smile, he said, "I wasn't going to harm you, miss. I just wanted to tell you to stay out of my territory."

Nancy did not comment. Instead she asked, "Where are the rest of Mrs Wabash's stone tablets?"

There was no answer.

"Okay," Nancy said. "If you won't talk, we'll take you to the police. There's a warrant out for your arrest back in River Heights, and the Las Vegas police have been alerted to find you."

Fleetfoot looked surprised. He knew he was cornered and said, "Why don't we strike up a little bargain? If you promise not to have me arrested, I'll tell you where the rest of the tablets are."

Nancy told him she had no control over what the police might do, even if she didn't turn him in. "So it's no use trying to evade the law," she added.

Again Fleetfoot seemed to be thinking about what to say next. To everyone's surprise he blurted out, "Mrs Wabash has the tablets!"

Suddenly a voice behind them in the darkness called out, "That's not true!"

A young Indian woman stepped forward. Wanna Antler!

She turned towards Nancy and said, "A little while ago I went to the kitchen and used the shortwave telephone to call Mrs Wabash. She said one tablet had been brought to her by a man who was not Fleetfoot and had offered to sell it.

"The price was pretty high, but she decided to buy it. Mrs Wabash recognized the tablet."

Bess exclaimed, "She bought something that actually belonged to her?"

Professor Maguire now stepped forward. "I think the sooner the police have this man in custody the safer we all will be. I'll call them at once."

Nancy whispered to him, "Fleetfoot is a slick person. Don't you think we should tie him up and put a guard over him until the police get here?"

The professor smiled. "I think it would be a very good idea."

While the boys tied up Fleetfoot, Wanna took Nancy's arm and they walked off together.

"I have a surprise for you," the Indian girl said. "The tablet Mrs Wabash bought was the copy you made!"

Nancy was amazed. "Evidently Fleetfoot and his buddies didn't recognize it as a forgery," she said, smiling. "Otherwise I'm sure Fleetfoot would have blurted out the truth."

"What about the rest of the tablets?" Nancy asked.

Wanna replied, "Mrs Wabash said that the caller had promised to return and bring them if she would pay the high price he wanted. Knowing their value, she agreed, but so far the man hasn't returned."

"It's my hunch," Nancy said, "that this man is a buddy of Fleetfoot's, and Fleetfoot isn't giving them up that easily. I'm sure if he gives them up at all, it will be only after he has had copies or drawings made. He'll sell them to Mrs Wabash one by one."

Wanna nodded in agreement. By this time she and

Nancy had reached their tent and were soon ready for bed.

Nancy was very happy at the turn of events. Not only had she uncovered something valuable for the dig, but she had helped to capture a wanted thief and was one step closer to solving the mystery of the valuable stone tablets, the golden plates, and the location of the Forgotten City.

She consulted Wanna, Bess, and George, asking if they didn't think it would be wise to go back to the Mouse's Tank and the Valley of Fire to make a more thorough search for the missing tablets.

"I do!" George called out.

"Yes," Bess echoed, yawning.

"Count me in," Wanna added.

The following morning Nancy asked Professor Maguire to go along with her group. He consented eagerly.

They started off in two cars. The professor rode with Wanna, Nancy, and Ned.

He said, "Suppose you call me Don. All year long I'm addressed as professor and it would be a relief to hear my own name."

"All right, Don," the others said.

When they approached the Valley of Fire area, Nancy said, "Let's start at the Mouse's Tank. We can separate and look inside and outside for anything Fleetfoot may have buried."

They reached the place so early that there were no tourists at the site. They examined the ground for recent digging and flashed their lights over every inch of the cave, but found nothing suspicious.

"I guess," said Nancy, "that if Fleetfoot had anything hidden here, he took it away after he saw Bess, George, and me."

They joined those in the other car, and together the eight went to investigate possible hiding places for the tablets in the Valley of Fire.

Nancy grinned and said to the other half of her party, "We've lost our professor temporarily. Meet Don, everybody."

They all laughed, and to make the change of name official, Bess, George, Burt, and Dave shook hands with Don.

Bess spoke up. "I'm glad you asked us to call you Don," she said. "I feel much more comfortable now. Professors always scare me!"

The others laughed, then Don said, "Where does the lady sleuth want us to start?"

Nancy suggested that they search in pairs. She handed out a whistle to each couple. "Every ten minutes I suggest we blow the whistles to be sure everyone is all right.

"Ned and I will be first to whistle, then George and Burt should answer, next Bess and Dave, and finally Wanna and Don."

They started up one of the trails, each searcher looking carefully in every crevice and depression for the missing tablets. Nothing was found, and in a few minutes the group separated, each pair taking a different route.

Nancy's imagination conjured up all sorts of ossified prehistoric animals. She pointed them out to Ned, who was amused.

"Yes," he said at one point, "if I concentrate real hard I can figure that the formation ahead was once a white polar bear turned red."

Nancy knew she was being teased and continued her search for the stolen tablets. Suddenly it occurred to her to glance at her wristwatch. Fifteen minutes had gone by.

"It's time for us to signal," she told Ned. "Would you like to blast a real long sound on the whistle?"

He put the whistle to his lips, and the shrill sound it emitted made Nancy put her hands over her ears.

A few seconds later they heard a blast from another whistle. Several seconds later there was a third. The couple listened for the fourth whistle. They heard nothing.

"That's strange," Nancy remarked. "Maybe Wanna and Don didn't understand. Let's try again."

The signal was repeated, but only two more whistles were blown. Nancy's forehead puckered. "I hope this doesn't mean Wanna and Don ran into trouble."

Still, there was no response from the missing couple.

"Ned, sound long, short, long on the whistle." This was a signal for the group to meet. "We should get together and start a hunt for the fourth couple."

This was done, and in a few minutes Bess, Dave, Burt, and George had joined Ned and Nancy.

"What's up?" Burt asked.

"You didn't hear a fourth whistle, did you?" Nancy asked.

The two couples shook their heads.

"Then we must start a hunt for Wanna and Don."

They looked round until Nancy spied Don helping Wanna climb a steep incline.

"Are you all right?" Nancy called down. "You didn't answer our signal."

Wanna replied, "Sorry. We didn't hear it. But come down here. We have a wonderful surprise for you!"

·18·

Surprise Gift

RELIEVED that the missing couple were all right, Nancy and her friends followed them down the rocky slope. At the foot of it was a deep recess.

"Here it is," said Wanna. She pulled out a package.

Nancy's eyes glistened. "Don't tell me——"

Wanna and Don smiled, and the young Indian woman said, "Yes it is—another one of the missing tablets. I'm sure."

She unwrapped the object, and Nancy looked at it eagerly.

"This certainly looks like the others," she said.

Taking her magnifying glass from a pocket, she trained it on the left- and right-hand corners of the stone tablet.

"This is one of the missing pieces, all right," she said. "Here's the chuckwalla in the left-hand corner, and in the right——" She stopped speaking.

The others waited for an explanation. Finally Bess asked, "Did you find something else?"

Nancy said she had a new theory about the markings in the right-hand corner. She wondered all along if there were some way of indicating the order in which the tablets should be placed to give a continuous story.

"This may be a wild theory," she said at last, "but I believe that the moon was used as a way of discerning how this puzzle worked. Seven phases could have been used. The new moon was number one. Number four was probably the full moon and five and six the waning moon."

Nancy's friends were used to her logical deductions, but Wanna and Don stared at the girl in amazement.

"That's very clever," Don remarked. "Which tablet do you think this one is?"

Nancy's guess was number three, the one just before the full moon.

"The mark on this part of each tablet is so faint, it's really difficult to decide what it was meant to be. But the petroglyphs on the three tablets I've seen so far are similar to the way we picture phases of the moon."

Everyone in the group wondered if more of the tablets might be hidden in this niche in the rocks. They hunted inside it and all around the area. Finally they gave up, sure that there was nothing more in that particular spot.

"I wish we could find Mrs Wabash's stolen dictionary," Nancy said.

"What do you make of this tablet?" Ned asked her.

She studied it for a minute, then replied, "Possibly it's the one right next to the tablet that wasn't stolen from Mrs Wabash. As I recall, that one had a full circle pictured on it, which could mean the full moon.

"A large group of people definitely trekked into this area and settled here. Then something happened and many of them died. Perhaps it was a war or a drought or some epidemic."

"But they didn't all die," Bess spoke up.

"I think not," Nancy replied, "but they probably fled from here."

She asked Don which of the four civilizations he thought had made the plaque.

"I believe every tablet will have to be carbon-dated to find out its age. The only thing certain is that all of them came from a peculiar sandstone type of rock in this area."

Dave noted that it was getting very hot. "And that means we should go back to camp and cool off."

Bess said she would be glad to get off her feet. "My ankle hurts a little," she admitted. "Maybe I won't join you this afternoon."

Nancy nodded. "It's a good idea. Why don't you spend most of the time lying down and reading?"

"I think I will."

They all returned to their cars and rode off. When they reached camp, the searchers found it buzzing with excitement. Many diggers had been lucky that morning, finding various artifacts. Now they proudly displayed them.

"Oh, see these beautiful shells!" Wanna remarked. "It's unusual to find them in the desert. I wonder if these could have been brought here from the coast by visiting or warring Indians."

Don had a different idea. "I am pretty well convinced that at one time what is now an underground river was aboveground. Wouldn't there have been all sorts of little creatures with shells in the water?"

Like so many of the questions that had been brought up in connection with the Forgotten City this one also had to go unanswered for the present.

Nancy and Ned had walked over to one of the

Nevada students. He was proudly displaying an ancient pipe. It was cylindrical in shape and had a hole in the middle.

"Not a very interesting way to smoke," Ned remarked. He picked it up. "This weighs a ton!"

The student said he wondered just how the ancient Indians used the pipe. "I understand they didn't smoke for pleasure, just for ceremonials. When two warring factions finally declared a truce, the elders of the tribe would gather round a pile of burning tobacco. Then each man would suck the smoke up through the stem of his own pipe."

Nancy recalled having heard that later generations of Indians had stopped wandering round as hunters and had become farmers.

"This gave them more leisure time, and they developed religious customs. The men had secret meetings down in great pits, which were called *kivas*. Smoking was part of their ceremonies."

As the campers were finishing their mid-day meal, someone called out, "Visitors for Nancy Drew!"

Nancy was surprised. Who could be calling on her? She hurried outside the tent. One of the Nevada girls pointed to a car standing nearby.

"There they are," she said.

Nancy walked over to it. The car was large and flashy. The couple inside were gaudily dressed, which seemed out of place in this desert landscape.

"You're Nancy Drew?" the man asked. When she nodded, he went on, "We're Mr and Mrs Horace Greene from Los Angeles. We've been spending a little time in Las Vegas and——"

His wife interrupted. "Nancy, it's very hot out there.

Please get into the back seat, where it's cool, so we can talk to you."

Nancy climbed in. The car was cool. It made her sneeze several times.

"Oh, I'm sorry," said Mrs Greene. "Horace and I don't mind the cold, but we positively cannot stand the heat!"

Nancy wondered who the couple were. Beyond the fact that they evidently had a great deal of money, she could not figure out anything about them.

Mr Greene seemed inclined to talk about the heat, the long drive, and his annoyance that he could not play golf.

Finally his wife interrupted him. "Why don't you show Miss Drew what you came here to talk to her about?"

"Oh yes, yes," he said. "Well, a man walked into our hotel. He said he was from the University of Nevada Museum. They had too many artifacts there and he had been given special permission to sell some of them."

Mr Greene paused and began to unwrap a box that lay on the front seat between the couple.

Mrs Greene turned around to face Nancy. "Horace paid a horribly big sum of money for this thing. But we just felt we couldn't pass it up."

By this time her husband had the box open. He unwrapped the object inside. Nancy stared at it in astonishment.

Another one of the missing tablets!

"Queer looking, isn't it?" Mr Greene asked Nancy. "We drove over to the Lost City Museum to find out what it said. The curator there couldn't tell us much, but he suggested that we come out here and find you. My, you look so young, Miss Drew. Are you a special student in this kind of work?"

Nancy took the tablet and looked at it carefully. There was no doubt in her mind but that this was one of the original collection of six stolen from Mrs Wabash.

She looked up and asked, "You say that the man who sold this was from the University of Nevada Museum?"

"That's what he said," Mrs Greene replied. "The way you ask that question sounds as if you don't believe it."

"No, I don't," Nancy replied. "I'm sorry to have to say this, but you have purchased stolen property. It belongs to a woman I know."

"What!" Mrs Greene shrieked.

Her husband asked, "How do you know this?"

Without going into too much detail, Nancy told the couple how she happened to become interested in the case and actually had helped to capture the thief, who was now in jail.

"I believe he's in Las Vegas. If you'd like me to, I can verify my story."

"Oh, I believe you," Mr Greene said, "but I am shocked to think that I was taken in so easily."

Suddenly Mrs Greene threw the box and papers on to the back seat with Nancy. "Horace, don't you have another thing to do with that! We've bought stolen property! We're liable!"

Nancy gathered that Mr Greene was used to taking orders from his wife and that he would now follow her advice.

He said to Nancy, "You know who the rightful owner is. Will you please give this to her? We want nothing more to do with it. Please wrap this up and take it. We will drive off at once."

Nancy was stunned by the announcement, but she made no protest. Quickly she got out of the car, taking the tablet, the box, and the wrapping paper with her. Mr Greene backed up, turned the car, and sped off across the desert.

Nancy stood looking after the Greenes. What an amazing way to receive stolen property! When she joined her friends and told them the story, they were perplexed.

"You're sure," George spoke up, "that this plaque is one of the set?"

Nancy laughed. "You think I might have been fooled and this is a clever copy? But remember, I didn't pay anything for it!"

After lunch Wanna and Don joined Nancy and her friends and gazed at the tablet. Nancy pointed out that it was almost entirely covered with wild animals, large and small, all the way from the giant sloth to the little chip fox.

She turned to Ned. "I think we should return our two tablets to Mrs Wabash immediately. Want to go to town with me? And how about anyone else?"

Burt and George decided to go. "You may need my judo protection in case of a hold-up," George stated, grinning.

"We'll go in the daylight so it won't be so risky," Nancy replied. "But I'd love to have you along."

The four set off in Nancy's rented car. They reached Mrs Wabash's house without incident at five o'clock. She was overjoyed to receive the tablets and kept reiterating how amazing the whole story was

"You're going to so much trouble for me," she told the young people. "I never could repay you."

Nancy smiled. "Let's just say that if we can be of use to our country by uncovering the secrets of the past, that will be a great big reward for us."

"Oh bless you!" the Indian woman said. "I'm sure my ancestors did not want the history of the people here forgotten entirely. It was pure luck that our paths crossed, but I am very happy about it."

"We all are," George assured her.

Mrs Wabash insisted that the young people stay to dinner. Later, after helping the woman tidy up, the visitors said they must leave.

Burt suggested that they park the car down-town and walk around a little. "I'd like to stretch and exercise after that big meal, and before our long trip back."

Ned left the car in a parking lot and took the key to the attendant.

As they walked along the main boulevard, he said, "Maybe I should go back and lock the car. I forgot to."

"Oh, don't bother," Nancy told him. "There's nothing in there worth stealing and we won't be gone long."

After covering several blocks, the group turned round and started back. When they reached the corner, they were held up by a red traffic light.

An instant later Burt said, "I really suspect we'd better go back. This tired man wants to go to the car. Please walk behind me, George."

Nancy and the others realized that this was a coded message, saying, "Suspect man behind."

The group turned so suddenly that they nearly knocked the man down. He balanced himself, then ran off along the crowded sidewalk.

"Shall we follow him?" Ned asked Nancy.

"I doubt that it would do any good," she said. "But I did recognize him. He's one of the two men whose picture Dave snapped that night in the motel garden."

"I wonder why he's here," George asked. "I'll bet he's up to something!"

Burt laughed. "If he is, we've nipped his idea in the bud."

The two couples reached their car and climbed in. Again Ned took the wheel with Nancy alongside him.

They had gone less than a block when suddenly George, who was sitting in the back, cried out, "Nancy, there's a snake beside you!"

George made a lunge for the reptile just as its fangs were ready to strike her friend!

·19·

Nancy Disappears

As George grabbed the back of the snake's head with one hand, she opened the car door with the other.

"Stop! Stop!" she cried out.

Ned pulled up short, and instantly George got out. She had a good grip on the snake, which was wriggling and trying to free itself. The snake was not large but it whipped its tail up over her hand.

"Turn the torch on it!" she requested.

By this time Burt had climbed out of the car too. He held the light on the snake, which seemed to be confused by it and stopped wriggling.

"Want me to kill it?" Burt asked.

George looked disdainful. "Certainly not. This little creature is needed in the desert. If he weren't around, the place might be overrun with rodents."

"Okay, lady professor," Burt replied. "Now tell me what it is."

George admitted she was not sure, but thought it was a sidewinder. "I'll know when I put it down, but I'm not going to do so here in town. We'll take it out in the desert and let the poor thing loose."

Still grasping the reptile, she got back into the car, and once more Ned drove off. When they reached the turn to go into the desert road, George asked him to let her out once more.

Burt trained his torch on the snake as George set it down on the ground. The little creature seemed stupefied for a few seconds; then it began to move. The snake progressed by looping its body as it slithered away.

"It's a sidewinder all right," Burt remarked.

There was a discussion as to how the snake had got into the car. All four young people agreed it could not have crawled inside by itself.

"Someone put it here," Nancy declared. "But who?"

Ned recalled that he had not locked the car, so it would have been easy for anyone to open the door.

George said, "If someone at camp was playing a joke, it was a mean one. Do you think Archie could be responsible?"

"No," Nancy replied. "Archie's a nuisance but he isn't bad. Besides, if the snake was in the car when we left camp, we would have seen it sooner."

Burt was more inclined to think that one of their enemies had done it. "Don't forget that man on the street. Nancy thought he was a buddy of Fleetfoot's."

"And he had plenty of time to put the snake in," Ned said. "He might have been watching us all the time and was following us back here, expecting to watch the fun."

Burt remarked that some people's idea of fun was warped. "Nancy, I'm glad you weren't bitten."

Ned had a new suggestion. "Suppose someone we don't know played this trick. The snake could have been in a torpid state and just revived in the parking lot."

When the four friends reached camp, they found Archie giving a dozen of the diggers a lecture on something he had found that afternoon. It was a small pottery bowl, which he had picked up in pieces but had mended nicely.

The bowl, an attractive one, was light tan in colour and had a black swastika-like design on it. Archie claimed that this had come from the very earliest civilization of the Moapa Valley.

Nancy and the others joined Bess and Dave. After listening for a while, they looked at one another. All of them knew from their studies and from what they had seen in the museum that this bowl was not that old and probably had been dropped recently where Archie had found it.

"Everything around here is red in colour," Nancy whispered to her friends. "Later civilizations of Indians far to the south of us had the tan clay, but there is none of it in this area."

She and her friends decided not to spoil Archie's lecture. As usual he was being eloquent and pompous and having a very good time.

Ned whispered, "I'm sure his listeners will find out the truth sooner or later, so let him have fun."

Nancy and her friends walked off and she said, "Well goodnight everybody. See you in the morning. I can't wait to get out to the Valley of Fire again to make another search."

By four the next morning the searchers were on their way. When they reached the spot where they always left their car, they were startled to find another car there. Mrs Wabash stepped out.

"What a wonderful surprise!" Nancy said, running

up to the Indian woman. "Good morning!"

Mrs Wabash greeted everyone, then said, "I have some very exciting news for you that you won't believe!"

"Fleetfoot didn't escape, did he?" Burt asked.

"No, that's not my news." The Indian woman smiled. "What I have to tell you is what you call a bombshell. The police found out where Fleetfoot had been living. In a closet in his bedroom behind his clothes, they found my missing petroglyph dictionary!"

"How wonderful!" Nancy exclaimed. "Now we can decipher what's on the four stone tablets we have, and get a connected story."

Again Mrs Wabash smiled. "I have not told you all my news," she said quietly. "Crayoned on to the walls of his closet, Fleetfoot had put marks. When the police took me there, I thought at once they might indicate places where Fleetfoot had hidden the rest of the tablets."

"Do you remember what the marks were?" Nancy asked.

Mrs Wabash said she had not trusted her memory. She had asked the police to take a photograph of the marks. She opened her purse. "Here is a copy." She handed it to Nancy.

The girl detective took it eagerly and looked at the various marks.

Suddenly she exclaimed excitedly, "I'm sure this one indicates the place where Wanna and Don found one of the tablets."

"Which just about proves," George said, "that the other marks are the rest of Fleetfoot's hiding places. Let's start our search!"

Mrs Wabash said that she did not feel equal to climbing around the rocks. "I'll wait for you here. With the hope that you find the rest of the tablets, I brought along the ones I have. I also have some magazines to read. I'll be all right. Don't worry about me."

The young people decided to divide their forces. Wanna stayed with Nancy and Ned. The other two couples each chose one of the other places to hunt. Again it was arranged for them to use whistles at fifteen-minute intervals to signify that everyone was all right.

"Let's change our signalling a little," Nancy suggested. "If you're just telling us you're all right, give one long blast. If you find a tablet, give two blasts. If you find two, use your whistle three times."

"This arithmetic is too much for me," Bess said. "Dave, you remember it."

The group separated and climbed to their various positions. Nancy, Ned, and Wanna had gone to a rock that looked like a poodle lying down. They hunted assiduously all around the stone animal but found nothing.

Nearly twenty minutes had gone by, and Nancy felt she should start signalling. She blew one long blast on her whistle. A few seconds later George and Burt replied with one blast. Several seconds went by. Then, to everyone's delight, they heard the third whistle give two long distinct blasts.

"That's Bess and Dave!" Nancy said. "They've found a tablet."

She assumed that the couple would return to Mrs Wabash's car. Burt and George and her own group would continue to search.

Wanna sighed. "Maybe there's more than one poodle around here," she said.

With this thought in mind, the three searchers spread out a little and began hunting for another rock formation that resembled the poodle. None of them found one and they were puzzled.

Nancy sat down on a somewhat flat rock to think. "What does a poodle resemble?" she asked herself.

Wanna and Ned came to the girl's side, and she asked them the same question. While each of them was trying to form a picture in his mind, Nancy realized that it was time for her to blow the whistle again. She gave a loud blast on it, then waited.

The answering signal soon came. To her delight there were two shrill responses.

"George and Burt have found a tablet!" she announced. "Fleetfoot's directions were perfect!"

Wanna and Ned looked at her and he said, "So we get the booby prize. What's the matter with us?"

In a flash the answer came to Nancy. "A poodle that hasn't been clipped could look like a baby mountain lamb that has no horns yet."

"You're right!" Ned exclaimed. "And there's one looking right at me."

He climbed to a stone figure that had one paw lifted. Under it was the tablet!

Nancy and Wanna quickly joined him and examined the stone plaque.

"It's one of them all right!" the young Indian student said gleefully.

Nancy checked it with her magnifying glass. "Yes," she agreed, "and here is another phase of the moon pictured."

"I'm glad the hunt is over," Ned said. "I'm tired of hunting for wild animals that aren't real."

The three successful searchers hurried down to Mrs Wabash's car, Ned waving the plaque in the air.

"You found the last one!" the woman exclaimed. "How wonderful!"

Nancy's friends were already there and had handed over the tablets they had found.

Tears formed in the Indian woman's eyes. "I can't believe it!" she exclaimed. "Oh you dear, dear people!"

Ned, who disliked tears, said, "Let's try to arrange these stones in order, Mrs Wabash. With the help of your dictionary we'll see if we can piece out the full story about your ancestors and the Forgotten City."

Everyone helped. With the aid of Nancy's magnifying glass, they were able to accomplish this by putting the tablets containing the phases of the moon in the correct order.

Mrs Wabash looked at the figures and kept consulting her paper, figuring out the probable translation of the petroglyphs.

After a while she heaved a sigh. "A complete analysis of this is going to take some time," she said. "As I see it now, one man centuries ago pictured the world of his day. It included life along the Muddy River and the finding of gold. He had gathered many nuggets and fashioned a series of gold plates. An enemy tribe came, so he hid them.

"Unfortunately I can't see that he told where they were," Mrs Wabash remarked. "It also says here that he had made other matching tablets on which future generations were to write their history."

"One thing that puzzles me," said Nancy, "is why

you call these different tribes your ancestors, Mrs Wabash."

The Indian woman said she figured that whenever a conquering tribe took over, there was intermarriage and part of her family had remained near the site of the Forgotten City.

"I wonder what its real name is," she mused.

Since it was becoming hot, Mrs Wabash said she thought she would go home. The young people felt that the Indian woman should not travel without an escort. Nancy suggested that they all go to the camp. From there the boys would follow her home.

"You're very kind," Mrs Wabash said. "I will accept your offer, since I will be carrying such a precious load in my car."

As soon as the girls were left at the camp, Nancy sought out Don. He had just returned from his dig. She told him of their unusual good fortune during the morning's expedition.

"Magnificent!" he said. "When the story becomes known, what a buzz there will be in the scientific world!"

It was hard for Nancy to relax during the hottest hours of the day. Having solved part of the mystery, she was eager to go on a further hunt for the plates of gold. At four o'clock her group was ready to start out again.

When they reached the deep hole that led down to the water, she said, "This time I'd like to go down."

"Okay, but take it easy," Ned warned.

An underarm sling was put over Nancy and the ropes lowered.

"Don't stay long," said Bess, who was fearful about Nancy's going at all.

When the young sleuth reached the bottom, she spotted an object in the wall of the watery tunnel opposite her. Wondering what it was, she tried to reach across. This was impossible.

"I guess the only way I can get there is to let myself out of this sling and reach over," she told herself, and slipped from the ropes.

Nancy was in the midst of wading across, when there was a rush of water through the tunnel towards her. It knocked the girl over, and the current swept her along into the foaming tunnel.

Nancy never panicked, but now she knew she was in serious trouble. If the tunnel remained as wide as it was, she might be carried outside and be able to save herself.

"But if the passageway gets too narrow to carry me through——" she thought. Nancy closed her eyes and prayed.

·20·

A Faggot of Treasure

AT the top of the hole, Ned and the others waited for Nancy to tug the rope. Nothing happened. Ten more minutes went by and still there was no signal.

Finally Ned called down, "Are you ready, Nancy?"

There was no answer.

"Are you sure she can hear you?" George asked, alarm showing on her face.

Ned got down on his knees, leaned over the hole, and shouted at the top of his lungs.

"Nancy! Nancy!"

The only reply was a hollow echo of his own voice.

"Oh I know something dreadful has happened to her!" Bess wailed. "What are we going to do?"

Ned was grim. He tugged the rope and realized there was nothing on the end of it.

"She's not there!" he announced.

Hoping Nancy had gone adventuring and sent up a note to explain, he pulled up the rope quickly. No note was attached. By this time everyone was frantic, and Bess was crying.

Ned tried to remain calm. "Nancy got out of this sling deliberately," he stated. "I'm going down there to find her! If I have any information, I'll send up a note."

148

He fastened himself into the harness, and the others let the rope down. When he reached the bottom, Ned looked up and down the tunnel. Nancy was nowhere in sight.

"Nancy! Nancy!" he called.

He repeated her name over and over. There was no sound except the rushing water.

"I must go after her," he thought, determined.

Ned wondered, however, which way to go. He decided that there was little likelihood that she had battled against the stream.

"She must have gone downstream," he decided.

Before getting out of the sling, Ned pulled a notebook and pencil from a pocket and wrote a message to the watchers above. It said:

Nancy not here. Does not answer. Going down-stream to try to find her. Suggest two of you go to water-hole and dig tunnel in case she's stuck.

Ned took off the harness, attached the note to it, then tugged on the rope. Quickly it was pulled up and the note read.

"We'll follow instructions," Burt called down. "George and I will go over to the water-hole. The others can stay here in case you send up more notes." They let the rope down again.

George and Burt grabbed picks and shovels and raced off. When they reached the spring, the two started digging furiously to enlarge the hole. Soon a larger flow of water was coming into the water-hole.

Meanwhile Nancy had been swept along the tunnel.

She had managed to keep her torch on and kept looking for a place where she could stop or find something she could cling to. At first she found nothing, and went on. The tunnel curved and was so narrow at times that she had to duck under the water to avoid being hit.

"I mustn't drown!" she kept telling herself.

Presently the tunnel widened and the roof sloped upwards again. Her torch revealed a large square niche on one side. It was slightly above water-level, and the young detective managed to drag herself up into it. To her delight and relief, the opening was high enough so she could stand up straight.

"Thank goodness!" she murmured.

Instead of wondering how she was going to get back, Nancy beamed her torch around the opening.

"What are these?"

At the back of the opening was a smaller niche, which formed a sort of shelf.

"Something's lying on it!" Nancy thought, excited.

A couple of steps brought her to the spot. On it lay a bundle made of tightly woven twigs. Nancy lifted the faggot. It was small, but very heavy.

Just as the girl detective was speculating breathlessly on whether or not the faggot contained the missing plates of gold, Ned swam up to her.

"Nancy! Nancy! How relieved I am to see you!" he exclaimed, pulling himself out of the water and standing beside her. "Are you all right? Why did you come here alone?"

She told him what had happened, and he frowned. "A rush of water! That could happen again. We'd better get out of here!"

"Not yet, Ned," she pleaded as she looked at her

friend fondly. "I'm terribly glad you came. I think perhaps I've made a great discovery." She pointed to the bundle on the shelf. "This may be the lost treasure of the Forgotten City!"

Ned's mind was still on the danger they were in. "Treasure or no treasure, do you realize what can happen to us if the water rises?"

Nancy realized that he had risked his life to save her. "You're right, Ned, but just give me half a minute. I do want to take that bundle with us. Then we'll get back somehow."

Ned told her that George and Burt were probably working frantically at the spot where the underground river came out through the bottom of the water hole, which was rather shallow.

"Listen!" he said tensely. "Do you hear a sound like digging?"

Nancy's face lit up. "I certainly do. And it doesn't seem far away."

Hand-in-hand the couple waited expectantly. Presently they could hear voices.

"We're saved!" Nancy said. "Your idea was an inspiration, Ned."

Within minutes there was a breakthrough and the hole was large enough for Nancy and Ned to swim to their friends.

"Let's go!" he said eagerly.

"Can you possibly take this package?" Nancy asked, handing it to him.

Ned lifted the faggot to his shoulders and held it there with one hand. Now he and Nancy let themselves back into the water, and he swam with one hand. Seconds later, the couple were swept out to the water-hole.

"Thank goodness you two are all right!" George cried out.

Burt, mud spattered but grinning said, "What an experience!"

"I confess," said Nancy, "that for a while I was scared. Thank you. Thank you a million."

Burt asked, "Ned, what's in that faggot on your shoulder?"

"We don't know yet," Nancy answered. "But I'm wishing it's the lost treasure of the Forgotten City."

"You mean the gold plates?" George asked sceptically.

Nancy nodded. "I'm hoping my guess is right, and that we won't all be fooled."

At this moment Wanna joined the group.

"Nancy," she said, "we were dreadfully worried about you and Ned. I'm so happy to see you're safe. Tell us what happened. And how did you get here?"

Nancy pointed to their escape route.

Wanna surveyed the large opening of the underground river and cried out with joy. "My theory has been proved!"

The others nodded. Ned smiled. "This should get you an extra college degree!"

Wanna smiled. "But I shall have to give all the credit to Nancy Drew."

"No, indeed," Nancy objected. "Everyone in our special group had a hand in this whole exciting adventure."

Wanna said she would summon Bess and Dave to join them. She blew a loud blast on her whistle. Within minutes the other couple arrived. Bess hugged Nancy and cried a little.

"It's so wonderful to see you alive and okay!"

Burt explained about the opening through which the underground river flowed. He said this no doubt would help speed the curator's dream that this would become a lush area in the desert. "Once more it can be a great farming spot for the Indians."

"Let's open the bundle!" Ned suggested. "I want to find out whether that golden treasure is really in it."

Unwinding the interlaced twigs was a tedious job. The whole group of young archaeologists realized that even the covering was valuable for historical purposes.

"This was certainly ingeniously woven," George remarked.

"And it's amazing," Wanna added, "that it is in such good shape. It's my guess that these twigs came from bushes by the Muddy River and the dampness inside the tunnel was like food for them."

Finally the outer covering came off in one piece. Underneath were several layers of bark. These were carefully removed.

When the contents of the bundle were finally revealed, everyone stared in amazement. There were four oblong plates of gold. They were in perfect condition and all were covered with fine-lined symbols. Had they been done with a stone or some sharp-pointed instrument? The answer would take a lot of study.

"The story of the golden treasure is true!" Bess burst out. "And Nancy and Ned risked their lives to find it!"

At the camp that night, Nancy found a few minutes to be alone. The usual feeling of emptiness came over her whenever she had solved a mystery. She longed for another, that came as *The Strange Message in the Parchment*.

People at the camp had been hurriedly summoned by telephone. Mrs Wabash drove out. The curator, his wife, and their daughter were there along with several State Police to guard the valuable find. Now the whole story was told to the group of young archaeologists.

Professor Don Maguire got up to speak. "Everyone on this dig has made a valuable contribution to science," he said, "but I think we should have a rousing cheer for Nancy Drew. Her discovery is invaluable!"

Nancy blushed at the applause and calls that filled the desert air.

The Strange Message in the Parchment

First published in a single volume in hardback in 1979 by
William Collins Sons & Co Ltd.
First published in paperback in Armada

·1·

Stolen!

"IT's perfectly beautiful!" Nancy exclaimed.

She was standing in front of a long mirror in the Drew hallway, admiring herself in a sheepskin jacket. Near her stood a girl of the same age, eighteen. The two were of identical height and slender, but Nancy was a strawberry blonde with blue eyes, while the other girl had brown hair and eyes.

"Junie Flockhart, you're a darling!" Nancy said, hugging her friend, a former schoolmate. Junie's family had moved many miles away, to a large sheep farm.

Junie smiled. "You know, Nancy, you were always one of my father's favourites. When I told him I was coming here to visit, he sent you this gift. By the way, how would you like to solve a mystery for him?"

Nancy's eyes sparkled. A mystery!

At this moment a motherly, middle-aged woman came into the hallway to greet Junie and admire the sheepskin jacket. She was Hannah Gruen, the Drews' housekeeper, who had been a mother to Nancy since the girl was three and her own mother had passed away.

"Did your father make the jacket?" Hannah asked Junie.

"Yes," she replied. "At one end of Triple Creek Farm he has a factory that produces sheepskin articles. Dad also makes parchment from the sheep's skins.

"He has a marvellous collection of parchments from all over the world," Junie went on. "Some are very old. A few have illuminated writing on them in foreign languages; others have beautiful painted pictures."

"I'd love to see them," Nancy put in.

"You will if you come home with me to solve the mystery. My father has a parchment that has four lovely small painting on it. He is intrigued by the parchment because of a strange phone call he received soon after he bought it. A man who didn't give his name said the picture had a message. Anyone who could figure it out would bring happiness and comfort to several people, and right an old wrong."

"That's strange," Nancy replied. "If the man knew this, why didn't he tell the whole story?"

"He hung up abruptly," Junie answered, "as if someone had approached him and he couldn't say any more. Everyone in our family has tried and failed to decipher the meaning of the picture."

"I'd like to try to solve the mystery," Nancy said. "When do I start?"

"As soon as you can get ready. And say, why don't we have a house party? Ned, Burt, Dave, Bess, George, and my date, Dan. I know you'll like him."

"That's a wonderful idea," Nancy replied. "What do you think, Hannah?"

Mrs Gruen smiled. "The instant I heard there was

a mystery to solve at Triple Creek Farm, I knew you'd want to go. I think the idea is great. If your father hasn't any special work for his sleuthing daughter, I'm sure he'll agree."

Nancy took off the sheepskin jacket and laid it on a chair in the living room for her father to see when he came home. Then she went upstairs with Hannah and Junie to look through her closet and select appropriate clothing for the trip.

"Don't bother with a lot of dresses," Junie said. "At the farm we just about live in jeans, shirts, and jackets."

All this time Hannah Gruen had been grinning. "Junie, you've never seen Nancy when she's trying to solve a mystery. She's like a hound on a scent and never gives up until she has caught the villain!"

Junie was about to say something, but just then Nancy whispered, "Listen! I heard the front door close softly. Let's find out who's there."

She and Junie hurried down the stairs. No one was in sight and when Nancy called out, asking who was in the house, there was no answer. Then she noticed something strange.

"My new jacket is gone!" Nancy cried.

The girls stared at the empty chair.

"My beautiful sheepskin jacket must have been stolen!" Nancy exclaimed.

She rushed to the front door and opened it wide, just in time to see a girl disappearing around the end of the curved driveway. She was wearing the sheepskin jacket!

"Let's chase her!" Nancy urged. She whistled for her little terrier, Togo, who hurried from the kitchen.

"Come on, old boy! We must catch a thief."

Togo followed her and Junie out the door. For a few seconds the dog ran alongside Nancy. As soon as they reached the street, however, and his mistress pointed to the fleeing thief, he knew what he was supposed to do and bounded off. The stranger had a good head start and was running like a trained athlete.

"We'll never catch her," Junie said.

"She must be a professional thief," Nancy added. "She was so quiet she didn't even disturb Togo."

Junie wondered how the girl had known about the coat. "Of course I carried it in a plastic see-through bag," she said. "That girl may have noticed it and followed me from the train to your house."

Nancy nodded. "She may have been spying and when we went upstairs, she came in. But how did she get in?"

By now Togo had almost caught up with the stranger. At the same moment all three girls saw a policeman in the distance. The thief, realizing it was useless to proceed, quickly turned into a driveway.

By the time Nancy and Junie reached the spot, the suspect was out of sight. Togo was returning, however, to present them with a chunk of cloth, which he held in his teeth. Nancy reached down and took it.

"This is a piece from that sneak thief's skirt!" she exclaimed. "What a great clue! Togo, you're a clever little dog."

Togo barked as though he were urging Nancy to continue the search. "Maybe the thief is hiding," Nancy said.

The girls raced down the driveway to the rear of

the property, where there was a hedge. Nancy's jacket lay on the ground in front of it! Togo pulled it along the ground, growling all the time.

Nancy picked it up. "Togo, you're marvellous! You scared that girl into discarding the jacket when you took a piece out of her skirt!"

"Let's go on!" Junie urged. "Maybe we can catch her."

The girls parted the hedge and went through. The thief was not in sight. Trying to guess which direction she had taken, they ran into the adjoining yard. Here the two searchers separated, one going along the left side of the house, the other to the right.

Within a few seconds they met on the front pavement and looked up and down the street. There was no sign of the person they wanted.

Nancy heaved a sigh. "Anyway," she said, "I'm thankful to have my beautiful jacket back. And Togo got a good clue we can take to the police."

The little dog was jumping and barking. Junie looked puzzled.

"Togo is asking for further instructions from me," Nancy explained. She leaned over and patted him once more. "He's eager to continue the case. I—"

Nancy stopped speaking abruptly when Togo barked again. This time he leaped to the pavement and ran alongside a car that was speeding down the street.

"What's Togo doing that for?" Junie asked.

Without replying, Nancy started running also. Her first thought was to keep Togo from being killed if the driver, either accidentally or deliberately, swerved across the street and hit him.

"Togo, come back!" she cried out.

The little dog paid no attention. Suddenly Nancy caught a glimpse of the young woman on the passenger side and realized why. The dress matched the sample Togo had snatched from the thief's skirt!

The car's driver, evidently sensing the situation, put on speed. Out of breath, Nancy stopped. She was in time to catch the number on the licence plate and memorize it. Togo had given up the chase, too, and returned to Nancy on the pavement.

"Thank you, Togo," she said, hugging him. "Now we'll go."

Junie hurried up to them and was told of Nancy's discovery. She was astounded at the rapidity with which clues were mounting.

"All you have to do," she said, "is report the licence number to the police. They'll learn who the car's owner is, the name of his passenger, and catch the thief."

"I hope it will be that easy," Nancy said. "But—"

"But what?" Junie asked.

"The driver may not be the owner of the car."

"You mean, he might have stolen it?"

"Right. If he did, he'll probably abandon it. Another possibility is that the driver does not know his passenger. She could have hitch-hiked and not given her name."

Junie's look of hope faded. "And here I thought it would be easy. Well, it may still be. Let's think positive, Nancy, and go to the police with a report."

·2·

Triple Creek Farm

"LET'S go back to the house first and get my car," Nancy suggested. "It's some distance to the police station. Then we'll show Chief McGinnis the shred from the thief's dress and the jacket. He's a good friend of mine."

Junie asked, "What can the police find out from the jacket?"

"Sometimes they discover the most amazing facts about the person who wore a garment."

"Like what?"

"Oh, the blood type, kind of skin, height, weight, male or female—"

By this time her friend from Triple Creek Farm was laughing. "Don't tell me any more. I'm lost already."

When they reached the house, Nancy took Togo inside and told Hannah where they were going. Then, taking along the new jacket, Nancy backed her sleek blue car out of the garage and drove to head-quarters. Chief McGinnis greeted the girls enthusiastically.

"Nancy, I know you have come to tell me about a mystery. I see it in your eyes. What is it this time?"

165

Nancy grinned, then introduced Junie. She told the middle-aged, good-natured man she was trying to track down a thief.

"Junie brought me this beautiful jacket from her father's sheep farm, but a short while later, a girl sneaked into our house and stole it."

Chief McGinnis looked puzzled. "You say *this* jacket was stolen?"

"It was. But we got it back." Nancy told him about the whole incident and produced the piece of material from the thief's skirt. Her eyes twinkled. "You see, Chief McGinnis, I even have Togo trained to be a detective."

"He's very clever. Maybe you ought to put him into our Canine Corps!" the chief replied. Then he promised to alert his men and have them track down the thief, using the shred of cloth she had brought as a clue. Nancy told him the licence number of the car in which the girl had escaped.

"I'll trace it at once," Chief McGinnis said.

Nancy explained that the thief had actually worn the coat and run in it for several blocks. "Then she saw a policeman ahead, and Togo was close to her heels. So she threw the jacket on to a hedge. Do you think you might find any clues to her from this?"

"I don't know. But if you'll leave it here, together with the cloth, I'll have our lab inspect them carefully."

Nancy thanked the officer and the two girls said goodbye. That evening Mr Drew was amazed to hear the story, and wondered how the thief had entered their home. Nobody could explain it and for several seconds there was silence in the living room, where the family had gathered with their guest.

Suddenly Togo, who had been lying on the floor with his ears cocked, jumped up, stood on his hind legs, and walked around.

Junie laughed. "How cute!" she remarked. "Not only is he a detective dog, but a trick dog!"

Nancy explained that there was more to the gesture than that. Whenever Togo was trying to convey a message to anyone in the family, he would do this. The little dog now dropped to all fours and hurried to the front door. Nancy followed and asked the others to join her.

As they watched, Togo got up again on his hind legs and held the handle of the door in his forepaws. Next he put his teeth around the handle and presto! the door opened. The Drews and Junie looked at the animal in astonishment.

"You little scamp!" Nancy said to him. "You're the one that left the door open so the thief could come in!"

Togo acted very pleased with himself. He danced around some more and gave several short barks.

"That was a neat trick," Mr Drew remarked, "but I think we'll have to put an extra lock on the door. One that Togo can't reach and open for burglars."

Togo seemed to understand. His tail dropped, a sad look came to his eyes, and he lay down.

As Nancy patted him, she told her father about the invitation to Triple Creek Farm. "Bess and George and also Ned, Dave, and Burt are to be invited for a house party up there."

The lawyer's eyes twinkled. "With a mystery to solve and a house party included, I don't see how you could refuse such an invitation."

Nancy kissed her father, then immediately went to call her friends and give them the exciting invitation. Nancy would go ahead with Junie; the other guests were to follow later.

While she was on the phone, Mr Drew said to Junie with boyish pride, "I have a few sheepskins of my own. Come with me and I'll show them to you."

He led her into his study. Between bookcases and pictures hung framed diplomas. One was from high school, another from college, and the third and most impressive was from law school.

"I see you graduated from all three places with honours," Junie said. "My congratulations!"

"Thank you," the lawyer replied. "The other day we were discussing the laws governing the ownership of sheep in your state. If you have a flock and any of the sheep are killed by wild animals, will the state reimburse the owner for his loss?"

"Yes," Junie replied. "And wild dogs are also classed under the heading of wild animals. It has always amazed me how dogs differ. Wild dogs will kill sheep and eat them, but those that have been reared from puppies by human beings love the sheep. They guard them and take care of them. We have several sheep dogs at the farm. My favourite is Rover."

The conversation was interrupted by Nancy, who reported that all of their friends would be able to visit Triple Creek Farm.

"Bess and George can make it next weekend," she said, "but the boys are uncertain when they can come. They'll try to visit at the same time as the girls."

Nancy went on to say that her friend Ned Nickerson had told her about an interesting artist who lived in the vicinity of Triple Creek Farm. She asked Junie if she had ever heard of Vincenzo Caspari.

Junie shook her head. "I never have, but my parents may know him. Why did Ned mention him?"

"I was telling Ned about the strange phone call regarding the parchment. He said this man might be able to help us."

The girls went to bed early and were up at seven o'clock, packing their bags. By nine they drove off, with good wishes from Mr Drew and Hannah Gruen. They took turns driving Nancy's car, since it was a long ride. Afternoon shadows were lengthening as the travellers finally reached the six-hundred-acre Triple Creek Farm.

"What a wonderful place!" Nancy exclaimed, as Junie turned into a long lane that led to the farmhouse.

Though the building had many wings and extensions in every direction, it was attractive and inviting. Mr and Mrs Flockhart were there to welcome the girls.

The owner was a large, handsome man with greying hair. Nancy thought his beautiful grey eyes looked as if they had stars shining in them.

Junie's mother was small and dainty. Although her daughter resembled her, Junie was already half a head taller than Mrs Flockhart.

After making Nancy feel very much at home in the roomy, comfortable house, which was furnished with beautiful antique furniture, Mr Flockhart tweaked Junie's chin. "It's high time you got home, young lady," he said. "The lambs are crying for you."

Junie laughed and explained to Nancy that she worked for her father. Her job was to look after the new-born sheep. These were kept in a special barn with individual stalls, so they would not be endangered by other animals..

As the group walked into the living room, Nancy noticed a framed, glass-covered picture hanging over the fireplace mantel. It measured about twelve by twenty inches.

"Is this the mystery picture?" she asked.

"Yes," Mr Flockhart replied. "Nancy, it's all yours to solve. We've given up."

"But let's not start now," Mrs Flockhart begged. "Dinner is ready."

After the meal was over, Nancy looked at the parchment paintings again. The first of the four was of a beautiful woman; the second a young man with his back to the viewer. Nancy was intrigued by the third picture. It portrayed a group of angels surrounded by clouds. The figure in the centre was holding an infant. The last painting depicted a collision between a steamer and a sailing vessel.

Junie and her father had walked up behind Nancy. "What thoughts are going through your mind, young lady?" Mr Flockhart asked. "I've never had the pleasure of being this close to a detective in action before. I'd be interested in hearing your ideas."

"I'm afraid I haven't much to offer at the moment," Nancy said. "My first reaction is that the picture tells a story about a family. There was happiness in the beginning, but then tragedy struck. I think there is a connection between the second and last paintings. Perhaps something happened to the man at the time of the accident."

"Do you have an inkling of what the strange message might be?" Junie queried.

"I haven't the faintest notion," the girl detective replied, "but give me a little time. When I'm on a case, the facts are foremost in my mind. I refer to them off and on. My best thinking hours seem to be late at night or early in the morning.

"By the way, Mr Flockhart, have you met an artist named Vincenzo Caspari, who lives in this area?"

The answer was no, and Junie's father asked why Nancy wanted to know.

"Ned Nickerson thought he might be able to help us," she said.

Mr Flockhart went to the phone and called the artist. A woman who answered said Mr Caspari would be out of town for a few days.

"I'll call again," Mr Flockhart said.

Nancy and Junie were weary from their long ride and retired early. The following morning they dressed in shirts and jeans, had a quick breakfast, then went to the barn where the newborn lambs were. Nancy fell in love with each baby as she came to it.

Suddenly she exclaimed, "Why, here's a pure black one lying down! Isn't he darling?"

The man in charge walked up to the girls, and Junie introduced him as Finney.

"Something happened to this poor little fellow," he reported. "Maybe he got stepped on. Anyway, he can't stand up. I guess we'll have to send him over to the slaughterhouse."

"Not yet," said Junie quickly. "Let me look at him."

She entered the stall. As Nancy and Finney watched her, she manipulated the lamb's legs, massaging them, then rubbing the little animal's body. To the onlookers' amazement the little black lamb stood up and bleated *"Baa!"*

"Well, I'll be—he's gonna be all right!" Finney exclaimed.

"I think he will be," Junie said jubilantly, watching the black lamb closely. Then she explained to Nancy that she had had some training in animal massage.

Nancy had noticed that outside there was a great deal of activity, carts and trucks going in both directions. Most of them contained full-grown sheep. Wishing to watch this part of the operation more closely, she walked out of the barn. Junie followed.

Just then a high-powered car roared around the corner of the barn, put on speed, and headed in the girls' direction. The driver made no attempt to swerve out of their path.

Horrified, Nancy and Junie jumped back against the wall to avoid being hit!

·3·

Plaintive Bleating

THE big car whizzed past Nancy and Junie, missing them by inches as they braced themselves against the wall of the barn. On the passenger side stood a little dog, who leaned out the window and gave quick staccato barks.

The driver yelled at him, "Shut up!" But the dog paid no attention.

The man stopped abruptly and jumped out of the car. He was short and stocky and had a swarthy complexion. He walked back to the girls, and without a greeting of any sort he said to Junie, "Where's your father?"

Before replying, Junie asked, "What was the idea of almost running us down? We might have been killed!"

When the man ignored her question, she went on, "Mr Rocco, this is my friend Nancy Drew from River Heights. Nancy, this is a neighbour of ours from across the hill."

Rocco did not acknowledge the introduction. His beady black eyes stared into Nancy's blue ones for a few seconds, then he said, "I've heard your name somewhere. In the papers, maybe? Have you ever

173

been in jail or in some other kind of trouble?"

Nancy was taken aback by this rudeness. She merely said, "No."

Junie squeezed her friend's hand and indicated she was to say no more. She herself addressed the man. "Mr Rocco, I think my father is at the factory. At least, that's where he usually goes in the morning."

Without another word, the crude visitor turned on his heel, went to his car, and jumped in. He drove off rapidly, his dog still yapping.

Junie said to Nancy, "Isn't he horrid? But we have to be nice to him because he's one of my father's clients. By the way, would you like to go to the factory and see how parchment is made?"

"Yes, I'd like that very much," Nancy said and the two girls got into the Triple Creek jeep and went off.

As they approached a string of one-storey buildings, Junie said, "Some of these places are pretty smelly from the animals. Think you can take it?"

Nancy assured her she could and in any case, she would put up with it in order to learn about parchment making.

The first place was the shearing room. Several men were cutting the thick wool from the sheep's bodies. They were using electric knives, which operated very quickly. Now and then one of the sheep bleated pleadingly and Nancy realized that a knife had gone too close and nipped the skin.

As soon as all the wool had been taken off, the sheep were driven into the next building through a fenced-in alleyway. The girls left the shearing room and walked to the slaughterhouse.

"I see what you mean by smelly," Nancy

remarked, holding her nose for a moment. "When Bess and George get here, I'll bet Bess won't come near this place. She not only can't stand bad odours, but she can't watch any living creature being killed."

Before the sheep were slaughtered, they showed great fright and their bleating caused a terrific din in the place. Junie told Nancy that after being killed, the animals were hung up to drain. Nancy nodded silently, not looking too happy.

"I guess you've had enough of this," Junie said understandingly. "Let's go in the next building. That's more civilized!"

Here the skins of the animals were skilfully removed so that the meat underneath would not be damaged. As soon as the carcasses were ready, they were carried to a waiting refrigerated truck.

"From here they go to wholesale meat plants," Junie explained. "My father is not involved with that part of the business."

"Now what happens?" Nancy asked.

"I'll show you how the hides are treated before it is possible to make them into parchment," her friend replied.

In the next building men were busy shaving and scraping the tough hairs from the skins of the sheep.

"When these are ready," Junie said, "the hides will be covered with lime. This is done to absorb excess fat. The next step is to douse the hides in a pure water bath, then hang them up to dry. You can see some of them over there being stretched on frames. This is to make them smooth."

"There's a lot of work involved," Nancy remarked.

"You're right," Junie agreed. And the farm girl

made Nancy laugh by reciting an original ditty:

> Junie had a little lamb.
> She kept it in a stall.
> But Daddy took the lamb away;
> Now it's a parchment on her wall.

"Junie, you're a great poet!" Nancy said. "Let's see if I can do as well." Nancy thought for a few seconds, and then she recited a rhyme of her own:

> Junie had a little lamb.
> It really got her goat
> When Daddy took the pet away
> And made her friend a sheepskin coat!

"Very clever!" Junie praised. "We're so good we should go into the poetry business."

"Not so fast, partner," Nancy cautioned. "First we will have to solve the mystery of your father's parchment."

"Righto. Well, back to my duties as a guide. The last process in making parchment is again scraping the hides and then sandpapering them. By that time they will look like your father's diplomas."

"What if a sheep has really thick skin?" Nancy asked.

"Then it's possible to separate the outer from the inner layers. Very fine vellum is made from the inner layer. That's the most expensive kind of what we normally call writing paper, but it's really not paper at all because it's not made from the wood of trees. Can you imagine going into a fine stationery store and asking for a box of sheepskin to use for letters?"

Nancy chuckled. "Right. The sales assistant would think you'd escaped from a funny farm. By the way, can you make parchment and vellum from other animal hides, too?"

"They use the hides of calves and goats, but they're coarser than sheepskin, so my dad doesn't bother with them."

Nancy said it had been a very interesting and enlightening tour.

"Oh, the sightseeing isn't over yet," Junie replied.

"Really? What else is there to visit?"

"I want you to meet a very interesting character who works for my dad. He has nothing to do with this factory, though. He's an elderly shepherd who lives high on one of our hills and takes care of a large flock of sheep. His name is Ezekiel Shaw, but everyone calls him Eezy. I won't tell you any more about him now, but you'll like him. I have a walkie-talkie in my car for him."

Junie drove the jeep part-way up the hill, then parked it. "We'd better walk from here. Sometimes the engine of this jeep disturbs the sheep. They're timid and scare easily."

Almost immediately a beautiful sheep dog came to meet them. "Hello, Rover!" Junie said to him, ruffling his thick fur. "Rover, this is Nancy Drew, who is visiting me. Make her welcome to Triple Creek Farm."

Rover sat down and put up his right paw to shake hands. Nancy responded and patted the dog lightly on the back of his head.

"I'm glad to meet you, Rover," said Nancy Drew.

"I take it you guard the sheep."

The dog seemed eager to be off. Junie said he probably felt he should get back to Eezy, his master. The girls followed him as quickly as they could, but could not worm their way among the sheep as easily as the dog did.

Nancy and Junie finally reached the top of the hill. Before them stood a small cabin with trees around it. The place was quiet and well-kept.

"Is that where Eezy lives?" Nancy asked.

"Yes. But when the weather is good, as it is today, he's usually outdoors. He must be around here somewhere. Often he's seated on that big rock over there. From that spot he can look all around and see if any of the sheep need attention, or if there are any prowlers."

"What kind of prowlers?" Nancy asked.

"Oh, rustlers who come to steal sheep, or sometimes wild dogs."

Julie began calling Eezy's name. There was no response from the elderly shepherd.

"This is strange," Junie said. "I wonder where he is."

Suddenly Rover began to bark wildly and to zigzag quickly among the sheep. He headed down the slope at a different angle from the direction the girls had taken to come up.

"Let's find out where Rover's going," Junie suggested. "I suspect trouble."

She and Nancy hurried down the hillside. By now all the sheep seemed disturbed. They began to move around, and a few started to run. Had the dog caused this, or was there some other reason?

Far down the hillside the girls could hear both Rover's bark and the sheep's loud bleats.

Junie looked worried. "Now I'm sure there's trouble of some kind down there. We'd better find out what it is—and fast!"

·4·

Eezy Shaw

NANCY followed her friend as fast as she could. The sheep were everywhere. Some were standing, others were lying down. In her haste to keep up with Junie, Nancy decided to hurdle some of the animals. Once, while jumping across an old sheep that was lying down, she stepped on the tiny tail of a younger one. Immediately there was a loud *baaaaa*.

"I'm sorry," Nancy called back, as she sped on.

When the girls neared the lower end of the hill, they noticed two men running as fast as they could towards a road at the foot.

"They must have caused the disturbance," Nancy called. She asked, "Do you know who they are?"

"No," Junie replied. "Maybe they were trying to rustle our sheep."

"That's bad," Nancy remarked.

The men were too far ahead for the girls to get a good look at them. Junie said she still did not recognize either one of them. A moment later the two intruders jumped into a waiting car that roared off.

Rover had been after the men, but could only scare them away. When he realized the girls were coming down, he turned and trotted up to their side.

180

"Good dog!" they both said, and Junie hugged him affectionately. As the three climbed the hill, Nancy asked, "I wonder where Eezy is?"

"I do, too," Junie replied. "It's not like him to leave his station, especially if there's any trouble and the sheep are disturbed."

As soon as the girls reached the top of the hill where Eezy's cabin stood, they began to call the shepherd's name. When there was no answer, Junie went inside the house. He was not there.

Puzzled, she said to Nancy, "I can't imagine what happened." She leaned down to the dog and said, "Rover, where is your master? Go find Eezy. Take us to Eezy."

The beautiful animal cocked his head. Then, as if understanding what was wanted of him, he sniffed along the ground, apparently trying to pick up the scent of Eezy's footprints. Presently he disappeared into a small copse of trees. Meanwhile, the girls looked all around the cabin and some distance beyond it. There was no sign of Eezy, nor any clue as to what had become of him.

"This is really strange," Junie remarked. "Eezy has never left this place since he became a shepherd here."

At this moment Rover began to bark wildly. Nancy and Junie followed the sound, which led them to an area in the copse of trees. The faithful dog was standing beside his master, who lay stretched out on the ground, unconscious!

"Oh!" the girls cried out and knelt down next to him.

The shepherd was just beginning to revive. He

mumbled and presently Nancy caught the words, *"I will seek that which was lost, and bring again that which was driven away."**

Nancy looked at her friend for an explanation. Junie said that Eezy was a very religious man, who often quoted the Bible to explain the philosophy behind some situation. "I think he's blaming himself, perhaps for letting some of the sheep be rustled."

"It looks as if you and I got here just in time," Nancy said.

Junie nodded and gave the stricken man some first aid to help him regain full consciousness. He did not respond at once, so Junie said, "Nancy, you try it."

Nancy did and in a short while the shepherd opened his eyes wide, then smiled wanly. Finally, with their help, he got to his feet.

"This is no kind of reception at all," the slender, elderly man said. "And, Junie, I see you've brought a beautiful young lady to meet me."

"Yes, this is my friend Nancy Drew," Junie told him.

"Sorry I was sleepin' when you came up," Eezy said. "Next time I'll be wide awake, I promise."

The girls looked at each other, then Junie said, "Eezy, you were not just asleep. You were unconscious. What happened to you?"

The shepherd hung his head. "I see I can't keep anythin' from you. Well, two men came up here to see me. We didn't quite hit it off. They got mad and knocked me out. Never gave me a chance to fight back."

Nancy explained that she and Junie had seen two

*Ezekiel: 34.16

men running very fast down the hill with Rover after them.

"But," Junie added, "before we got close enough to identify them and see their licence plate, they sped away in a car."

"That's just as well," Eezy said. "They're tough, bad people. Take my word for it. And don't get involved with 'em."

Junie begged the elderly shepherd to tell them why the men had been there. Eezy shook his head. "I'm not goin' to say anything more about 'em 'cept that they wanted me to do somethin' I don't approve of. We had just better let it go at that."

By now Eezy seemed to have recovered his strength, and he walked back with the girls to his cabin. "May I invite you lovely ladies to join me in a glass of cool lemonade?" he asked. "This is the time of day I like to wet my whistle."

Nancy and Junie accepted and followed the shepherd inside. The place was immaculate and attractively decorated with furniture Eezy had made. He was pleased that the girls were interested in his handicraft.

He did not refer to the unfortunate incident, except to say that he was mighty thankful to Rover for having run the men off the premises.

Nancy asked, "Where was Rover when the men were here?"

"I think he was off chasin' a wild dog, maybe. I heard another dog bark."

"I have something for you in the jeep," Junie said. "My father asked me yesterday to bring you a walkie-talkie. If you have any more unwanted visitors here, just call the farmhouse and reinforcements will come at once to help you."

"That's very kind of you," Eezy said. "I hope I won't have to use it."

As the girls walked to the car to get the instrument, Junie said, "It's too bad Eezy didn't have the walkie-talkie sooner."

"I wonder if he would have had a chance to use it," Nancy said. "Obviously he talked to the men first, but didn't realize they would beat him up."

Junie nodded. "Now that he knows, he can call if he sees them in the distance."

When the girls returned to the çabin, Junie showed the shepherd how to use the walkie-talkie.

Eezy's eyes twinkled. "I can call you now and ask you to come up and keep me company!"

'You do that," Junie said, then the girls bade him goodbye. On the way home they discussed the incident.

"Have you any idea what the men could have wanted that Eezy didn't approve of?" Nancy asked.

"Not the slightest," her friend replied. "Of course, I suspect that they might have been trying to bribe him into helping them rustle sheep. But then it might have been something more personal that Eezy didn't want to talk about."

Nancy asked if there was much sheep rustling in the rest of the neighbourhood.

"No," Junie replied. "There are only a few sheep farms around here besides Dad's. More than likely, since they had only a car with them and planned to steal sheep, they would have taken only one or two for food."

"Then it's more of a puzzle than ever what they wanted Eezy to do that he wouldn't, and his refusal made them so mad they knocked him out."

Junie suggested that perhaps her father might have some ideas on the subject, so after dinner that evening she asked him. He thought for some time and wrinkled his brow. "I don't like this. There are so many miles of unguarded fields in this area that all kinds of things could happen. The attack on Eezy bothers me. It's too bad you didn't get a better glimpse of those men."

Nancy said they were of medium height and build. Both wore hats pulled far down, so she could not see the colour of their hair or their skin.

"Hm," Mr Flockhart said, "I'll alert the State Police to keep an eye open." He went to the hall telephone to call them.

While he was gone, Nancy stared at the parchment over the mantel. Then she got up and stood beneath it, taking in every detail.

When Mr Flockhart returned to the room, he said, "I see you have already started looking for clues to solve the mystery of my parchment."

Nancy admitted that she had noticed only one thing so far. She could not find an artist's name on it.

"That's right," he agreed.

"The first picture," Nancy went on, "is of a lovely woman but she's not doing anything to indicate what part she is playing in the message."

"That's true," Mr Flockhart replied. "What about the second one?"

Nancy studied it for several seconds. "A portrait of the upper part of a man, but a rear view," she said.

"All I can see is that he seems stocky and has dark hair. That's not much help."

"No, it isn't."

"The third picture is the most intriguing of all," Nancy went on. "See that group of angels in flowing robes floating in the heavens? And the one in the centre is holding an infant. All the others are looking at it adoringly. It's just beautiful. Only a very fine artist could have painted that."

Nancy now concentrated on the fourth painting, the scene of a sailing ship being rammed by a steamer.

"I think it's an accident that really happened," Junie said. "Nancy, what's your guess?"

"I don't know. Perhaps the steamer is wrecking the sailing ship intentionally. I'm sure there's a message here. But what?"

Turning to Mr Flockhart, she asked, "From whom did you buy this parchment?"

"From my neighbour, Sal Rocco," Junie's father replied.

Nancy instantly remembered the unpleasant man and became very thoughtful. "Did he tell you where he got it?"

"He said he bought it at an auction, but was tired of it and agreed to sell the parchment painting to me."

"Does he know what it means?"

"No. I asked him if there was any story to it, and he said not as far as he knew."

"Have you ever taken this parchment out of its frame?" Nancy went on.

"No," Mr Flockhart replied. "Why?"

"There might be a message on the back, or at least a clue to one."

"Good idea," Mr Flockhart said. "Let's take it out right now!"

·5·

Bird Attack

THE mystery picture was carefully framed, and looked as if it had never been opened. Mr Flockhart removed the backing, then slid out the parchment. He held it up for the others to see.

"It's even more beautiful out of the frame!" Junie exclaimed.

Mr Flockhart handed the picture to Nancy, who turned it over.

"Here's an initial," she noted. "It's an A." She flipped the picture over to look at the front again. In a moment she exclaimed, "The A is directly behind the baby who is being held by the angel!"

Mr Flockhart said, "I wonder if it has anything to do with St Anthony."

The others doubted this, and Junie asked, "Is there another notation on the back?"

Nancy looked closely. "Yes, there is," she said, excited. "In the lower right-hand corner are the initials DB, and under it is printed *Milano*."

"Milano?" Mr Flockhart repeated. "That must mean Milano, Italy, although there is one in Texas."

Nancy turned to him. "I assume Mr Rocco is Italian. Perhaps he brought the parchment from Italy."

"That's a logical guess," Mr Flockhart replied. "He might have bought it at an auction over there." He smiled at Nancy. "I can see why you are known as such a good detective. Just by taking the parchment out of the frame you've come up with a couple of clues already!"

"Oh, don't compliment me now," she answered modestly. "Wait until I've solved the case."

Junie teased, "Your next stop may be Milano!"

"I think we should go and see Mr Rocco," Nancy said. "He might be able to tell us more."

Junie's father agreed, but said, "Not tonight, please. Wait until morning."

Nancy asked Junie if she knew the way to the Rocco farm. The girl shook her head. "I've never been there. Dad, can you tell us how to get to Mr Rocco's?"

"Sure," Mr Flockhart said and gave the girls explicit directions. "As you know," he added, "I don't care for the man. Please be very careful while you're there. He may become suspicious that I'm sending you over to see him with some ulterior motive in mind. I don't want that to happen. After all he is a good customer and I'd hate to lose his business."

Nancy and Junie said they understood and would follow his instructions. Then they went to bed early so they would be well rested for their mission.

The following morning after breakfast they drove to the Rocco farm. When they arrived, the girls noticed that the house and grounds were surrounded by a high fence. There were two iron gates blocking the entrance.

The friends looked at each other in dismay. "Your

father was right," Nancy said. "This man must be suspicious of everyone in the area to barricade himself like this. What a terrible way to live!"

Junie tried to open the gates, but found that they were locked. "Stymied already," she said.

"Here's a bell," Nancy said, pushing the button. "We're not done yet. Where there's a will, there's a way!"

The girls waited, but no one came to answer their call. Nancy pressed the button again, holding it firmly in place for several seconds. Still there was no response of any kind.

"I can't imagine that there's no one around," Junie remarked. "Surely there must be someone to come and let us in."

Nancy said that perhaps the owner did not want any visitors. "Or maybe the bell doesn't work," she added. "Are you game to climb over the fence with me, Junie?"

"Sure."

Since both girls were wearing jeans and shirts, it was not much trouble for them to get over the enclosure. In front of them was a long lane, bordered on both sides by a stone wall.

'Not a very inviting place," Junie remarked, gazing ahead. "Soon we'll see a sign saying, 'Beware of the people who live here. They may bite.'"

Nancy laughed, then said, "Let's keep our eyes and ears open. We don't want to miss anything. Look over there. Several cars are parked near the house. That proves somebody is home. Probably Mr Rocco is having a very private meeting and doesn't want any outsiders around. That's why he wouldn't answer the bell."

The girls went on. They had almost reached the stone farmhouse when they became aware of a great fluttering overhead. Startled, they looked up. The next second a huge flock of black birds descended and attacked the visitors viciously!

"Ouch!" Junie cried out. "That hurts. Get away from me!"

She and Nancy tried hard to fight off their unfriendly attackers. The large birds had long claws and prominent beaks. Each girl put one arm over her face and with her free hand tried batting at the birds to make them fly away. But their efforts seemed hopeless, and the battle to beat off the birds' attacks continued.

Making no headway, Nancy and Junie began to scream as loudly as they could. "Help! Help! Someone please help us!"

Their cries were almost drowned out by the raucous noise made by the birds. No one answered the girls' pleas, so in desperation they dropped to the ground and doubled up, putting their heads and arms under their bodies. This seemed to anger the birds, who made more noise than ever and pecked mercilessly at the helpless visitors.

Once Nancy raised her head and screamed at the top of her lungs. "Help us! Quick! We need help! Hurry!"

Whether it was her cry that was heard by the men in the house or the frightening noise of the birds, the girls did not know. Several men rushed out, yelling. Finally the birds flew off.

One man walked up to Nancy and Junie and asked in an unpleasant, demanding voice, "What are you doing here? Don't you know this is private prop-erty?"

Junie explained that her family were neighbours of Mr Rocco and that she had come to see him on an important matter. "Please take us to him."

"You can't visit him now," the man replied. "He's in conference. How did you get into the grounds?"

Neither girl answered. They were staring at their interrogator and at the other men who by now had arrived at the scene. All of them looked tough and unfriendly. Rocco's pals resembled underworld characters, Junie and Nancy thought.

"Who owns those birds?" Nancy asked. "Mr Rocco?"

In a surly voice one of the group replied, "What makes you think anybody owns them? In any case, it's none of your business. What right do you have to ask questions? Now get out of here before you cause any more trouble."

Junie asked him, "Will you please unlock the gate?"

The man squinted at the girls and said, "No, I won't, and neither will anybody else. We've had enough guff from you smart alecks. You got in here; now get out. But don't try any funny stuff, because I'll be watching you!"

With no choice Nancy and Junie hurried down the lane. The man who had ordered them out followed at a distance. He made no move to open the gate, so once more the girls were forced to climb the fence.

Junie then drove towards Triple Creek, but took a road traversing the neighbouring village. "Let's stop at the general store and get some ice cream," she said. "All that exercise has made me hungry. Besides, when I get mad I get hot, and something cool will taste good."

The girls went into the store, which included a few tables where customers could eat sandwiches, cakes and ice cream.

Nancy and Junie sat down. Presently a woman came to wait on them, and after serving heaped saucers of vanilla ice cream topped with whipped cream and nuts, she stopped to talk to them. Junie introduced her as Mrs Potter, and said she managed the store for a friend. She then told the woman of their recent experience.

"You know Mr Rocco, don't you?" Junie said. "What can you tell us about him?"

The woman stiffened. "Nothing good," she replied. "Besides, he has some men working for him that I don't like. They were in here one day, talking to me. I couldn't agree with a thing they said. I never want to see them again and I hope from now on they'll all shop in another store."

"Could you tell us why you don't like him?" Junie asked.

"No, I'd rather not. It was something concerning my work, and I don't care to discuss it. Sorry."

The girls respected the woman's wishes and said no more. As soon as they had finished their ice cream, they left the store.

After they were in the car and on the way home, Nancy asked Junie if Mrs Potter was always so abrupt.

"Oh, no," Junie replied. "She's a very nice person and usually full of fun. I can't understand why she acted in the way that she did."

Nancy was silent for a few minutes, then said, "It's my guess she has been intimidated, perhaps by the same men and in the same way that Eezy was!"

·6·

"No Speak English!"

LATER, when Nancy thought Mr Rocco would be free, she called his home. Another man answered and said he would get the owner. Several minutes passed but no one returned to the phone.

"Maybe he had to go a long way to find Mr Rocco," Nancy reasoned.

A few minutes later, she thought, "It wouldn't surprise me if Mr Rocco didn't want to talk to me after I climbed his fence!" She could not understand, however, why her call had not been disconnected. Over and over she said into the phone, "Hello? Hello? Hello!"

Finally she heard Mr Rocco, who was not very cordial. He said, "If you want to see me, I'm glad you called up for an appointment. I don't like people who climb over my fence uninvited!"

Nancy apologized for having done this but added in a pleading voice, "Junie Flockhart and I were eager to see you. When we thought the bell didn't work, we took a chance. Please forgive us."

"What do you want?" Rocco asked abruptly without acknowledging the apology.

"I have come across some very interesting information that I would like to discuss with you—but not over the phone."

After a moment of silence on the other end of the line, Mr Rocco said, "You know I am a very busy man."

"Oh, yes," Nancy replied, "but we won't take up very much of your time. Please. We'd like to talk to you as soon as possible."

"How about next week some time?" the man asked.

Nancy's heart sank. Next week! She could not wait that long. "We were hoping that perhaps we could see you tomorrow," she said.

There was another long pause, then Mr. Rocco said, "What's the hurry?"

"I'll be able to tell you that when we get together," Nancy answered. "Couldn't you spare a few minutes tomorrow morning, say at nine o'clock?"

"Nine o'clock! I make my workers get up at six!" the man said.

"Any time you say will be all right with us," Nancy told him.

Mr Rocco reluctantly agreed to eight o'clock and added, "Don't be late. I can't stand unpunctuality."

Nancy thanked him and cradled the phone. She went to tell Junie of their early appointment.

"Oh, Mr Rocco is impossible, just as my father said!" Junie exclaimed. "But we'll be there. In fact, I suggest we arrive at his home by quarter to eight so he won't get mad. By the way, congratulations for persuading him."

Nancy smiled. "It was a bit of a problem, but it worked."

The two agreed to go to bed early in order to awaken in time for their conference.

The following morning they arrived promptly at quarter to eight. In response to the bell the gate swung free. A man opened the door to the house and said he would see if Mr Rocco had finished his breakfast. Nancy and Junie looked at each other but said nothing. What about Mr Rocco's bragging that he made his workers get up at six o'clock?

Nancy thought, "He's a bit of a slave-driver."

In a few minutes the farm owner appeared. He neither smiled nor shook hands. Instead he growled at them, "I told you not to be late but I didn't want you to come so far ahead of our appointment, either!"

Junie said that the girls would wait until he was ready. Both she and Nancy felt that this unpleasant man tried to intimidate anyone with whom he came in contact. When Rocco realized that his method did not work on the girls, he scowled and paused for several seconds before replying to his callers.

"You don't have to wait. But be quick about what you want. I haven't much time, you know."

Without hesitation Nancy said, "We are very interested in the parchment you sold to Mr Flockhart. Did you bring it from Italy?"

"Yes," Rocco replied. "I bought it at an auction there."

"Can you tell us anything about it?" Nancy went on.

"I don't know anything about it. At first I liked the figures painted on the parchment, but a while ago I got tired of looking at them, so I decided to sell the picture. It's very fine work and brought a nice price. I guess Mr Flockhart recognized a good thing when he saw it."

"The parchment's lovely," Nancy agreed. Then she asked Mr Rocco if he had ever taken the parchment out of its frame to look for anything of interest that might have been written on the back.

The man stared at his visitors intently. "No," he said. "It never occurred to me. Did you find something?"

The two girls glanced at each other. They thought it best not to tell him what they had discovered.

"Oh, we studied it, but there wasn't much on the back," Nancy said lightly.

Rocco did not inquire just what they had discovered, and the girls were glad. Suddenly the man bombarded them with questions.

"Why this great interest in the parchment? Do you feel there is something wrong with it? Is your father sorry he bought the painting? Does he expect me to buy it back?"

Mr Rocco paused, but only long enough to catch his breath. "You young whippersnappers come barging into my home and hammer me with questions. What's going on? I think I have a right to know."

By this time the man was very excited, and for a short time Nancy felt guilty about upsetting him. Then she thought of several things that had happened and her attitude changed. She said she was sorry if she and Junie had harassed the farm owner. They meant no harm. Their main interest was to learn the background of the parchment. This seemed to satisfy Mr Rocco for the time being.

Junie changed the subject and asked Rocco, "Were you ever married?"

"No!" Rocco said quickly, and did not volunteer any more information. Instead, he stood up as if he were afraid Nancy or Junie might ask more questions he did not want to answer. He indicated that the visit was over.

The girls walked to the front door, with Rocco following them stiffly. On the way home in the car, Junie said, "I wonder why Mr Rocco was so unwilling to give us anything but the barest information about either the parchment or himself."

Nancy said she thought he was a man with many secrets, which he had no intention of divulging.

Junie remarked, "I just think he's an old grouch. How are we going to find out anything about the picture he brought from Italy if he won't talk?"

Nancy thought for a few seconds, then replied. "Let's try to get the information in spite of him! We'll leave the car on the road and hike across the fields until we meet one of his workmen. Maybe he'll talk, and we can learn more about Rocco."

"His first name is Salvatore, by the way," Junie said.

It was several minutes before they saw a man working in one of the vegetable fields. The girls went up to him and smiled.

"Good morning," Nancy said.

The man remained silent, though he smiled at her. She wondered if he were deaf, so this time she shouted her "good morning". Still there was no response and the farmhand went on working.

Junie walked close to the man and shouted at him,

"Do you live here and work for Mr Rocco?"

The man shrugged. "No speak English," he finally said.

Nancy and Junie looked at each other and walked on. Across the field they saw another worker and headed in his direction. They put the same question to him and received the same answer, "No speak English!"

Junie sighed. "No one around here seems to speak our language. We're getting nowhere fast."

As the girls walked on Nancy suddenly spotted something and pointed. "I see a boy over there. Maybe we'll have better luck with him."

They walked towards the lad, who appeared to be about ten years old. He was handsome with large brown eyes and black curly hair.

The boy was seated on the ground in the shade of a large branch, and was holding a sketching pad and coloured pencils. He was drawing a picture of the landscape spread before him. Against a tree nearby stood a hoe.

"That's very good, sonny," Junie told him, looking closely at the sketch. "What is your name?"

The little boy smiled but said nothing.

"Do you speak English?" Nancy asked.

The boy shook his head. "No English. Italian."

Suddenly the young artist jumped up. He hid his sketching pad and pencils under a sweater and grabbed the hoe. He moved off a little distance and began to work furiously. Nancy and Junie looked at him in surprise. Since they made no attempt to move, he pointed into the distance. They followed the direction of his finger. Mr Rocco was coming towards them.

"We'd better scoot," Junie warned. "I doubt that Mr Rocco would like our being here."

Nancy nodded and the girls hurried off in the opposite direction. On the way home, Nancy said, "I believe if young Tony could speak English he might give us some clues."

"How do you know the boy's name is Tony?" Junie asked.

Nancy grinned. "I saw it on his sweater!"

"Good observation!" Junie praised. "I didn't even notice his sweater."

As soon as the girls reached the farmhouse, Nancy called her father's office. He was there and asked how she was progressing with the mystery.

"Not very well," she replied. "I need your help."

"Sure thing. What can I do for you?"

"Will you please find out from the Immigration Department all you can about Salvatore Rocco, who came to the United States from Italy several years ago?" She told her father all she had learned so far.

"I see you've been busy," he said. "I'll check with Immigration and let you know the answer."

After the call, the girls went to look at the mysterious parchment again. They puzzled over it for some time before Junie asked Nancy if she had come up with any new theories.

Nancy's eyes sparkled. "I have a wild guess!" she said.

·7·

A Mean Ram

"I THINK we can assume," Nancy said to Junie, "that Mr Salvatore Rocco knows more about the parchment than he is telling. The initial A on it could stand for Anthony, and a common nickname for Anthony is Tony."

Junie knit her brows. "Are you trying to say that Tony, the little boy we met on Mr Rocco's farm, might be the baby in this parchment picture?"

Nancy nodded. "I told you it was a wild guess."

"It sure is," Junie agreed, "but I respect your hunches."

Mr Flockhart walked into the room and was told Nancy's latest theory. He chuckled, but said he was impressed with the idea. "Nancy, please continue with your suppositions. It sounds like an intriguing story, and the first hypothesis that has been made so far in the mystery of the parchment."

Junie remarked that the man pictured on the parchment, who had his back to the viewer, could be the boy's father. "But why wouldn't he be facing the viewer? Was the artist ashamed of him?"

"That's a possible answer," her father agreed. "On the other hand, maybe the artist just didn't like

202

the person and turned him around so nobody could recognize him." He said to Nancy, "Have you any more guesses?"

"Not yet," she replied, "but I may have after I learn more about little Tony and Mr Salvatore Rocco."

Mr Flockhart reminded the girls that it was generally believed in the community that Mr Rocco was the child's uncle and that the boy's parents had died.

"That gives me an idea," Nancy said. "The last picture on the parchment portrays the collision of a sailing ship and a steamer. Maybe," she added, "Tony's parents were killed in the accident."

"Very reasonable assumption," Mr Flockhart said. "I wonder if Mr Rocco legally adopted his nephew."

"I guess," said Junie, "that we'd have to go to Italy to find out." She teased, "Nancy Drew, detective, Milano is getting closer and closer."

Nancy grinned. "Maybe, but I have a hunch I'll solve the mystery right here at Triple Creek Farm."

Junie and her father looked at their guest, then Junie said, "Nancy Drew, you're holding back one of your hunches, or theories, or wild guesses. Come on, what is it?"

Nancy nodded. "You're right. In the first place, I'm not convinced that Mr Rocco's story to Mr Flockhart and to us about buying the painting at an auction is true. I've been thinking of poor Tony. He has so much talent as an artist, and so does the person who made these paintings, whose initials are DB. That person could be a close relative of Tony's. By the way, what's his last name?"

"I don't know," Junie's father replied. "I have

always supposed it was Rocco."

Mr Flockhart said he thought the girls should try to find out what DB stood for. "It might be the initials of the artist, or an art school, or a museum, or even a dealer's initials."

"One thing is sure," Nancy said, "Milano is Milano, Italy, so that's as good a place to start as any, but I guess we can't go there."

Junie's father said, "Leaving the mystery for a moment, Nancy, I have a little favour to ask of you. In your spare moments, try your hand at creating an attractive symbol for Triple Creek Farm. I don't like the one I've been using."

"I'll be glad to try," Nancy replied.

As soon as he left the room, she went to the hall table, where the telephone was, and picked up several sheets of paper and a pencil. Junie watched intently as Nancy made sketch after sketch. The girls laughed at some of them.

"This one looks like a three-legged monkey," Junie remarked. "No offence meant."

"And this one like a broken harp with all the strings missing," Nancy added. "Junie, let's do something else. By the time we come back, maybe my imagination will return. Right now I've run out of ideas for a Triple Creek symbol."

"What would you like to do?" Junie asked.

The girl detective thought they should call on Eezy as soon as Junie finished her chores, with Nancy's help. "Maybe he'll be willing to tell us more about those two men who knocked him out, and also what he knows about Mr Rocco."

Junie agreed. After two hours of work with the

new-born sheep, the girls changed clothes and were ready to set off for the shepherd's cabin.

As before, they drove part of the way, then climbed up the hillside among the sheep. Eezy was there, sitting on a log in front of his little cottage and casting an eye over the hundreds of healthy-looking sheep in his flock.

"Howdy, girls!" he greeted them. "I had a feelin' maybe you'd run up here today. Glad to see you."

When Nancy said, "I hope we're not interrupting your work," the shepherd chuckled and immediately answered. "As it says in the book of Hebrews, *'Be not forgetful to entertain strangers: for thereby some have entertained angels unawares.'"*

The two girls smiled at the compliment, then Junie said, "I'm not an angel, but I do like to help people. Nancy does too. That's why we're here."

"Eezy," Nancy said, "did the two men who attacked you ever return?"

"No."

She asked him if he was still unwilling to talk about what his attackers wanted him to do for them.

"I'm afraid I am," the shepherd replied. "Sorry, but it might get some innocent people into trouble."

Nancy now asked Eezy to tell them all he knew about Mr Rocco. The herdsman repeated the story Mr Flockhart had told, then added, "I don't know anythin' else about the Italian, because he's a man without a civil tongue.

"Not one of his workers can speak English, and somebody told me he pushes them very, very hard in the fields. He overworks his men on the produce

* Hebrews 13:2

farm. Besides, he is often cruel. I understand that sometimes he beats that little boy who lives with him. Rocco says he's his uncle, but I don't believe him. He sure doesn't look like the boy or have his disposition."

"Mr Rocco beats the boy? How dreadful!" Nancy remarked. "Don't the authorities get after him?"

"Guess not," Eezy replied. "But there's a proverb in the Bible that says, *'The merciful man doeth good to his own soul: but he that is cruel troubleth his own body.'"*

The girls thought about this and decided the proverb was indeed true. They wondered what punishment might come to Rocco for his cruel and unwarranted actions to others.

At this moment a cute and friendly little lamb came up to the girls and stood patiently waiting for their affection. Both of them leaned down and hugged the young animal.

"You're a cutie all right," said Junie. "I'm going to call you 'Cheerio'."

"Oh, I hope it won't have to be slaughtered," Nancy said, worried.

Eezy smiled. "I won't recommend it, 'cause the little sheep is a real comfort to me. You know it gets mighty lonely up on this hilltop. This little critter comes and sits by my side and listens to all my woes."

"That's something that shouldn't be changed," Nancy said. "I suggest you put a sign around Cheerio's neck saying, 'Private Property. I belong to Eezy.'"

The shepherd smiled and said he would certainly like that.

* Proverbs 11:17

In a few minutes the visitors left and started down the hillside. They had not gone far when Junie called Nancy's attention to a large ram standing close by, silhouetted against the cloudless skyline.

"Sometimes he's mean," Junie said. "We'll avoid him."

The girls kept walking but their eyes were on the ram. He looked at them balefully, tossed his head into the air, then lowered his horns before charging at the girls.

"He's going to attack you!" Junie cried out. "Run! Nancy, run! Follow me!"

Both girls sped off like a couple of deer, but the ram was also quick. Nancy and Junie managed to stay ahead of him until, without warning, a strange dog began barking nearby.

"Maybe that will frighten the ram away," Nancy suggested.

Junie said there was not a chance of that happening. "This ram is not afraid of dogs," she explained. "One day I saw him toss a big black one high into the air. He almost killed it!"

Nancy was thinking, "This mustn't happen to me!" and ran faster.

She was finally outdistancing the ram when a large sheep, frightened by the strange dog, ran directly in front of Nancy. She tried to leap over the broad-backed, woolly animal, but could not make it. The next moment she fell flat!

By now the ram had caught up to her. The next moment Nancy felt his curved horns reach speedily under her body.

Wild thoughts went through the trapped girl's

mind. Would the ram toss her into the air as he had the dog?

·8·

The Mystery Boy's Story

As the ram got ready to toss Nancy into the air, a desperate thought came to her on how she might save herself. She reached out to grasp the animal's curved horns, caught one with each hand, and hung on.

The animal, angered, tried again and again to throw the girl off, but she kept her grip on the horns, and braced herself against his body. Nancy swung crazily from side to side but did not lose her hold, as the animal endeavoured desperately to shake her off.

After one more try, the ram stood still. Was he exhausted or defeated? No matter what the answer was, Nancy regained her balance and stood up, but kept a wary eye on the unfriendly animal.

Junie came running up. "What a dreadful experience!" she exclaimed. "Oh, Nancy, I'm so sorry."

The ram, though mean, knew Junie and made no attempt to attack her. She gave him a resounding slap and sent him galloping off.

The girls had counted on their luck too soon. The ram had not gone far when he suddenly turned around and made a bee-line for the girls, horns lowered. At the same moment a loud commanding voice came to their ears.

"Eezy is using his giant megaphone!" Junie said. "He's chastising the ram."

The command lasted for a few seconds, then the insistent animal started moving forward again. At once the strains of beautiful music could be heard. Nancy looked at Junie, puzzled.

"Eezy plays an Irish harp to calm the sheep," her friend explained. "It has never failed yet to halt fights."

This time was no exception. The ram stopped short, sniffed the air, then lay down. All the other sheep on the hillside that were not already resting slowly dropped to the grass.

"That's remarkable!" Nancy exclaimed. "I'd like to go back and thank Eezy. In a way he saved my life."

"All right," Junie agreed. "I'm sure we'll have no more trouble with that ram. No doubt by this time he knows that you and I and Eezy are friends."

When the girls reached the shepherd's cabin, they found him seated outdoors, strumming his harp. As soon as he finished the number, Nancy complimented him on his playing. "You're like David in the Bible," she said.

The elderly man smiled. "Thank you," he said. "You know it says in the book of Amos, *'Chant to the sound of the harp, and invent to themselves instruments of music, like David.'"*

The girls nodded and Nancy said, "Your small Irish harp is a good tuneful substitute for David's lyre."

"That's what I decided," Eezy replied. "And to tell the truth, I think I can get a lot more music out

* Amos 6:5

of it than David did out of his lyre!" He chuckled.

Nancy thanked him for helping her ward off a second attack by the ram. She begged for an encore of his harp playing. The shepherd obliged, then put down his instrument.

He picked up his megaphone and called out, "Rest period is over, boys and girls. Stand up and get to work!" He winked at the girls. "The sheep's only work is to eat grass!"

Nancy unexpectedly asked Eezy if he had a pad and pencil in the cabin. The shepherd went to get them, and at once Nancy started sketching. In a few minutes she drew three streams with a woolly sheep superimposed over them. Under the sketch Nancy printed TRIPLE CREEK FARM.

"How do you like that as a trademark?" she asked.

"It's great," Junie replied.

"Mighty good work,' Eezy added. "And it's real picturesque."

Nancy said she hoped Mr Flockhart would like it. She folded the paper and put it into her pocket. Then she and Junie said goodbye to the shepherd and walked down the hill towards the car.

As it carried them towards Triple Creek, Nancy asked, "Junie, do you know anyone around here who speaks Italian?"

Junie said she knew no one in the immediate vicinity, but that her boyfriend, Dan White, was studying Italian at a nearby university. "Why do you ask?"

Nancy replied, "Would he be willing to come here and secretly talk with some of Mr Rocco's farm workers?"

Junie laughed. "There goes that detective mind of

yours again," she said. "I'm sure Dan would love the assignment. I'll try to get him on the phone as soon as we reach home."

Fortunately Dan was in his room, studying. When Junie gave him the message, he expressed surprise. "If you think I can speak the language well enough, I'll be over. I'd certainly like to try acting as interpreter."

It was arranged that he would arrive the next morning around ten o'clock, since he had no classes at that time. Nancy liked him. The tall, red-haired young man was intelligent-looking and had a great sense of humour. He was intrigued to hear that Nancy was a girl detective.

"Junie didn't mention this to me," he said. "I'll never be able to match you in tracking down clues."

Nancy grinned. "You won't find that hard."

Dan asked for instructions on the part he was to play. Nancy started by telling him they were becoming more suspicious each day of Mr Rocco, who seemed to be carrying out some wicked scheme in the area and mistreating the little boy he said was his nephew. "Besides, we're sure that the parchment hanging over the mantel, which Mr Flockhart bought from Mr Rocco, holds some special significance. If we could discover the meaning of it, we might solve a couple of mysteries."

Dan asked, "What makes you suspicious of Mr Rocco?"

Junie told him about the insolent men who had talked to Mrs Potter at the store; how Eezy was attacked by two strangers who, they suspected, were henchmen of Rocco's; of his reported cruelty to little

Tony; and about his unwillingness to permit visitors on to his grounds or into his home.

"Sounds complicated to me," Dan said. "But if I can do anything to help unravel the mystery, I'll be at your service. Shall we go to the Rocco farm at once?"

"Oh yes," Nancy replied. "All right with you, Junie?"

"You bet."

The three set off. Junie took a route that led them through the small nearby village. She pointed out the general store and said, "That's one of our clues!"

Nancy told Dan that she thought clue number two was about four miles away. When they reached the area, Junie turned down a side road.

"I think it best if we are not seen near the gate of the Rocco house," she said. "I'll park down here, under some trees, and we'll walk across the fields until we locate the workmen."

As they started off, hoping to find the Italian labourers, Dan and the girls found most of the terrain hilly. It was a long trek before they saw the first workman. The three detectives walked up to him. Dan smiled and said good morning in English, but the man did not reply, nor even smile. Were these Rocco's orders?

"Try it in Italian," Junie urged Dan.

He did so, but the man shook his head. Puzzled, Dan said a few more things to him. Finally the labourer answered but hopelessly Dan threw up his hands. "This man speaks one of the dialects used in Italy, but he doesn't understand my college Italian, and I don't understand his regional Italian."

The three visitors said goodbye, although they knew the listener did not understand them, and went on.

Nancy said, "I see another man way over at the end of this field."

The three trekkers headed in that direction. After a long walk in the hot sun, they reached the farmhand's side. Once more Dan tried his college Italian. All he received in reply was a blank stare.

"This is maddening," Junie burst out.

The workman went on with his hoeing. In a last desperate attempt to get some information, Dan said several things to him in the Italian he knew. The labourer merely shook his head.

"I guess we'll have to give up," Dan said. "I'm terribly sorry."

"Let's make one more try," Nancy suggested. "It's possible these men are under orders from Rocco not to talk."

"There's no one else in sight," Junie Flockhart pointed out.

"That's true," Nancy replied, "but how about little Tony?"

Both Dan and Junie felt they had nothing to lose by trying, so the three set off across the field. It was a long walk to where the little boy was at work. This time he was busy with a hoe. His drawing pad and pencils were not in sight.

As the visitors arrived, Tony politely stopped working and bowed. At once Dan said to him in his college Italian, "Good morning!"

Tony replied, a great smile breaking over his face. Then, as he and Dan talked, Junie's friend translated. "Tony says he is an orphan and that Mr Rocco is his uncle, but that he has to work very hard and has no chance to play.

"Tony tells me he loves to draw but has to do this on the sly. After you girls were here the other day, his uncle caught him and tore up a drawing pad one of the men had given him secretly. Rocco even burned the pencils."

Nancy was furious. There was no doubt that the boy had great talent. It was shameful that the tools for his art should have been destroyed!

Dan translated further. "After Tony's parents died, he was brought to this country as a baby. He has been reared by Italians from Rome and never allowed to mingle with anyone else. He has had good schooling, but only from an Italian college tutor who comes in the evening. Poor Tony says he is so tired sometimes from working hard all day that the print blurs before his eyes."

Dan went on to explain that Tony had never been away from the farm since the day he was brought there. "His uncle says that some day, when they get rich, the two of them will return to Italy."

Further conversation was interrupted when Tony cried out and spoke excitedly in Italian. Dan translated, "Run fast! My uncle is coming! He will be very angry! He doesn't like trespassers and may harm you. But come to see me again. Oh, please come to see me again!"

·9·
Midnight Thief

TONY started working furiously with his hoe and the visitors left quickly, running towards a nearby down-hill slope so they would not be seen.

But it was too late. From not far away came a loud shout. Angry words were hurled at them in English, and at Tony in Italian.

"Get out of here! I told you to stay away from this farm!"

Everyone turned to look. Rocco kept yelling. "You girls got no business here! Don't come back or you'll get hurt!"

So Rocco had recognized Nancy and Junie.

Without waiting to be caught by Mr Rocco, Nancy and her friends fled down the hillside. They reached the car, jumped in, and sped off.

It was not until then that anyone spoke. Dan asked, "What are you going to do now?"

Nancy thought for a few moments while she caught her breath, and finally said, "I believe I should get in touch with Mr Vincenzo Caspari. He should be home by now."

"Who is he?" Dan asked.

"An acquaintance of my friend Ned Nickerson,"

the young sleuth replied. "Ned gave me his address over the phone and thought perhaps he could help us. He's a well-known painter."

Junie and Dan thought this would be a good idea. Nancy went on to tell them that the man had been born in America but his parents had come from Italy. "No doubt Mr Caspari speaks Italian. I understand he studied in Italy for several years."

Dan grinned. "He probably speaks better Italian than I do! Perhaps he should talk to little Tony."

"I think," said Nancy, "that you did very well and got a lot of important information for us."

"I'll tell that to my Italian professor," Dan replied. "Maybe he'll give me a better grade!"

The university student said he must leave in order to attend a class later that day. He promised to return soon. "Call me if you need me," he added.

As soon as he had gone, Nancy went to the phone and called Vincenzo Caspari. She introduced herself and said Ned Nickerson had suggested that perhaps the artist could help her solve a mystery posed by a puzzling group of pictures on a parchment. "They're supposed to contain a great secret," she concluded.

"That sounds most intriguing," the artist replied. "Ned has told me that you like to solve mysteries. I presume there is more to this story than you're telling me."

"Oh, yes," Nancy replied.

But before she could go on, the man interjected, "I can't imagine how I might be able to help you. When I look at a picture, that is all I see—the composition, the colour. I do not look for anything beyond that. It is up to the artist who painted it to reveal whatever hidden meanings he intended."

"Please, Mr Caspari," Nancy said, "don't say no until you've seen the parchment. I have no real proof my guesses are correct, but perhaps after you see the pictures, you can give me some clues that will help solve the mystery."

"You flatter me," Vincenzo Caspari said. "After all, I am only an artist, not a detective."

Nancy said quickly, "You may find yourself becoming a sleuth before you know it!"

They exchanged a few more words before the artist consented to meet the young detective. Nancy inquired if it would be possible for him to come over some time soon.

He replied, "I can make it tomorrow morning. Is that soon enough?"

"It would be wonderful," Nancy told him. "What time shall we say?"

Ten o'clock was decided upon. The conversation ceased, and the artist hung up. Nancy did too, but she stood there, deep in thought. Finally she was interrupted by Junie, who was going outside to do some work.

"I want to see if that little fellow whose legs I massaged is getting along all right," she said. "How about coming with me?"

Nancy was glad to. She had been wondering about the little black lamb herself. The girls hurried out to the barn where he was kept.

"I see several new lambs have been brought in since yesterday," Junie remarked. "Oh, and here are twins."

Two snow-white bundles lay sound asleep together. Their mother stood nearby. The ewe looked at the girls with a warning eye.

Junie laughed. "I'm not going to hurt your babies. I just want to congratulate you." The ewe seemed to understand and gave a loud *baa*.

"They are darlings!" Nancy remarked. "Don't tell me they're likely to be taken away and their skins made into parchment or vellum."

Junie put a hand on Nancy's arm. "That's for my father to decide. After all, this is his livelihood, and business is business."

Nancy realized how necessary the slaughtering of domesticated sheep, cows, goats, and hogs was. Otherwise the countryside would be overrun with animals. She also thought, "As long as people want to eat meat, this practice will go on."

In a few moments they reached the pen where the injured black lamb was. Both Nancy and Junie were delighted to see that he was walking around quite normally. They plucked some freshly-cut hay from a nearby cart and held it for him to munch. He took it gratefully, then looked at the girls with his bright eyes as if asking for more.

Junie laughed. "You didn't know that I was trying an experiment on you," she said. "I just wanted to see if you had a good appetite and could swallow all right." She turned to Nancy, "I think I'll have to report that this little fellow is ready to be put out in a field." She went to a book fastened with a cord to a small desk and wrote down her report.

After lunch Junie got the jeep and the girls rode all around the farm. This time Nancy had a chance to see other fields of sheep. Each one had a shepherd.

"Eezy is my favourite of them all," Junie told her friend.

The day wore on and Nancy could not help thinking how quickly it had gone by, when Junie reminded her it was time to go to bed. All the lights were extinguished and everyone went upstairs. In a short time the house became very quiet.

Junie fell asleep at once, but Nancy lay awake, going over the whole mystery in her mind. Each time her thoughts would lead to Tony. She became incensed at Mr Rocco and thought, "He might cause a permanent injury to that boy! Tony should be taken away from him!"

Presently Nancy became fidgety. Not only was she wide awake, but questions were going round and round in her head.

"It's no use staying here," the girl detective told herself finally. "I'll go downstairs and study the parchment for a while."

Nancy put on her robe and slippers, picked up her flashlight, and tiptoed from the room. She closed the door and walked softly along the hallway to the stairs, descending noiselessly so as not to awaken anyone. Then she crossed the big hall.

Nancy was about to turn on a light switch, when she was startled by a thin shaft of light moving across the living room. She saw no one, but realized that it was impossible for the light to move by itself.

She strained her eyes and finally discerned the dim figure of a man holding a flashlight. Presently the light stopped moving and was beamed directly on the parchment hanging over the mantel.

Nancy's heart was beating very fast. Was some

member of the household holding the flashlight? Suddenly she realized he was an intruder. The man was wearing a stocking mask!

The girl sleuth stood perfectly still, hardly daring to breathe. Suddenly the masked figure reached up and took down the picture.

Nancy decided it was time to act. "Leave that alone!" she commanded.

In response the man turned around and threw the picture at Nancy. It missed her by a fraction of an inch and crashed against the door jamb. It fell to the floor, the glass broken to bits.

Nancy tried to reach the light switch, but before she could do so, her assailant shone his brilliant light directly in her face. She could see nothing!

The thief leaped across the room and grabbed the parchment and frame. He dashed to the front door.

"Stop! Stop!" Nancy cried at the top of her voice.

As the intruder started to open the front door, Nancy reached him. He tried to ward her off with his free hand, but she managed to get hold of it and rip off the glove he was wearing.

The girl's movement had been quick, but it gave the thief a chance to fend her off. With a great shove he sent her reeling across the hallway. As she was regaining her balance, the man opened the door and rushed out, carrying the precious parchment with him!

Just as Nancy recovered her wits, the house was flooded with lights. Mr and Mrs Flockhart and Junie hurried down the stairs, each asking what had happened. Nancy quickly explained. At once Junie's father set off an ear-splitting alarm. He explained that it would awaken the workers in their cottages so they would be on the lookout for the burglar.

Mrs Flockhart said, "Shouldn't we alert the police, also?"

Her husband agreed, so Junie hurried to the phone and called. Meanwhile, Mrs Flockhart took Nancy into the living room and made her sit down on the couch.

"This was a dreadful experience for you," she said. "Now I want you to take it easy."

The girl detective was much too excited to take it easy. Besides, she felt all right and tried to reassure Junie's mother.

"I'm furious at myself for letting the thief get away!" she said. "That was bad enough, but to think he took the parchment with him!"

Nancy was on the verge of tears. Apparently Mrs Flockhart realized this. Giving the girl a hug, she said, "I think we should be thankful that you weren't hurt!"

Nancy appreciated the concern and tried to smile, but she said, "I came here at Junie's invitation to solve the mystery of the paintings on that parchment. I didn't do it and now the parchment is gone! I may as well go home," she finished with a sigh.

"Oh, no, no!" Junie's mother said, holding Nancy tighter. "I'm sure my husband and daughter wouldn't hear of such a thing. As a matter of fact, Nancy, now you have a double mystery to solve. You must first find the parchment and then tell us its meaning."

·10·

Running Footprints

FOR a while Nancy and Mrs Flockhart wondered who the parchment thief might have been.

"Have you any ideas at all?" the woman asked the girl detective when they came to no conclusion.

"No, not really," she replied. "Of course I think our first idea would be Mr Rocco, but the man who was here was too tall."

"Anyway," said Mrs Flockhart, "why should Mr Rocco feel he had to steal the parchment? All he had to do was come and ask Mr Flockhart to sell it back to him."

"That's true," Nancy agreed. "But I think Mr Rocco became worried after I quizzed him about the pictures. Buying back the parchment might make it too obvious that he wanted it, so he had someone take it."

"That's good reasoning," Mrs Flockhart said. "On the other hand, a person who knows the true story of the parchment may have stolen it, and will do some blackmailing."

At this moment Mr Flockhart and Junie walked in with a State Policeman. They all sat down together in the living room.

"Any luck?" Mrs Flockhart asked her husband.

He shook his head, then introduced the State Policeman, Officer Browning. Mr Flockhart said that his chase and that of the police and the many workers on Triple Creek Farm had yielded no sign of the fugitive.

"It is unfortunate," the officer said. "We'll have to hunt for clues."

Nancy produced the glove she had torn from the thief's hand and gave it to the officer. "I grabbed this from the burglar's left hand," she explained.

"This is an excellent clue," Browning said. When he was told by Junie that Nancy was an amateur detective, he asked her, "What is your guess as to the kind of glove it is?"

The young sleuth was flattered and not a bit dismayed. She replied, "It's not a workman's glove. Therefore, I doubt that it belongs either to a sheepherder or to a farmer of any kind."

Officer Browning nodded. "You're right. This could mean that the thief is a professional burglar who is not native to these parts. He may even be from the city."

Junie spoke. "Then it may be very difficult to find him," she said. "Like looking for a raindrop in a pond."

"Not necessarily," the officer told her. "The man could have been hired to do this job and may still be in the neighbourhood, delivering it."

He told the others that he would take the glove to the police laboratory and have it thoroughly examined.

Nancy asked, "Can you find clear fingerprints

inside the glove?"

The officer shook his head. "No, because the material is textured and porous. But we may get some clue from the glove."

He asked if anyone had touched the front door since the burglar had had his bare hand on it. No one had, so Browning said he would get a fingerprint kit from his car and try to take impressions of the newest set of fingerprints.

Although Nancy had watched fingerprint work by police many times, she never tired of looking at the process. But presently she walked outside. Her eyes picked up a clear imprint of half a shoe. Nancy hurried over to look at it, crouched down, and studied the print intently. Then she got up and looked for another. Using her flashlight, she discovered a series of similar ones for left and right feet in turn. They led across a field to a road. Here the prints ended, and Nancy assumed from tracks in the pavement dust that the thief had gone off in a car.

Nancy quickly returned to the house. By this time the officer had finished his fingerprint work. She asked him to come over and look at the shoe marks. Nancy told him she believed they belonged to the burglar.

"Since they are only of the front half of each foot, they were made by someone running."

Officer Browning nodded. "You're absolutely right, Miss Detective. Now tell me, what kind of shoes was the man wearing?"

"Sandshoes," Nancy responded promptly.

The State Policeman shook his head. "You sure know your stuff." he said, "I won't tease you any more. I'll just continue to ask your help."

Junie, who had been indoors, heard the last few remarks and at once told the officer that Nancy Drew had a fine reputation for solving the most difficult mysteries imaginable.

"Oh, stop bragging about me," Nancy pleaded with her friend. She explained to the officer, "I came here to find the meaning of four paintings on the parchment that was stolen, and now it's gone. I've botched the case."

Junie said, "Officer Browning, Nancy says she might go home because she hasn't solved the mystery. Can't you do something to make her stay?"

The husky-looking man smiled. "I tell you what, Nancy. Suppose I find the parchment for you; then you can keep the job of solving the mystery of the paintings."

At once Nancy's old eagerness to win the case returned. She said, "I wish you the best of luck and try to make it soon. I can't stay here much longer; I will wear out my welcome!"

The officer got a camera and took pictures of the footprints. Finally he stepped into his car and drove off.

Junie turned to Nancy. "Maybe, just maybe," she said, as she locked arms with her friend and went into the house, "maybe you'll solve both parts of this mystery yourself before the police do!"

Before the girl detective could reply, Mr Flockhart ordered everyone back to bed. He put out the lights and followed the others upstairs.

Nancy was up early the next day, hunting for further clues to the intruder. First she searched the

living room, dining room, and kitchen thoroughly.
She could find nothing to indicate how the burglar
had gained admittance to the house. She felt he must
be a professional with a master key.

Next Nancy went outdoors and again looked at the
running footsteps. Satisfied that this was the only
clue outside the house, she returned indoors. The
Flockharts were there and they all sat down to breakfast.

Nancy had nearly finished eating, when suddenly
she said, "Oh!"

"What's the matter, dear?" Mrs Flockhart asked.

Nancy said she had just remembered that Mr Vincenzo Caspari was coming to look at the parchment.
"And the parchment is not here!"

Junie suggested that Nancy go at once to call the
man so he would not make the trip in vain. Nancy
hurried to the phone and dialled the artist's number.
A woman answered. When Nancy asked for Mr Caspari, she was told that he had already left. The young
detective, worried, came back to report this to the
others at the table.

"That's too bad," Mrs Flockhart said. "What will
you do?"

Nancy thought a moment, then said, "I'll try to
make a sketch of the paintings on the parchment as
nearly as I remember them. You can help. I'll recite
what I know and you add to it."

She described the first picture of a beautiful
woman. "I hope I can make her look as much like
the original as possible."

Junie spoke up, saying the woman had shiny
coal-black hair, large brown eyes with long lashes,

a rosebud-shaped mouth, and a lovely olive complexion.

"That's absolutely right," Nancy agreed. "Besides, she had a sad smile."

The others nodded and she went on to mention the man with his back to the viewer, the cluster of angels with one of them holding a baby, and the collision of a sailing ship and a steamer.

Mr Flockhart laughed. "You don't need our help," he said. "Now scoot upstairs and draw the pictures before your guest comes."

"But what if I don't finish them in time?" Nancy replied, worried.

"Don't get so uptight. Just relax," Junie said. "If he arrives while you're upstairs, Dad and I will talk to him."

Nancy darted to the stairs, then stopped. "I don't have any paper or coloured pencils with me."

Without saying a word, her friend left briefly and returned with a large, unlined pad and a box of crayons. "Sorry I can't supply pencils."

"Thanks," Nancy said, then hastened to her room. She took a deep sigh as she stared at the blank sheet before her. Then, as if the images on the parchment had suddenly flooded her memory, she began to draw them.

In about twenty minutes she had finished rough sketches of the four paintings. Then, on the back of the one with the baby in it, she printed an A. In the lower left-hand corner of the sheet she put in the initials DB and under it the word *Milano*.

Nancy had just finished when she heard a car drive in. She looked out of the window to be sure that the person arriving was Mr Caspari.

The man who alighted was in his forties and was alone. Was he the great Vincenzo Caspari?

Before Nancy could decide, she noticed something that horrified her. The man's car had begun to roll slowly. If it kept going it would crash into a tree!

·11·

A Tough Suspect

TAKING two steps at a time, Nancy leaped down the stairway of the Flockhart farmhouse and raced out of the front door. Could she stop the rolling car before it crashed into the tree?

The owner, who seemed to be unaware of what was happening, was walking towards the house. Nancy passed him in a flash. He turned to find out why she was in such a hurry, then gasped at what he saw.

Fortunately, his big car was rolling slowly. It had not yet gathered momentum. Nancy was able to yank the front door open, jump in, and jam on the brake. The automobile stopped within an inch of the tree.

"Oh thank you, thank you!" the man exclaimed, catching up to the car. "I am so sorry to have caused you all this trouble." He spoke with an Italian accent.

"I'm glad I saw the car moving," Nancy said. "By any chance, are you Mr Caspari?"

"*Si, si,*" the middle-aged man replied, bowing slightly. "And you are Miss Nancy Drew?"

"Yes, I am," she answered, stepping from the car, with his assistance. The two walked towards the open front door of the farmhouse.

The artist was a charming person, but by his own admission, a bit forgetful. "I should have remembered to put on the brake," he said.

Nancy merely smiled and made no comment. She led her visitor into the living room and they sat down.

"I tried to reach you on the phone this morning, but was told you had already left your house," she said. "I have a horrible confession to make to you."

"Confession?" Mr Caspari repeated. "You do not seem like the kind of girl who would have to make confessions."

Nancy made no response to this. "I'll get right to the point," she said. "The parchment that I asked you to come and look at was stolen last night!"

"Stolen?" he repeated. "From this house?"

"From right above that fireplace mantel," Nancy explained.

She told him the whole story, then said that she had attempted to draw something that looked like the original. "I'll show it to you. Perhaps you can give us a clue to the painter of the original."

She excused herself and went upstairs to get the drawing. After she came down and handed it to the artist, he studied the front of the paper for a long time. He even turned it upside down, but quickly put it back into position.

Finally he looked up and said to Nancy, "Did you draw this from memory?" When she said yes, he went on, "It is an excellent drawing, especially the picture of the angels with the baby."

Nancy thanked him and said, "Maybe that's

because I think it may be the most significant picture in the group. I'll show you why I think so." She turned the paper over and pointed out that the printed A on it was directly behind the picture of the angels. "This is just the way it was on the original."

The artist rubbed his chin. "And none of the other pictures had initials at the back of them?"

"No."

Mr Caspari told Nancy, "I think you are very observing, as an artist should be. Now please tell me what your theory is."

"My guess is that the A stands for Anthony. We met a boy who is an artist. He is the nephew of the man who sold the parchment to Mr Flockhart," she explained. "It may be a long and wild guess, but I am wondering if by any chance that boy could be this baby. His nickname is Tony."

The artist wanted to know if Nancy had ever questioned the former owner about the picture. She nodded. "I tried to, but didn't get very far. He is very secretive and unco-operative. By the way, do you know him—Salvatore Rocco?"

"No. I never heard of him. Tell me more about the boy."

Nancy explained the situation, and ended by saying that Mr Rocco had said he knew nothing about the origin of the parchment . He had purchased it at an auction.

"It is an interesting story," Mr Caspari remarked. "There's a chance, of course, that his story isn't true."

Just then he spotted the initials DB in the corner with the word *Milano* under them.

"Have you any ideas about what these initials stand for?" he asked Nancy.

"No, I haven't."

Mr Caspari said that on this point he might be able to help her out. "I brought with me a directory of European artists." He took it from a pocket and began turning the pages. "I'll look under the section for Italy and see if we can find a DB in Milano."

Nancy sat watching quietly as the man flipped page after page.

Finally he said, "No one with those initials is listed in Milano, but I see three in Rome. Their addresses are here. Do you want them?"

"Yes. I would like to have them, but does it say anything about the people?"

The artist told her that two of them were men and one a woman. Nancy was thoughtful for several seconds, then remarked, "Another one of my hunches—I have a feeling, because of the style of the painting of the angels and the baby, that the artist may be a woman."

"That's a good deduction," her caller said.

"Mr Caspari," Nancy continued, "do you think that this Miss or Mrs DB could have studied in Milano and painted on the parchment when she was there?"

"That's very likely," he agreed.

Reading from his directory, the artist said that the woman's name was Diana Bolardo. Suddenly he snapped his fingers. "I have the perfect solution!" he exclaimed. "My grandparents live in Rome."

Vincenzo Caspari offered to get in touch with them. "I'll phone and ask them to try to find Diana Bolardo."

Nancy was thrilled. How she wished she might go to Rome and investigate herself! She realized, however, that this would be expensive and the clue might lead to a dead end.

"I appreciate this great favour," Nancy told the artist, "and I can hardly wait to hear the answer."

The man smiled. "To tell you the truth, I'm excited to be part of the team trying to solve this mystery."

After Mr Caspari had left, Junie came in to catch up on the news. After telling her, Nancy said, "Junie, would you drive downtown with me?"

"Of course. But why?"

Nancy told her she thought the person who had smashed the glass in the frame of the parchment picture might have brought the frame to a shop to have the glass replaced. "Or else, he might just have taken the measurements and will put the glass in himself. Let's go first to a hardware shop."

Junie said there were three in town. They would go directly to the best one.

Nancy tried to explain to a salesman what she was trying to find out. He said no one had brought a broken picture in for him to fix, or bought a twelve by twenty-inch piece of glass.

Not discouraged, the girls went outside and Junie drove to the next hardware store. As they walked in, Nancy thought this was a likely place for the thief to have brought the parchment picture. One half of the store was devoted to hardware, the other half to pictures and picture framing.

A pleasant woman listened to Nancy's story, but shook her head. No one had brought in any pictures that morning to have new glass put in, and no one had bought a piece of glass to use himself.

"Thank you very much," Nancy said, and the girls walked out.

"There is one place left," Junie said. "It's not very attractive and it's in a shabby part of town, but I believe it's just the kind of place that a thief might go to."

She drove a few blocks until she came to an older section of town. Finally she parked in front of what had once been a house and was now a store. A gaudy sign in the window read: IF YOU CAN'T FIND IT HERE, YOU CAN'T FIND IT ANYWHERE. The two shoppers smiled.

Nancy remarked, "That's a pretty broad claim. I wonder if the owner can live up to it!"

Junie giggled. "If he can, your quest is over."

The interior of the shop was untidy and badly in need of dusting. A middle-aged man came from the rear room, slid behind the counter, and asked what the girls wanted.

Nancy noted that he eyed them up and down, as if he were asking the question, "What are girls like you doing in this part of town?"

Nancy made her request. At first the proprietor shook his head, saying no one had brought in a picture that morning. Then suddenly he added, "Oh, I forgot. A young fellow from town was in to buy some glass."

"What size was it?" Nancy asked quickly.

The man looked at a piece of wrapping paper lying on the counter not far from his telephone. On it was scribbled 12x20 inches. He repeated this to the girls.

"That's just the size we're interested in!" Nancy said. "Who was this young man?"

The proprietor said he did not know, and Nancy wondered whether he was telling the truth or covering up for the thief. Acting as if she believed him, she asked, "What did he look like?"

"Oh, he was of medium height and kind of tough-looking. I did notice one thing about him, though. His right hand had been bandaged as if he'd cut it. I asked him about it. He told me he had injured his hand on some broken glass that he wanted to replace."

Nancy and Junie were exuberant. They were sure they had tracked down the thief! But the question was, where was he?

"You say you don't know him?" Nancy asked the owner again.

The man shook his head. "I've seen him hanging around town with some other tough guys, but I don't know who he is. In fact, I don't want to know.

The girls felt that the least they could do for all this information was to buy a few articles from the shop. Junie selected a small hammer, an awl, and a package of assorted nails. Nancy found a new type of lawn sprinkler and purchased it to take home to her father. As soon as the articles had been wrapped and paid for, she and Junie left the store.

As they got into the car, Junie teased Nancy. "Now I suppose you will ask me to drive around to where the tough guys hang out!"

Nancy smiled and said, "You're wrong this time. Take me to a chemist's in this neighbourhood."

She explained that she wanted to find out where

the young man with the cut hand bought the bandage he was wearing.

"It's a long chance, I know," she added, "but, Junie, a good detective tracks down every possible little clue."

Junie said she was beginning to see that. "It amazes me how much trouble you have to go to for one itsy-bitsy clue."

The girls went into the chemist's and approached the counter where first-aid accessories were sold. A pleasant woman waited on them. Nancy asked her if a young man had been in that morning to purchase a fresh bandage for a cut hand.

She was elated when the woman said, "Yes, there was. He was in early. Said he had been in a car accident but didn't have to go to a doctor. He could bandage his own hand."

"Do you know who he is?" Nancy asked hopefully.

"Of course I do. He comes in here a lot. His name is Sid Zikes. I'm surprised that girls like you would be interested in trying to find out about him."

Nancy thought it best not to explain her reason. She merely asked where he lived. This time she received an "I don't know" for an answer.

"But I understand he doesn't have a very good reputation," the woman said. "If you aren't aware of that, I think it's my duty to warn you to stay away from him."

"Thank you for the advice," Nancy said, smiling. "Why does he have a bad reputation?"

The woman said she had been told that upon several occasions when there had been a theft in town, young Sid Zikes had suddenly disappeared. "But the funny thing is that after a while he comes back and nothing ever happens to him. I guess he has been suspected many times but never arrested."

Nancy asked the woman if Sid Zikes ever wore gloves. She said she did not know. "But it wouldn't surprise me. Sid, in his own flashy way, can be quite a dandy."

Both girls thanked the woman for her helpful information. Then they bought some powder and perfume. Nancy decided that hers would go to Hannah Gruen.

A few minutes later, as the young detectives were driving off, Nancy said, "Junie, I think we should report our suspicions to Officer Browning. Let's stop at State Police headquarters and tell him or at least leave a message for him." He was not there, so Nancy wrote a note to the absent officer.

When she and Junie finally reached home, Mrs Flockhart met them. After she had kissed the two girls, she said, "Nancy, you are to call home at once. Your father phoned and said he has some very special news for you!"

·12·

Tell-tale Glove

WHEN Mr Drew answered the phone, he asked how Nancy was, and how she was progressing with the mystery. Hearing that she was very enthusiastic about her work, he added, "Hannah Gruen and I are both very busy and we keep well, but I must say we miss you very much."

He now began to tell her about his interview with the United States Immigration Department. He said they had made a thorough search and could not find a Salvatore Rocco who had come into the United States from Italy about ten years before, with or without the baby he claimed was his nephew. The lawyer said he was sorry he did not have better news for his daughter.

"Oh, I'm not discouraged," Nancy assured him quickly. "I assume that Mr Rocco either sneaked into the country with the baby, or came here under an assumed name."

"No doubt you're right," her father agreed, "and it would be almost hopeless to track down this man under such circumstances. But let me know if you get any more clues I can help with," he added.

Nancy now brought him up to date on the mystery

and ended by telling him about Diana Bolardo. "Do you think it would be a good idea to find out if anyone by that name entered this country either to stay or to visit during the past ten years?"

The lawyer thought it was a good idea. "However, if the woman is living in Rome, it won't be necessary."

Nancy said she would let her father know the instant Mr Caspari told her what his grandparents had found out.

"And now," Mr Drew said, "I have a surprise for you. The police caught the girl who stole your jacket."

"Really? How wonderful! What did she say?"

The lawyer reported that the girl had noticed Junie carrying the coat in a see-through bag and felt she had to have it. She followed Junie from the station, found the Drews' door open and tiptoed in. "Her case comes up in two weeks. I guess you'll have to testify against her. Incidentally, she's a known petty thief. She wasn't acquainted with the man in whose car you saw her."

"Too bad," Nancy said with a sigh.

By the time she had finished her call, Junie had gone outdoors to visit the barn where the newborn lambs were kept. As Nancy sat thinking about the case and what to do next, Mr Flockhart came in.

"Why so pensive?" he teased. "Did the phone call upset you?"

Nancy told him about the conversation, and then changed the subject. "I was thinking about something else. Would it be possible for me to obtain a piece of parchment the size of the one that was stolen? I'd like to try painting on it to see how close I can come to imitating the four original paintings."

The owner of Triple Creek Farm said he would be glad to let Nancy have a piece of his finest parchment. With a twinkle in his eyes he added, "If you make a really good duplicate of the stolen picture, I'll have it framed and hang it up!"

Nancy grinned. "I don't expect to do anything so wonderful as the original artist did, but I'd like to try. It's just possible it might help us solve the mystery."

Mr Flockhart said he would take her to the factory at once and choose exactly the right piece. He escorted her outside to his car and they drove off. Since Nancy had never tried painting on parchment, she did not know what to choose, but Mr Flockhart showed her the different grades of parchment and told her which was the best variety for what she wanted to do.

Nancy thanked him and said she could hardly wait to get started on the painting. She had expected to return home at once, but Mr Flockhart wanted to speak to Eezy, so they rode back to the house the longer way.

He parked the car where Junie had on previous occasions and walked up the hillside with Nancy. Eezy greeted them with a big grin. The shepherd did not wait to hear any message that might be brought to him.

At once he said, "Howdy, boss! Howdy, Nancy Drew!" Then as he picked up his Irish harp, he quoted from the Bible, "'Now I can make a joyful noise unto the Lord.'"*

* Psalms 98:4

At once he began to accompany himself in a song telling about a lamb that had wandered far from home. Finally though, the little sheep had become so lonesome he could not stand it and turned around and went back. Eventually he rejoined his flock and the ditty ended with a series of *baas* in various pitches.

Nancy and Mr Flockhart laughed and clapped appreciatively. Nancy now went to pat her favourite lamb, who nudged her affectionately. She noticed that he was growing stronger daily. She had to brace herself to avoid being shoved over.

In a few minutes Mr Flockhart finished talking with his herdsman and called to Nancy that he was ready to leave.

"What's the rush?" Eezy asked. "I got somethin' in the cabin I want to show Nancy."

He disappeared inside his shack but soon returned, holding up a glove. The girl detective was amazed. The glove looked exactly like the one she had torn from the hand of the thief who had stolen the parchment painting.

Excited, she asked Eezy, "Where did you get this?"

As the shepherd slipped the glove on to one hand, he said, "You know, this fits perfectly. Rover brought it to me. You're a good detective, Nancy. Do you think you could find me the mate to this?" He began to sing loudly.

Before the callers could answer the question, one of the nearby sheep, apparently unused to his singing, gave a loud *baa*, which made everyone laugh.

It was Nancy's turn to surprise the shepherd. "I

think maybe I know where the mate to this glove is. If I'm right, I'll tell you."

Eezy wagged his head from side to side. "You're the most amazing girl I ever met! You take this glove and see if it matches the one you know about."

Nancy now changed the subject and asked Eezy if the two men who had attacked him had ever returned. "I was afraid they might attempt to attack you again."

"Oh, no, nothing like that," the shepherd said emphatically. "I'm keeping that mean ram penned up behind my cabin. If there is any disturbance around here, I'll just turn the old fellow loose on anybody who bothers me!"

"That's a good idea," Mr Flockhart said.

Nancy was thinking of the walkie-talkie that she and Junie had brought to the shepherd. Apparently he thought the ram would be a quicker and more effective means of warding off an attack!

"And after what happened to me," she thought, "I guess he's right!"

In the meantime Eezy had picked up his harp and began playing a pretty little tune on it. He finished in a few minutes, then Nancy and Mr Flockhart said good-bye and trudged down the hill. When they got into the car, he drove at once to State Police headquarters and turned over the glove Rover had brought to Eezy.

Officer Browning was there and was thunderstruck to see Nancy holding the matching glove.

"There is no question but that this is the mate," he said. "Where did you find it?"

Nancy told him how Rover had picked it up on the

Triple Creek property and brought the glove to his master, Eezy.

"I have a strong feeling," Nancy said, "that the thief wanted to get rid of the mate of the tell-tale glove. He deliberately planted it on Mr Flockhart's farm to throw suspicion on Eezy or some of the other shepherds or helpers. What do you think, Officer Browning?"

"That you have made a reasonable deduction," he said. "Of course it would be hard to prove, but we may get some other evidence to support your theory."

Mr Flockhart spoke. "It didn't do that thief a bit of good to try making any of my men look guilty. I trust every one of them, and I am sure all are innocent of any wrongdoing."

The officer nodded. "I would certainly take your word against any other person's," he said. "The police are convinced that the intruder in your home was a stranger, and the theft of the parchment picture was an outside job. Don't worry, there will never be any charge against your men, I'm sure."

After a little more conversation about the mystery, the phone rang, so the visitors stood up to leave.

"Don't go yet," Browning said. "I've been expecting a call. I think it may be of great interest to you."

Nancy and Mr Flockhart stood still while the officer answered the phone. He said, "Very good. Bring him in here. I have two visitors who would be glad to see him."

The officer put down his phone, but gave no explanation of the conversation. Nancy and Mr Flockhart looked at each other, puzzled.

A full minute went by, then the door opened. Two policemen walked in with a handcuffed prisoner. A sullen-looking youth glanced at the visitors, then his eyes dropped.

Officer Browning said, "Mr Flockhart, Miss Nancy Drew, I want you to meet Sid Zikes!"

·13·

A Paint Disaster

Sɪᴅ Zikes! The young man they had been trying to find! His right hand was still bandaged.

Officer Browning said, "Sid is being charged with petty larceny and will be booked on that count."

Sid Zikes spoke up. "I got a right to bail!"

He was told that this was a judge's decision and he would have to remain behind bars until the amount was decided upon.

The prisoner's eyes roamed from one person to another in the room. Finally they rested on Nancy. The girl detective felt uncomfortable. Was he blaming her for his arrest?

Officer Browning asked Nancy and Mr Flockhart if they would like to question the prisoner. The sheep-farm owner said he would defer to Nancy. "She knows better than I do what to ask."

Addressing Sid Zikes, the girl detective began. "Why did you steal the parchment picture from Mr Flockhart's home?"

Sid looked at the floor and replied, "I didn't."

Nancy told him that she knew he had purchased a new piece of glass exactly the right size to replace the one that had been smashed when he had thrown the picture. The young man made no comment, and looked out of a window.

Nancy decided to change her line of questioning. She said, "Did you threaten the shepherd Eezy and knock him out?"

The prisoner shouted, "No!"

"When you went up the hillside to his cabin, who was the person with you? A friend or a stranger?"

Sid Zikes said defiantly, "I don't know what you're talking about, and I don't have to listen to this kind of questioning. Officer, take me away. But I warn every one of you, I won't be in jail long! I'll prove my innocence!"

As Mr Flockhart and Nancy left State Police headquarters, he said to her, "Do you think Sid Zikes is guilty?"

Nancy replied that she was sure he was the burglar who had taken the parchment picture. "He was about the size and build of the person I caught a glimpse of in your house. But I think it may be true that he had nothing to do with the attack on Eezy."

Mr Flockhart was inclined to agree. "But I doubt that Sid Zikes wanted the picture for himself. I believe he was paid by somebody to sneak in and get it."

Nancy asked the Triple Creek owner if he had any guesses about who that person might be. Mr Flockhart shook his head. "Unfortunately I understand there is a gang in town that will do such jobs for people who would not think of committing the act themselves. So far the police haven't been able to apprehend them."

Nancy remarked, "The person who puts anyone

up to stealing to gain something for himself is even worse than the thief, don't you think?"

"I agree," Mr Flockhart said.

He and Nancy went to his car and drove off. She asked him if he would mind going into town so she could purchase some fine coloured pencils to make sketches on the parchment.

"I'll be glad to," he said, "but don't ask my advice on the best colours. The truth is, I'm colour blind."

"That's too bad," Nancy said.

The farmer laughed. "It doesn't bother me. So far all my customers who plan to paint on parchment seem to know everything about colours."

After the purchases had been made, Nancy and Mr Flockhart rode home. He dropped her at the front door of the house, then drove off to his factory.

Junie and her mother were there and were amazed to hear the story of Sid Zikes's capture and imprisonment.

"I'd say the police are very efficient," Mrs Flockhart remarked.

Junie spoke up. "But Nancy had some excellent information to give them."

Nancy brushed aside the compliment and asked where she might work on the parchment. "I'm eager to get started," she said.

Junie's mother said she knew the perfect spot. "At the rear of the garden behind the farmhouse there's a lovely summerhouse. It's an attractive little place. I think you'll like the nice, shady spot. It's quiet and nobody will disturb you."

Junie offered to get an easel from the attic and bring it downstairs. The two girls walked out to the summerhouse and set up the easel. Nancy got out her paint brushes. Next she stretched the parchment across a frame and pinned it tightly. Then she set it on the easel and said, "I guess I'm ready to start."

Junie watched as her friend meticulously began her work.

The girl artist thought, "I'll do the hardest thing first. That will be the sketch of the beautiful young woman."

She closed her eyes for several seconds, so that she might recall the original picture exactly. Finally she opened them and began to paint.

Junie watched Nancy for several minutes, fascinated, then said she must do her own chores. "I'll be back as soon as possible," she told Nancy.

The young sleuth worked diligently for some time. Secretly she was pleased with the result of her work. "It really does look like the original," she thought.

Nancy had told no one, but what she had in mind was making a parchment picture resembling the original so closely that Mr Flockhart would indeed want to hang it over the fireplace in the living room.

She smiled to herself. "Maybe I have nerve even to try to do this, but I'll attempt it anyway."

By the time Junie returned, Nancy had almost completed the entire group of pictures. She was working on the sketch of the collision between the sailing ship and the steamer.

Junie was astounded. "Nancy, that's simply marvellous!" she exclaimed.

The words were hardly out of her mouth when the girls became aware of something sailing through the air behind them. The next instant their heads and the parchment were covered with paint!

Nancy and Junie had turned quickly. They were just in time to see two shadowy figures throw down cans of paint and run away. All thoughts of trying to follow the two men vanished from the girls' minds. The paint was running down from their hair, and they did not dare let it get into their eyes.

Both of them picked up pieces of cloth, which Nancy had handy to use for her work. They wiped off their spattered faces as best they could and then tried to remove the paint from their hair. In seconds they had used up all the available cloths and decided they had better hurry into the house to finish the job.

Nancy paused a moment, however, to look at the parchment. It was ruined! She was on the verge of tears as she picked up the parchment and coloured pencils, and followed Junie to the house.

Mrs Flockhart was near the door when the girls rushed in. She cried out, "What in the world happened to you?"

Junie explained and together they opened a kitchen drawer and took out a roll of cheesecloth. Mrs Flockhart quickly cut it into sections and handed pieces to the girls. While they worked on their hair, she mopped the paint off their clothing.

"We'd better shampoo right away," Junie advised.

"That won't get off all the paint," her mother said. "It has an oil base. What you should use is paint thinner. Wait here while I run out to the garage for some. I know there's a large can of it there."

She was gone only a couple of minutes. When she returned, Mrs Flockhart told the two girls to lean their foreheads against the rim of the sink and let their hair fall inside. Then she poured out the paint thinner, and in a little while the combination of the red and blue splotches had vanished.

"Now go upstairs and take hot showers and shampoos," she said.

The girls went to the first floor and reappeared an hour later, looking as if nothing had happened to them. Meanwhile Mrs Flockhart had tried to remove the paint from the parchment, but had found it impossible. The blue and red liquids had mingled with Nancy's sketches to such an extent that there was no chance of separating them.

"I'm dreadfully sorry this happened," the distressed woman said. "Did you girls see who threw the paint?"

Nancy replied that they had had a glimpse of two figures, but did not see the intruders clearly enough to identify them.

Suddenly she had an idea. "Junie, do you recall that those men threw down their cans of paint?"

"No, all I remember is wanting to get away from them as fast as possible."

"Well, it seems to me they did leave those containers behind. Maybe we can find some clue to where they came from—a brand name or some other kind of identification. Let's look!"

Overhearing Nancy's comments, Mrs Flockhart spoke before her daughter could. "Those men could still be on our property. They could be lurking behind the summerhouse."

"Oh, Mother," Junie said, laughing. "They ran off."

"I know you said that. But if Nancy is right about the paint cans, perhaps they returned for them." She paused a moment. "No, I would prefer that you remain here."

The girl detective, however, was not willing to let such a valuable clue slip past her so easily. "Mrs Flockhart, would you go with us? I'm sure that two men would not want to tackle three women."

Reluctantly the woman agreed. "All right, but let's be quick about it."

Nancy and Junie hurried outdoors with Mrs Flockhart behind them and headed for the summerhouse. Not far from it lay the two empty cans.

"These are the Acme brand," Junie said. "Maybe that will be a clue."

"I think it's a good one," Nancy replied.

She and Junie picked up the two cans and the three went back to the house. At Nancy's suggestion, Junie telephoned each store in town where paint was sold. The first one did not carry this brand.

Nancy waited expectantly, but as someone in each shop said he did not sell the Acme brand, she became more and more discouraged. Her beautiful clue was coming to nothing!

When Junie finished telephoning, she turned to Nancy. "What's the next move? I'm determined to find out who threw that paint at us and ruined your picture!"

"I'm just as determined," Nancy told her. "As you know, Junie, I have never trusted Mr Rocco from the beginning, and I trust him less now that I know he entered this country under an assumed name or sneaked in. I suggest that we go to his place and look around his barns while avoiding him. Maybe we can find some Acme paint cans."

Junie looked at her friend in astonishment. "That's the last thing in the world I thought you would say, but I agree it's a good idea. I'll get the car."

In a short time Junie parked far from the entrance to Rocco's farm and the two girls walked across the fields towards the barns, which were outside the fenced-in area. They entered one building, which was empty. There were many tools hanging up and shelves on which stood cans of various products, including paint. The girls tiptoed forward to examine them.

"Acme paint!" Nancy whispered. "And, Junie, look! Here is one of blue and one of red in exactly the same shades that were thrown at us."

"So two of Mr Rocco's workers are guilty!" Junie said in a low tone. "Maybe we'd better hurry away and report the incident before we get caught."

The girls were about to walk outside when they heard voices close by. Two men were speaking in Italian, and they seemed to be arguing.

This went on for a few minutes, then suddenly one of them spoke in English. The girls did not recognize the voice that cried out in a snarl. "If they won't join, they won't! And don't ask me to pull any rough stuff to make them do it!"

·14·

Important Information

ASTOUNDED at what they had just heard, Nancy and Junie stood stock-still, staring at each other. They had not recognized the voice of either man.

Instead of tiptoeing away at once, the girls waited to hear more conversation by the two unseen men. There was none, however, and their footsteps faded away.

Nancy at once thought of Eezy and Mrs Potter, the shopkeeper. Were they being coerced to join some association they wanted to have nothing to do with? Nancy signalled Junie, and the girls walked quickly out of the barn and returned to the car.

As they drove away, Nancy told Junie her suspicions and said, "Let's stop at the general store and see what we can find out from Mrs Potter."

When they arrived, several people were going in and out of the store, so Nancy suggested that they wait. "I'd rather talk to Mrs Potter when no one else is around," she told Junie.

Ten minutes later there seemed to be fewer customers, so the two girls walked into the country store. Mrs Potter greeted them cordially and asked, "What can I do for you?"

Nancy did not hesitate to tell her the whole story. She asked if her guess had been right about what the two men wanted her to do.

The woman suddenly blushed. "How did you ever figure that out? The whole matter was supposed to be kept secret, otherwise we'd be harmed."

The girl detective smiled. "Junie and I heard it from one of Mr Rocco's men. Please tell us more."

Mrs Potter heaved a great sigh and then told the girls that their guess was half right. "There's a lot more to it. Those men who, I suspect, are tools of Mr Rocco, found out that I knew the scheme was phony, and threatened me if I told anyone."

"What is the scheme?" Nancy asked.

"They are secretly trying to organize farm workers and employees in small businesses to form a vast association. They are going to fight for higher wages and fringe benefits and all sorts of advantages for the workers."

Junie looked amazed. "Does it include my father's workers?"

"I don't know but I think not. What made me suspicious was that the men demanded money in advance. I suspect they have collected a good bit already. This part I couldn't agree to. But I don't mind telling you that at times I'm afraid those men or some of their pals will come in here and injure me."

Nancy and Junie looked at each other, their thoughts on the attack of Flockhart's shepherd Eezy. As two customers walked into the shop at this moment, the girls quickly purchased some sugarless chewing gum and said goodbye to Mrs Potter.

"Let me hear from you if you find out anything," she called, as they started for the door.

"We will!" Junie replied. After she and Nancy had climbed into the car, she added, "Next stop Eezy's cabin."

As usual they found the elderly shepherd seated in front of his little cabin. He was not playing his Irish harp, but gazing intently over the large flock of sheep he was tending. Near him was the little lamb Nancy liked so much.

Eezy saw the girls trudging up the hillside and waved to them. He spoke to the lamb and apparently it understood what he had said. The animal loped down the slope to meet the girls. They stopped to pet and hug it, then the lamb trotted alongside as they went up the rest of the way to speak to Eezy.

"Cheerio, you get cuter every day," Nancy told the lamb.

When they reached the top of the hillside, Eezy had a treat for them. He had brought out some biscuits and glasses of iced lemonade. His visitors thanked him and declared it would taste good after their long hike. As soon as Nancy had finished hers, she got on to the subject she had come to quizz him about.

The shepherd listened intently, then suddenly slapped his thigh. "It beats me how you found out, but every word you say is true. I don't go along with the proposition and I don't think anybody else should. I too suspect those men are working for Rocco. I don't trust him and I don't like the idea of collecting money in advance—bah!"

Nancy asked him if he had any idea how far the

proposition had succeeded. Eezy said he did not know, but he thought many people had paid and signed up to join the organization.

"But nobody's supposed to talk about it, and I guess that's why no news gets around. The thing that bothers me most is that I think those men may be making progress with some of Mr Flockhart's workers. He pays us all well, and we're happy at what we're doing. Why should somebody come in here and upset things?

"Besides," he went on, "you know it says in the Good Book, *'Keep thee far from a false matter: for I will not justify the wicked.'*"*

Junie was alarmed by Eezy's theory that many of Mr Flockhart's workers had been approached and had already secretly joined the organization, giving them an advance payment. She suggested that they return at once to the house to talk with her father. The girl detective agreed and the two hurried down the hillside.

Junie's father had just come in. Together the girls told him the startling news.

The man's face became grave. "We can't let this go on!" he declared. "But I must admit that at the moment I don't know exactly how to cope with the situation. I wish I had more data on the subject. Then I'd know how to approach my men."

Nancy had been thinking hard. Now she said to him. "I have a suggestion, Mr Flockhart. You know my friends are coming here soon for a visit. No one in this neighbourhood knows them. How would it be if Ned, Burt, and Dave act as undercover men and find out what they can for you?"

* Exodus 23:7

Mr Flockhart smiled. "That sounds like an excellent idea," he agreed. "I will welcome your friends and ask them to do this detective work, but on one condition."

"What is that?" Nancy asked.

The big man looked intently at her and said, "I will permit it as long as the work is under the direction of Detective Nancy Drew!"

Nancy laughed. "It's a bargain," she said, and he went off.

A few minutes later a car drove up to the house. Dan White jumped out. Junie rushed outside to greet him, but in a few minutes called to Nancy to join them.

"Danny has a surprise for us," Junie said. "Dan, you tell her."

The college student who was majoring in Italian said that since seeing the girls he had delved into a study of the dialects used in various parts of Italy. "I particularly worked on those spoken by many peasants over forty-five years old, living in different areas of the country. I finally found one that I think Mr Rocco's workers use. I thought maybe we could run over there and I'll talk to some of the men."

Nancy was thrilled with the idea, so the three set off in Dan's car.

"Let's go to see Tony first," Nancy suggested. "I'd like to know how he's making out with his uncle."

Dan parked the car. He and the girls walked across the fields to the spot where Tony had been hoeing and drawing pictures. He was not there. They looked all over, but did not see him.

"I wonder where he is," Dan said.

"His uncle must have moved him to another field," Junie suggested.

Dan said he could see one of the workmen in the distance and suggested that they walk over so he could talk to him. It was a long trek but finally they reached the man. This time Dan did not say good day in his college Italian, but instead spoke in the dialect he assumed the farmhand might use.

The labourer turned quickly and looked in amazement at the young man. Then he began to speak in a torrent of words. Nancy and Junie wondered how much of it Dan understood. To their delight, he seemed to understand a good bit and answered the man intermittently.

Presently Dan turned to the girls. "What questions do you want me to ask him?"

Nancy said, "Ask him first if he knows where Tony is."

Dan did so and as he listened his brow furrowed. Nancy and Junie wondered what he was being told. Finally Dan turned and translated for the girls.

"This man tells me some very unfortunate news. Tony has run away!"

"Run away!" the girls exclaimed.

Dan said Mr Rocco had discovered the boy early that morning with a drawing pad and pencil, making sketches instead of hoeing rows of corn.

"His uncle became enraged. He tore the pad to bits and then gave Tony a terrible beating."

"How awful!" Junie said. "I don't blame the poor boy for running away!"

Nancy asked Dan to inquire of the man if he knew where Tony had gone. In response the labourer lifted his arm and pointed towards the Flockhart property.

"We must go after him!" Nancy declared at once. "I'll walk in the direction this man pointed out."

Junie said, "Not alone! After what has happened it would be too dangerous! Dan, how about your going with Nancy? I'll return to your car and drive it home. May I have the keys?"

Dan agreed. He and Nancy set off at a fast pace. They began to run in the direction where Tony was supposed to have gone. Presently the two searchers crossed the boundary between the Rocco farm and Triple Creek.

It seemed to Nancy that there were sheep everywhere but no sign of the boy Tony. Once they stopped to ask a shepherd, but the man declared he had not seen the child.

The couple walked on and presently came to a small ravine with a stream of water at the base. There were no animals in the area, and Nancy assumed that the shepherds tried to keep their flocks away from the dangerous spot.

Suddenly she stopped short. Dan looked at her and said, "Is something the matter?"

"Listen!" she urged. "I heard something."

They both listened and Dan said, "It could be a lamb crying."

Nancy replied, "Yes, it could be. But it sounds more like a child sobbing. Let's head in that direction!"

By listening carefully, the couple decided that it was a human cry coming from near the water at the foot of the ravine. Carefully they descended the steep embankment. In a few minutes they found Tony huddled in a heap and sobbing beside a large rock.

"Tony! Tony!" Nancy exclaimed as she ran towards the boy.

He lifted his tear-stained face and blinked as if he could not believe that Nancy Drew had found his hiding place. He smiled wanly first at her and then at Dan. Then politely he got up and shook hands with each of them.

Dan spoke to him in Italian, repeating what he had heard from the workman on the Rocco farm. Tony replied and Dan translated for Nancy.

"The story is true. Tony says he cannot stand any more of his uncle's cruel treatment. He wants to go to Italy to find his own family."

Nancy suggested that Dan ask him if he knew who they were and if any of them were living. Dan did so and the reply was, "Somebody must be and wouldn't be so mean to me!"

Nancy was touched. What should she do? Take Tony home with her? Or perhaps she should deliver the boy to State Police headquarters. But they might return him to his uncle!

The Nancy's eyes glistened as she thought of something. "Dan, I have an idea about what we should do about Tony!"

·15·

Secret Notes

"WHAT is your great idea about helping Tony?" Dan asked Nancy.

Excited, she told him of a plan she had suddenly devised. "How would it be if we take him to Eezy for tonight?"

Dan agreed that this would be better than leaving the boy out in the open. "Then what?" he asked.

"We'll get Tony to write a note to his uncle. He can assure Mr Rocco that he's safe and happy."

Dan urged Nancy to continue. So far he liked her plan.

"I think the note should also say that Tony will return home if his uncle will promise to tell him where the rest of the boy's family is and send him back to Italy."

Dan remarked that this sounded fair enough, but would Rocco keep his word? Then he added, "What about Tony's desire to draw? Isn't it wrong for Mr Rocco to keep him from doing this?"

Nancy agreed, but said, "I think that solution can come later. We'd better not overdo the request at this time."

Dan felt her decision was a wise one. He added,

however, "I can't help but feel that we're letting Mr Rocco off too easy. I think Tony's note should also warn his uncle that if he doesn't agree to the arrangement, the boy will go at once to the police and report him."

Nancy smiled. "That should throw a scare into the cruel man!"

Dan asked if Nancy intended to take the note to Mr Rocco herself.

"Oh, no," she replied. "This should be done secretly. He shouldn't know I have anything to do with the case. When I was at the general store, I noticed an old oak tree across the road. It had a deep hollow in the trunk. A note would fit in there perfectly."

Dan wagged his head and grinned. "It's very refreshing and interesting to see a real live detective at work!"

Nancy asked him if he would speak to Tony in Italian and tell him what they had been talking about. Before Dan translated the boy's answers, there was a good bit of conversation between the two. At times Tony would shake his head, at others he would look up at Dan and smile broadly.

Finally Dan was ready to translate. "Tony has agreed to everything," he reported. "He likes the idea of staying with Eezy and knows he will be comfortable and safe there. The only thing he was not sure he wanted to do was threaten his uncle about going to the police. But finally he has agreed to do it. Shall we get started?"

Nancy nodded. The three rose from the ground and walked up the canyon wall. This was difficult. Treacherous, loose stones skidded under their feet.

Dan kept a tight grip on Nancy's arm so that she would not fall. He tried to take Tony's arm with his other hand, but the boy scooted up the precipice with the agility and speed of a mountain goat.

They finally reached the top and walked quickly across the fields to Eezy's cabin. The elderly shepherd was standing up, shading his eyes with one hand, and looking all around. The young people wondered if some of his sheep might have strayed away.

As they drew closer, Eezy's eyes grew large. When they were still a hundred yards away, he shouted at them, "Well, howdy! Howdy! And who is this boy with you?"

Nancy shouted back, "Don't you recognize him? Look closely."

The shepherd shook his head. As Nancy walked closer, she introduced Tony Rocco, then Dan White.

The shepherd laughed. "Oh, Dan and I are old friends. Miss Junie often brings him up here to see me." Then, looking straight at Nancy, he added, "I'll bet you have something interesting to tell me. What is it?"

The girl detective asked him, "How would you like a temporary guest?" The elderly man looked puzzled. Then Nancy explained the plan she and Dan had worked out.

When she told Eezy how Mr Rocco beat the child, the herdsman scowled. "Fits right in with what I've heard all along about that man. You know I don't like him. I wouldn't trust him a quarter of an acre away."

All this time Tony had stood by, silent and motionless. Now he asked Dan a question in Italian.

Instead of replying, Dan asked Eezy what his answer was. "Why of course I'll take this boy in. I don't get much company up here and it will be fun for me." He asked, "Doesn't Tony speak English?"

"No," Dan replied.

Eezy snapped his fingers. "Then I'm going to start right in teaching him some. Any boy who lives in these United States should speak our language!"

Eezy produced pencil and paper, and Dan helped Tony compose a note to his uncle.

While he was doing this Eezy talked to Nancy. "So the boy was born in Italy and has been here ten years, but has never been allowed to speak anything but Italian."

The shepherd looked off into the clouds, then said, "You know, Nancy, it says in the Good Book, *'It is an ancient nation, whose language thou knowest not, neither understandeth what they say.'''*

Nancy made no comment but she agreed entirely. It would be interesting to see how fast Eezy could teach Tony some English. "He seems very bright and I'm sure he'll catch on quickly," the girl detective thought.

She reminded Eezy that Tony apparently had great talent as an artist. "While he's here, why don't you give him some paper and pencils and let him sketch? I'm sure that will make the boy very happy."

"I'll start as soon as you folks leave," the shepherd promised.

By this time Tony had finished the note. Dan folded it and put the message into his pocket. As he and Nancy started off, she called back, "We'll return

* Jeremiah 5:15

tomorrow." Dan repeated the message in Italian and Tony smiled.

When the two hikers reached the Flockhart farmhouse, they found Junie waiting there with Dan's car. "Tell me what happened!" she urged.

Nancy and Dan told her the whole story. Then they went on to say that they had not discussed Mr Rocco's possible underhand deals with Eezy because of Tony's presence.

"When are you going to get in touch with Mr Rocco?" she asked Dan.

"Right now. I hope he will be at home."

Someone else answered Dan's call. He asked for Mr Rocco in Italian and wondered what the man on the other end of the line was thinking. "I'm sure he's puzzled," Dan decided, smiling at the situation.

This was confirmed when Mr Rocco answered. He inquired who the speaker was and where he was from.

Dan did not reply. Instead he said, "Go to the big oak tree opposite the general store for a note to you from Tony." He hung up.

When Dan returned to the girls, Junie asked him, "How soon do you think we should go look for an answer?"

"Not until tomorrow morning," he said. "What do you think, Nancy?"

The girl detective nodded. "For one thing there might be trouble when someone picks up the answer to Tony's message. If so, it would be much better to have it happen in the daylight."

Dan stayed at the Flockharts' overnight. He and the girls were up early to drive to town for a possible answer to Tony's note. They had decided to use his car and to park it some distance from the oak tree, yet close enough so those remaining inside could have a clear view of what was happening.

When they reached the spot, Dan got out and walked quickly up the road to the tree. The girls, who were watching carefully for any attack on him, merely saw him take an envelope from the hollow in the tree, wrinkle his forehead, and then start back to the car.

He jumped in, then said, "What do you make of this?"

The envelope he had picked up had printed words on it, which said, "To the kidnappers of Tony Rocco."

"Kidnappers!" Junie cried out. "We're not kidnappers! We're only trying to help the mistreated boy!"

Nancy d d not comment, but was thinking hard. "This is a new angle. If Mr Rocco has some spies around, they may track us right to Triple Creek Farm and demand the return of the boy or go to the police and charge the Flockharts and Dan and me with kidnapping!"

This was a twist Nancy had not counted on. By this time Junie had torn open the envelope and removed a slip of paper inside. Again it was addressed to Tony's kidnappers, and read:

If you are looking for a ransom, forget it. I have nothing to fear from the police, but you certainly have.

Sal Rocco.

While Junie read the note aloud, Nancy looked in all directions to see if she could find any spies. Her eyes became riveted on some heavy bushes some distance behind the oak tree. Was she mistaken, or did she detect some movement behind it? As she continued to stare, she was positive that two men stood there, peering through the bushes and up the road towards the car.

"Mr Rocco did have spies!" she decided.

Nancy relayed her thoughts to the others and suggested that Dan take a circuitous route to Triple Creek Farm to throw off pursuit by their enemies. Junie directed Dan to drive down one road and up another and finally all the way through a farm, which had a long lane that exited on to another main road. From here they went home.

As the trio walked into the house, the phone rang. Junie answered it and called Nancy. "It's for you," she said.

To the young sleuth's delight Ned Nickerson was calling. After a cheery greeting, he said, "If the invitation is still good, Burt, Dave, and I will come up very soon with Bess and George. I hope you have some detective work for us to do."

"Indeed I have," Nancy replied. "A big important job is waiting for you!"

·16·

Reinforcements

ALL that day there was a flurry of excitement in the Flockhart farmhouse. Rooms were prepared for the guests and the refrigerators were filled from the well-stocked cold-storage rooms.

The task was almost completed when the telephone rang. Nancy was closest to the instrument, so she answered the call. It was from Vincenzo Caspari.

"Is that you, Nancy?" he asked. When she told him it was, he said, "I'm so glad I found you at home. I have some very important and exciting news to tell you!"

"Good! What is it?" Nancy asked eagerly.

The artist said he had been in touch with his grandparents in Rome. They in turn had tracked down Diana Bolardo!

"Marvellous!" Nancy exclaimed.

She was tempted to ask him a lot of questions, but she listened silently as Mr Caspari gave her the rest of his message.

"The young woman is indeed the person who painted the parchment Mr Flockhart purchased. Incidentally, I did not tell them it had been stolen. They would have wanted to know all the details and

I would not have been able to explain." Nancy thought this was probably wise.

"My grandparents reported that *Signora* Bolardo admitted she had painted the parchment picture, but otherwise had been very secretive. One thing she mentioned will surprise and, I am sure, delight you. Diana Bolardo plans to leave at once for the United States. She'll fly over, so she should arrive soon."

Nancy was amazed and delighted to hear this. "Where will she stay in the United States?"

The girl detective could hear Mr Caspari chuckle at the other end of the phone. "This will be a really big surprise to you," he replied. "She is coming directly to my home and then going to the Flockhart farmhouse!"

Nancy could hardly believe her ears. She was actually going to see and talk to the woman who had made the parchment picture! Again the thought flashed through her mind that the baby in *Signora* Bolardo's picture might be Tony!

Since Vincenzo Caspari had no more to report, she thanked him for doing this valuable bit of sleuthing, then they said goodbye. She rushed off to inform Mrs Flockhart and Junie of the latest development.

Both of them looked at her unbelievingly. Then a sudden thought occurred to Mrs Flockhart. She threw up her hands. "One more guest!" she exclaimed. "And she'll want her own room, I'm sure! This house is large but does not have rubber sides! It's going to take some figuring to decide where to put so many people!"

At this moment Mr Flockhart walked in. He was told the latest news. First Nancy revealed that Bess and George were coming with Ned, Burt, and Dave, then surprised him with the announcement that *Signora* Diana Bolardo was also arriving.

The big man stood in the centre of the floor with his feet far apart. He chuckled. "I'd say we're going to have a houseful. How would it be if we put the boys out in a vacant tenant house?"

Junie spoke up. "Oh, Nancy, they are darling houses. I wouldn't mind living in one of them myself."

"That sounds great," Nancy said. "I'm sure the boys will be happy there."

The house cleaning continued for more than an hour, then Nancy and Junie went to one of the tenant houses.

"This place looks spick and span to me," Nancy remarked, walking in.

Junie smiled. "My father is very strict about that. When tenant families move, they are required to leave it clean and tidy."

There was nothing for the girls to do but a little dusting. As soon as this was finished they left. Nancy helped Junie with her farm chores, but all the time she kept thinking about the mystery and the turn it would take when *Signora* Bolardo arrived. It would be exciting, she was sure.

The following morning Ned, Burt, and Dave drove in with Bess and George. As Nancy introduced them to the Flockharts and Dan, she realized how proud she was of her friends.

Ned was tall and good-looking. Burt and Dave were a little shorter. All of them were athletic. Bess and George were cousins but quite different from each other. Bess was a slightly plump blonde with dimples. George wore her hair short and was a brunette. She liked plain clothes, whereas Bess tended to admire frills.

"What a wonderful place this is!" Bess exclaimed enthusiastically. "Land, land, as far as you can see."

Dave said, "How would you like to mow six hundred acres of it?"

Junie replied, "We let the sheep do it."

Ned asked, "With a tractor?"

"Sure," said Junie, her eyes twinkling, "We train all our sheep to ride mowers, rake and bail hay, and store it—!"

"Enough!" cried Ned.

After a hearty second breakfast, Dan took the boys to their own house. They changed into farm clothes, then joined the girls, who also were in shirts and jeans.

The boys were eager to be off on their mission. Mr Flockhart had explained the situation to them and asked that they try to have a full report for him at least by the following evening. Dan joined them and the four drove off, with the girls wishing them luck.

Junie asked Bess and George, "How would you like to have a tour of my father's barns and his factory?"

"Great!" they answered.

Everything went well and the visitors were extremely interested in the work until they came to the slaughterhouse. Then Bess rebelled. She covered her ears with her hands and said, "I can't stand that bleating! Oh those poor things! Why, oh why do they have to be killed?"

Junie, used to this since childhood, smiled. She replied, "They're killed so you and others will have lamb to eat, Bess. Don't you like it?"

Bess said, "Oh, yes, I love it. But don't ask me to watch the slaughter in this barn."

She walked off and returned to the barn where the baby lambs were. Meanwhile the other three girls went into the slaughterhouse, but after watching the operation for a few minutes came out and joined Bess.

'Let's go to the place where your father sells articles made from sheepskins," Bess suggested to Junie.

Nancy said, "I must warn you, Bess. You're going to lose your heart to a lot of things you see in this shop. Watch your pocketbook!"

George was just as intrigued by the sheepskin articles as Bess was. The cousins bought gloves for their parents and treated themselves to after-ski bootees.

The tour continued for some time, then the girls drove up the hillside to see Eezy. Though the shepherd was in front of his cabin, Tony was nowhere to be seen. Nancy asked the sheepherder where he was.

After being introduced to Bess and George, Eezy said, "In his schoolroom."

Nancy looked puzzled. "Where is that?"

Eezy took his visitors to a well-camouflaged bower beyond the rear of his cabin. They walked inside. Tony was seated on the ground, writing English words.

The boy jumped up and when he was introduced made a low bow to the newcomers. To the amazement of Nancy and Junie he said in perfect English, "Good morning. I am very glad to see you."

"How wonderful!" Nancy said. "You learn very fast."

Tony was pleased. "Mr Eezy good teacher," he told the girls.

Bess whispered to George, "Isn't he absolutely darling?"

Shyly Tony opened his notebook and showed the girls a sketch of Eezy, which he had made. Nancy and Junie exclaimed in amazement. "It's a marvellous likeness!" Junie remarked, smiling at Tony. "You have a lot of talent."

At this moment Rover came bounding up. He stood still, looking at the group and barking furiously.

"This means," said Junie, "that there is a disturbance somewhere among the sheep. Perhaps some strangers are arriving."

Tony looked frightened. Quickly he gathered up his books and papers and disappeared behind a screen of trees, bushes, and vines.

By this time Eezy had started to follow Rover among the sheep. George puckered her mouth and quipped, "He ought to be called Uneasy!"

Nancy and Junie had already started running after the shepherd, so Bess and George followed. Soon they could see two men trudging up the hill. Their clothes indicated they were law officers. Both wore badges.

When Eezy and his group met the two men, the shepherd asked, "What do you want?"

Without answering him, one of the men asked,

"Which of you girls is Nancy Drew?"

When the young sleuth answered, "I am," the same officer said, "Then you are accused of kidnapping Tony Rocco!"

·17·

A Denial and a Chase

THE accusation against Nancy astounded everyone. George, incensed, cried out, "Nancy Drew is not a kidnapper! That's crazy! You'd better leave!"

Nancy herself, having recovered from the shock, said, "Where are you men from? Show me your credentials."

The spokesman for the two said, "We're from the County Welfare Association and we have the power to make a charge against you and have you arrested!"

All this time Rover was growling at the men. He made a sudden jump towards one of them. The officer kicked him viciously, lifting the dog into the air. Rover came down with a thud and whimpered, but a moment later he was back, ready to attack.

Eezy, who had grabbed his shepherd's crook when they left the cabin, brandished it in the air. Then he said, "Nancy Drew is not a kidnapper, and I think you two had better get out of here quick before my dog Rover chews you up!"

The man who had not spoken now urged his companion to leave, but the other one stood his ground. "We're taking the guilty girl along with us!" he shouted.

Nancy spoke up. "I am not a kidnapper and I am not going with you!" she declared.

"Oh yes you are!" one of the men snarled and grabbed Nancy's arm. "You're coming with us whether you want to or not!"

His strong fingers dug into Nancy's skin as she tried to wrench herself away. "Let go of me!" she cried, as the man's partner took her other arm.

"Stop it! Stop it!" George shouted at the pair, pulling hard on the second man's wrist.

He released his hold briefly and swung his fist at the girl, who ducked. As she dodged his attack, she got a closer view of his badge.

"C'mon," he said to his companion, "let's get out of here before I really lose my temper."

"Just a minute!" George cried. "I think your badge is phony!"

"Aw, now who's crazy!" her attacker exclaimed.

His partner quickly loosened his grip on Nancy, allowing her to retreat towards Eezy. The other girls stepped forward to look at the badges.

"They certainly look like play badges and not real ones," Junie remarked, scrutinizing them closely.

The men glanced nervously at each other and tried to sidestep her. "I've got better things to do than play games with a bunch of teenagers!" one man snapped.

Rover was still growling and trying to get out of Eezy's grasp to attack the two strangers. Eezy straightened himself to his full height, brandished his shepherd's crook and bellowed, "Get out of here! And don't ever show your faces here again!"

The intruders, apparently bewildered at this point,

suddenly turned and ran down the hillside. Rover tried to get loose from his master and follow them, but Eezy kept a tight hold on his collar.

Suddenly one of the men turned and cried out, "Nancy Drew, don't think you're free! We'll get you yet!"

Nancy was glad to see the men go, but would have liked to find out more about them. She felt sure they were working for Mr Rocco.

"Let's follow those men!" she urged the others. "Eezy, please let us take Rover. I promise I won't let him hurt them. But I'd like to see where they go."

The shepherd agreed and said he would go back to the cabin. The chase started and the girls managed to get within shouting distance of the men.

Suddenly one of them turned round. He cupped his hands to his lips and shouted, "You give us back Tony and we'll drop the charge!" Nancy did not answer. With another thought in mind, she shouted back, "You tell me where the stolen parchment is hidden, and maybe we can manage some kind of a deal!"

There was no answer, although the two men looked at each other as if wondering what to say. They kept quiet, however, and soon reached the foot of the hillside. At the road a car with a driver was waiting for them. The motor was running, and as soon as the men jumped into the vehicle, it took off in a hurry.

Nancy memorized the letters and numbers of the licence plate. "It's an out-of-state car! This complicates matters," she thought. "If those men were from some local welfare association, I'm sure they wouldn't be driving an out-of-state car." Then she argued with herself, "But maybe they did it on purpose to avoid identification."

Nancy, Junie, and George had reached the road and stood looking after the fleeing car. Bess had followed at a slower pace. She had seen something glistening on the ground and stooped to pick it up. When she reached the girls, she showed them the shiny object.

"It's one of the phony badges!" Junie cried out. "What a clue!"

Nancy examined it and remarked that there was no identification on it. "I think we should take the badge to the police and tell them what happened here."

"Besides," she added, as they started to climb the hillside with Rover, "I noticed that the man who did the talking had a lot of fresh-looking scars on his hand." She paused. "Here's another one of my wild hunches: Do you suppose he could have handled the parchment picture with the broken glass in it? He may be a friend of Sid Zikes."

Junie declared it was worth investigating. When they reached the top of the hill, Nancy showed the badge to Eezy.

He became angry and said, "Those men are nothin' but a couple o' crooks! I've been thinkin' about what they said. I never heard o' any welfare committee around here. They weren't talkin' sense."

Nancy said, "At least we know they're a couple of fakers. My guess is that these are real badges and the men stole them."

At this point Bess heaved a sigh. "Do you realize

that George and I have been here less than twenty-four hours, and already we're in the midst of one of Nancy Drew's mysteries? And what a mix-up! We were supposed to help figure out some paintings on a parchment. Instead we are learning the secret of a runaway boy; waiting for the woman who painted the parchment to come from Italy, and looking on as Nancy is accused of being a kidnapper!"

The other girls laughed and George said there was a lot of truth in what Bess had said.

Nancy added, "And now more excitement. I'm going to introduce you to a real thief! Our next stop will be the jail to interview one Sid Zikes!"

·18·

The First Confession

ALTHOUGH George was intrigued by the idea of meeting a real thief face to face, Bess demurred. "There's no telling what he might do to us," she said. "Besides, he's probably a horrible person with a long record and I don't even want to meet him."

George looked disgusted. "Don't be such a cissy, Bess. The man can't possibly hurt you if he's in jail."

Bess said no more, but when they reached headquarters and were introduced to Officer Browning, she at once changed the subject. Handing him the badge, she asked if it was real or a fake. The officer examined it carefully and even got a magnifying glass.

"This was a police badge," he said, "until someone got hold of it and obliterated all the identification. Where did you find it?"

Nancy told him she had been threatened with "arrest" for kidnapping by two apparently phony county agents. The officer looked grave.

Bess asked, "Why would they tamper with the badges if they were pretending to have authority to take Nancy away?"

Officer Browning said he thought the men were

trying to fool the girls, not the police. "But fortunately it didn't work."

George asked, "Then we can assume this badge and the other one were stolen from some policemen?"

"It's a good guess," the officer said. "Suppose you leave the badge here. We'll give it an acid bath and see if we can determine anything about the owner or the phony who was wearing it."

Nancy now asked permission to talk with Sid Zikes. Browning said he had been transferred to the county jail until the date of his trial.

"But I'll be glad to give you a letter to the warden there, and he'll let you in." He looked at the four girls. "Only two visitors are allowed at a time," he remarked.

"You can count me out," Bess said quickly, and George added politely, "And I'll be glad to stay away too," although she was disappointed.

As soon as the note was ready, the four girls rode off. On the way to the county jail, the group became quiet, each girl thinking about some angle of the mystery. Bess's mind was still on the badge, George was intrigued by Eezy and his influence over the intruders, while Junie kept thinking of young Tony. "How wonderful it would be," she told herself, "if Mrs Bolardo should turn out to be his mother! But I mustn't get my hopes up too high."

Nancy was alarmed by Mr Rocco's power and his underhand methods of using other people to extract money from farm workers and swearing them to secrecy.

"He's a sly, untrustworthy person!" she decided. "The sooner we can prove something against him and have him arrested, the better it will be for the whole community."

In a little while the girls reached the county jail and went inside. Almost at once Bess said the atmosphere was too depressing and she would wait outside in the car. She got up and George followed.

"Don't run off with the car and leave us here," Nancy teased.

"It's only a ten-mile walk back," George retorted.

When Nancy and Junie were admitted to Sid Zikes' cell, he looked at them but said nothing. They tried to talk to him but he acted very childishly. The young man pouted and declared he had done nothing wrong. "I wouldn't be here if it hadn't been for you, Nancy Drew!" he told her bitterly.

The young detective had decided to talk to the prisoner in a completely different way than she had before. In a gentle voice she said, "Sid, I want to tell you that in case you don't know it, there's a big fraud going on in this area. It won't be long before the whole thing will be known.

"It would be best for you to admit any connection you have with it and act right now rather than wait. We already know of some thefts you have committed. That's bad enough, but to be involved in a really big scheme to defraud is something else again."

Sid looked at the two girls as if he were going to cry. A moment later he began to shake violently. He grabbed a blanket from his cot and wound it around his body.

Finally he said, "I'm not ill. I'm not really cold. I'm shaking from fear. If you'll promise not to tell anyone something I know, which might be part of the fraud you were talking about, I'll tell you a secret."

Nancy and Junie said nothing and apparently Sid Zikes interpreted this as an assent to his request. He went on, "Mr Rocco has several men working for him—I don't know their names. Two of them came to me and said they wanted the parchment picture that hung over the fireplace in Mr Flockhart's living room.

"At first I said I wasn't a thief and wouldn't go for any burglarizing. They just laughed and told me they already knew my record. If I didn't do this for them, they would harm me. I guess I'm chicken, but I don't like to be hurt."

Sid went on to say that he had finally agreed to the arrangement. He was to get the picture and take it to the two men at a designated place on the edge of the Rocco farm. He had done this and been paid well for his part in the scheme.

Nancy asked, "Did you deliver it before or after you ordered the new glass?"

"After. I couldn't deliver the picture with the glass broken."

Junie asked him, "Have you any idea where the parchment is now?"

Sid shook his head. "It means nothing to me. The whole point in taking it was that Mr Flockhart didn't need the picture, but somebody else did. I can't see what's wrong about that."

It flashed through Nancy's mind that here was a person who firmly believed robbing the rich and giving to the poor was perfectly all right. Laws, conscience, and possible harm to an innocent party meant nothing to him!

Nancy looked Sid straight in the eye. He lowered his head but she asked him please to lift it and look at her. She said, "Did it ever occur to you that there's always somebody poorer than yourself?"

The prisoner said no. Nancy went on, "What you have just told me proves that you think it is all right to take something from a person who has a little more than you have yourself." She stared at his right hand. "I see you have on a very good-looking ring."

"The police let me keep it. It's special."

"How would you feel if some really poor boy were to steal it from you?" Nancy asked him.

Sid sat up on the cot. "I'd feel awful. My girl friend gave this to me."

Suddenly the young man looked at Nancy with a totally different expression on his long, lean face. "Hey, I see what you mean. You know, Miss Drew, you've given me an idea. I think maybe I'll go straight from now on."

Nancy and Junie could have leaped for joy. There was something in the tone of Sid's voice that made them think he really meant this. Both of them walked over and shook hands with him and said how glad they were that he had come to this decision.

The prisoner actually smiled. "Hey, thanks an awful lot," he said. "Maybe staying in jail for a short time won't be so bad after all."

At this moment the jailer came and told the girls their visiting time was up. He let them out of the cell. The two waved to Sid, then walked off.

As soon as they reached the street, Junie congratulated Nancy. "It was absolutely marvellous the way you handled Sid."

The girl detective smiled. "Making a prisoner turn over a new leaf is something I've never done before," she admitted. "I feel good about it myself."

When they reached the car and jumped in, Junie immediately told Bess and George what Nancy had accomplished.

"That's super!" Bess remarked.

"A grand job, Nancy," George commented.

Just before dinner time at Triple Creek Farm, the four boys arrived. They looked weary but were exuberant over the day's achievements.

Ned said, "Mr Flockhart gave us until tomorrow evening to do our job, but we accomplished so much today, I'm sure it won't be necessary to take tomorrow too."

From a pocket he pulled out a sheet of paper. "Here is a list of people who secretly gave Mr Rocco money to start his agricultural society. So far we've been told of cash payments for Rocco of fifty to three hundred dollars. We even saw some receipts. When we examined them though, we realized the farmers and a few employees in small businesses never could prove anything from them."

Dan added, "Across the top of the sheet was printed Brotherhood of Agriculturists. It listed the amounts correctly, but the signature at the bottom was a scrawl that nobody could decipher." Nancy wanted to know if the signature was supposed to be Mr Rocco's.

"The victims all thought it was that of his top man," Ned replied.

Burt spoke up. "This man Rocco is quite an organizer, I'd say. When we totalled up the amount, it proved to be thousands of dollars."

Dave remarked, "If Mr Flockhart wants us to go ahead, we still have a long list of people to see."

Nancy thought their work was astounding and said so. "But how did you get the people to talk?"

All the boys grinned and Ned said, "Oh, it was easy." He turned to his fellow workers and said, "Shall we tell our secret?"

·19·

A Strange Reunion

As Ned and the other boys delayed telling the story of obtaining statements from people who had given Sal Rocco's henchmen money, Nancy urged them to begin.

"All right," Ned said. "The boys and I pretended without saying so that we were already members of the association." He grinned. "We must be pretty convincing because nobody questioned us."

Burt took up the story. "We said we were becoming very suspicious of Mr Rocco because we had heard nothing from him. We learned that nobody else had, either."

"In fact," Dave put in, "by the time we had talked to each one for a while, we felt convinced that most of the people were ready to protest. Each person was reluctant to be the one to organize a march on Rocco's men."

Dan said that a few people had telephoned the Rocco home and had tried to get some information. "The owner either was not there or refused to come to the phone."

Nancy asked, "So they didn't learn anything?"

Ned shook his head. "The farmers who did talk to

one of Rocco's men were assured that everything was fine and that they would hear about an organization meeting soon."

Dan added, "Each of those callers got a lecture on helping unfortunate people, which was the same one they had received when being asked to join the association."

Burt remarked, "It's quite a lingo that Rocco has worked up. At first I was inclined to believe it myself!"

George asked, "What I'd like to know is, where is Mr Rocco keeping all the money he had his men collect?"

"Good question," Dan replied. "I know the president of the local bank. How about my phoning him to see if Mr Rocco made a lot of deposits there?"

The others thought this was a good idea, so Dan called. The answer, however, was disappointing. Mr Rocco kept an account there from which he drew cheques to pay bills and get small amounts of cash, but he had never deposited large amounts. Most of the income was from products sold from his farm.

Junie heaved a sigh. "Another dead-end clue!"

The others laughed, then Bess asked Nancy, "Have you any hunches about what Mr Rocco might have done with the money?"

"I've been thinking about it," the young sleuth replied. "It's possible that he has hidden the cash right on his own farm."

"On his own farm?" Bess repeated.

"Sure, there are a million places he could hide his money—in an old suitcase, in the loft of the barn—"

"He could've planted it in the cornfield!" the plump girl quipped.

"Or in the bottom of a well!" her cousin added.

"Stop teasing Nancy," Ned said, circling his arm around her shoulder. "She's trying to solve a mystery and—"

Nancy smiled warmly at her friend. "I can always count on you for help, though," she said, causing the boy's face to redden.

"Maybe we ought to leave the lovebirds alone, Bess, to figure out this case," George put in.

"Now, now," Nancy replied. "I need everybody's ideas."

Further conversation was interrupted by the ring of the telephone. Junie went to answer it. During her absence the others began asking one another questions on angles of the mystery.

"What I can't understand," said Bess, "is why Mr Rocco is so mean and cruel to his young nephew."

They all decided that this was an important part of the mystery and they hoped it would soon be cleared up.

Dan said, "I'm sure the authorities will take this boy away and put him in a school or a home where he will be given kindness."

At this moment Junie rushed back into the room. "Guess what?" she said. "Mrs Bolardo has arrived in this country. Right now she is at Mr Caspari's house. She wants to come over here at once so she can see her son."

"Her son!" the others in the room cried out.

Junie said the artist had told her that the full story had to wait until Mrs Bolardo arrived at the Flockhart farm. "He's going to bring her right over, but it's a fairly long drive."

The girl's announcement had come like a real bombshell to the listeners. So Tony's real name was Tony Bolardo! While waiting for Mr Caspari to drive in, the group of young people tried to work, but found themselves gathering to discuss the mystery.

Bess remarked, "It's getting more exciting by the minute!"

Finally Mr Caspari arrived with the woman artist from Italy. She proved to be beautiful and charming. Both Mr and Mrs Flockhart had come to meet her, and she returned their welcome in perfect English. After the pleasantries were over, her expression changed.

"My son! Where is he? I want to see him at once! He was stolen from me!" she cried out.

Mrs Flockhart sat down on the sofa beside her and took the woman's hand in hers. "Please tell us the whole story from beginning to end," she requested.

If she had hoped to calm Mrs Bolardo, she failed. With each sentence the artist uttered, she became more emotional. "What does my son Tony look like?" she asked.

Nancy told her that he was a handsome child. "He looks like you and he shows great promise as an artist."

"Oh, I am so glad, I am so glad!" Mrs Bolardo said. "But tell me where he is. I want to see him!"

Junie told her that they had Tony hidden away and would go to see him in a little while.

"We took him away from his uncle because the man was mean and cruel to him."

"That dreadful man!" Mrs Bolardo exclaimed. "I

will tell you the whole story. My husband and I were
very happily married and excited beyond words
when little Tony was born. My husband had some
business to take care of, so he went off on a steamer.
Unfortunately it was in an accident with a sailing
vessel, and he was killed."

"That's terrible!" Bess murmured.

Mrs Bolardo went on to say that her husband's
brother, Salvatore, was the executor of her husband's
estate.

"Sal wanted me to marry him but I refused. In
revenge Sal took all the money that was left to me,
stole my precious baby, and disappeared. I have
searched and searched for them, but until now, never
had a lead."

Tears began to trickle down Bess's cheeks. She
wiped her eyes with a handkerchief and remarked,
"For ten years you never heard about them?"

Mrs Bolardo shook her head.

George mentioned that Tony's name was not really
Tony Rocco, but Tony Bolardo. His mother said that
actually his full name was Antonio Rocco Bolardo.
The name Rocco was his paternal grandmother's
before she married.

The woman artist continued, "Right after my husband's death I painted four pictures on parchment to
tell the story. Little Tony's abductor also took that."

"So you are the woman in one painting!" Junie
exclaimed, and Mrs Bolardo nodded.

Nancy said she was sorry she could not show the
parchment to the woman because it had been stolen.
"I made some rough sketches in imitation of it," she
said. "But the real clues to finding you were the in-

itials on the back of your picture."

Mrs Bolardo suddenly stood up. "Please take me to my boy!" she pleaded. "Where is he?"

Everyone felt convinced that the woman was not an impostor. It was decided that she and Nancy would go alone to Eezy's cabin.

Mr Flockhart added, "I think it best if we form ourselves into a group of guards. We can station ourselves around the hillside among the sheep, so that if any of Mr Rocco's men follow Mrs Bolardo and Nancy, we can head them off."

Nancy said, "Wouldn't it be a good idea also to inform the police of what has happened and to send men out to keep track of Mr Rocco?"

The farm owner thought this was a very good suggestion and went at once to phone the police. He talked to Officer Browning, who promised to take care of all the details.

Junie spoke up. "Dad, wouldn't it be a good idea to try getting Mr Rocco into his own house and to be there when we all come with Tony and his mother?"

"I'll mention that to Officer Browning," her father agreed.

Several cars were to be used in the operation. Nancy and Mrs Bolardo rode in one, in the centre of the line. Each car parked at a different place, and the group walked up the hillside in twos and threes.

"This is lovely country," Mrs Bolardo remarked to Nancy when they got out. "I guess it has been a good healthy place to bring up Tony. But it is dreadful that he has never been to a school or made any friends."

Most of the sheep were lying down, and the two

climbers walking among them did not seem to disturb the animals. It was so quiet that Nancy mentioned it to her companion.

"I don't see the shepherd either," Nancy said as she gazed around, realizing the man was not at his usual station in front of the cabin. They walked up and called out his name, but there was no answer.

Nancy peered inside the cabin. No one was there! The girl thought this was very strange, and suddenly began to worry that something had happened to the elderly man. And what about Tony?

Without showing the agitation she felt, the girl detective told Mrs Bolardo that Tony worked and studied in a well-hidden bower behind the cabin. Carefully they proceeded, parting branches of trees and shrubbery as they went.

Finally they reached the arbor and looked in. Mrs Bolardo screamed and Nancy caught her breath. Eezy and Tony had been trussed up, and were lying inert on the ground!

"Oh, how dreadful!" Mrs Bolardo cried out. "My son! My beloved boy! What have they done to you?"

Nancy jumped forward to remove the gags and ropes that bound the two tightly. Before she could reach them, strong arms came around her and yanked the girl backwards. Mrs Bolardo received the same treatment.

"Let me go!" Nancy cried out, struggling to pull free of her captor.

"Be quiet or you'll get something worse!" her unknown assailant hissed into her ear.

Nancy glanced at Mrs Bolardo. A man was holding one hand tightly over the woman's chest and was stuffing a gag into her mouth!

·20·

Found Money

THE men who had captured Nancy and Mrs Bolardo were masked and wore dark overalls. She could not identify her assailants.

They trussed up Nancy and the Italian woman as they had Eezy and Tony. No doubt they had just finished their work on the shepherd and the boy when they heard voices and spotted the girl and her companion coming up the hillside.

Nancy could hardly wait for the two men to leave. Surely the boys would capture the attackers somewhere among the sheep as they hurried away. Besides, she wanted to try untying some of the knots that bound Eezy's wrists.

There was a moment of panic for the prisoners when one of the captors lifted Tony and swung the boy over his shoulder. He was going to take him away! The other captor whispered something in his ear, however, and the man laid down his victim. "We'll come back for you after dark," he told Tony.

"Evidently they're afraid to go any farther at this time," Nancy thought.

Finally the dark-clothed figures left. At once Nancy wriggled over to Eezy's side. He understood what she

296

wanted to do, and rolled over. It took her several minutes to free his hands. In turn, he untied the knots of the ropes that bound her wrists. After that it did not take long to remove all the gags and untie their ankles.

Mrs Bolardo had been so frightened she seemed speechless, but Nancy said, "Tony, I have a wonderful surprise for you. This is your mother!"

The boy stared, unbelieving, but Mrs Bolardo rushed to him and hugged her child. "Tonio! Tonio!" she exclaimed, and then went on, speaking rapidly in Italian.

At first Tony could not believe what he had heard, but as his mother talked and told him about his own kidnapping and his thieving uncle, he believed her story and put his arms around her.

All this time Eezy had stood by, speechless. He swung his head from side to side, and kept mumbling, "I can't believe it!"

Mrs Bolardo heard him. She let go of Tony and addressed herself to the shepherd. "It is true! And the main part of the credit goes to wonderful Nancy Drew!"

Tony now surprised them all by saying in perfect English, "Thank you. Thank you very much. This is a very happy day for me and my mother."

Nancy asked if she might use Eezy's walkie-talkie. "I'd like to tell the good news to everyone down at Triple Creek."

The little group walked back to the cabin and Nancy called. Mrs Flockhart answered and was thrilled to hear that mother and son were together after all these years. She was not happy, however, to learn that the four of them had been attacked by men who apparently were in Mr Rocco's employ.

"I'll notify the police at once about what has happened," she said.

Nancy had just finished the conversation, when she saw Bess, George, Ned, Burt, Dave, Dan, and Junie coming up the hillside. They waved gaily and Ned called out. "We captured your attackers! They've confessed!"

When the group drew close, Ned explained that the young people were hiding at various posts behind the sheep and trees, and saw the two overalled men racing down the hillside. They were speaking in Italian but Dan could understand them.

"We realized from their conversation what had happened up here, so we ran after them," he said. "Right now they're in the hands of the police."

"That's great!" Nancy exclaimed, then properly introduced those present.

Mrs Bolardo and Tony stood together, arm in arm, looking delighted at the turn of events. Then a walkie-talkie message came from Mr Flockhart, advising that everyone except Eezy was to proceed at once to the Rocco home. He did not explain why, but everyone assumed that Rocco had been arrested.

Tony, excited, said in Italian, "I know a shortcut." He bid Eezy goodbye and thanked him for his good care and fine meals. Then the boy led the others down a different section of the hillside.

It was not long before the Rocco farmhouse was in sight. Ned, who had been walking with Nancy, had been very quiet, but now he said, "See all those people down there? Burt, Dave, and I got hold of the farmers and others who had joined the association. We suggested they come to Rocco's place."

Now the farmers and other residents of the area were milling around, talking. As Nancy and her companions came closer, she noticed that some of the crowd looked angry and a few were trying to get into the house. Police guarded the door and kept them out. By the time Nancy and her friends reached it, Mr Flockhart was there and told the guard to admit them.

They found Mr Rocco seated on his living-room couch, being quizzed by a police officer. He had denied every accusation.

Suddenly he looked up and blinked as he saw Tony and Diana Bolardo, arm in arm, standing before him.

Without speaking to them, the man jumped from the couch and dashed for the door. He was caught by a policeman and escorted back into the living room.

Finally he managed to say, "Diana! Diana! How did you get here? How did you find me? I meant no harm taking your baby. I felt that you would not be able to take care of him."

"That was because you stole all my money!" the woman cried out. "Salvatore, you are a wicked man. How glad I am that these good people here were able to bring Tony and me together again so you can't do him any more harm!"

Rocco looked defiant. "I did not harm him, and have brought him up right. I hope you will find it in your heart to forgive me for taking Tony."

His sister-in-law made no response. At this moment there was a great shout from outside, and voices calling, "We want Rocco! We want Rocco!"

"I'm not going out there!" the man declared.

"Oh yes you are," one of the police guards said.

He took Rocco by the arm and walked him on to the porch so that he could face his accusers. Rocco still denied any wrongdoing, but they insisted upon his returning their money.

Rocco, livid, shouted, "All right! You can have your money back if you can find it!" He turned and went back into the living room.

Ned whispered to Nancy, "It's my guess that the money is hidden on the premises. How would it be if the other boys and I help these farm workers find it?"

"Good idea," Nancy said, and the great search started.

She went inside, where Rocco was again seated on the couch, with police guards on either side of him. He looked sullen and angry. His black eyes kept darting towards his sister-in-law as if he could not believe she was really there.

Nancy noticed that between glances, the man's eyes kept roving towards a table with a large drawer in it. The girl detective wondered if there might be something in it that he did not want anybody to see.

She called one of the policemen aside and asked him to investigate. As the two walked towards the table, Rocco suddenly got up and tried to escape. He was soon stopped and brought back. The second guard rejoined Nancy, and they opened the long drawer in the table.

Inside lay the stolen parchment picture!

"Oh!" Nancy exclaimed. She turned to Rocco. "You had Sid Zikes steal this picture, hoping the secret it contains wouldn't be found out!"

Rocco shouted, "I never should have sold the picture! I should have destroyed it long ago! I never saw the initials on the back, but when I heard Nancy Drew was working on the case, I decided to steal it!"

At this moment one of the men who lived in the house came into the room. He went over and addressed Rocco.

"You fooled a lot of people, Sal, but you didn't fool me, although I admit your threats frightened me into being your puppet. I haven't forgotten how you cheated me and my family years ago, and I was determined to get even at some time. You knew the secret locked in the parchment picture and I knew it too! But I didn't know where Tony's mother was and whether she was alive or not. When you sold the picture I saw a good chance for somebody else to figure out the secret and bring you to justice.

"After you sold the picture to Mr Flockhart, I telephoned him that if he could decipher the meaning of the paintings, he would learn a great secret and right an old wrong."

No one in the room was more surprised at this revelation than Nancy Drew. Now all the questions concerning the strange mystery had been solved.

Nancy looked at the informer quizzically. "How much did you have to do with getting money from farmers to join an association?"

"Nothing," he replied. "My name is Hapgood. I have been telling Sal that he ought to get the association started or give back the money. But he wouldn't pay any attention to me."

Suddenly Rocco screamed at him, "Hapgood, get

out of here and never let me see you again! You are a cheat and a double-crosser!"

Hapgood did not move. He turned to the police guard and said, "I am innocent and I hope to get some credit for helping to straighten out matters at this place and restore Tony to his rightful mother. Most of the field workers, as well as Sal, sneaked into this country illegally."

One of the policemen said, "That's not for me to decide. You will be questioned with all the other men who work here."

Just then there was a great shout from outdoors. Everyone rushed to the porch except Rocco and his guards. Ned Nickerson ran up to Nancy.

"All the stolen money and the names of the people have been discovered!"

"Where?" Nancy asked.

Ned told her that some of it had been found in an abandoned well, other cash in the hayloft, under the car seat of Rocco's automobile, and the account book in one of the barns.

Farmers and others involved had appointed Mrs Potter their chairman. Now she was busy giving out the proper amounts of money to each person who had contributed to the fake association.

Burt and Dave came up and said they had located a cage of mechanical birds, which had attacked Nancy and Junie on their first visit to the Rocco farm.

"We understand from the man who worked the mechanism by remote control that Mr Rocco believed the lifelike birds would drive off intruders. He would not be blamed, however, because the victims would think the birds were alive."

Finally the crowd outdoors dispersed, happy at the outcome. Mrs Potter spoke for them all and thanked Nancy for her part in keeping them from losing so much money.

Nancy was thoughtful for a moment as she realized this mystery was solved. Little did she know that she would soon become involved in the exciting *Mystery of Crocodile Island*.

In the meantime, more police arrived. Every worker on the Rocco farm was rounded up and word came that other henchmen of Rocco's were being sought.

After everyone had gone, Mr Flockhart came into the house and talked with Mrs Bolardo about her plans.

"Oh, as soon as we can get Antonio's clothes packed and buy him some new ones, we'll set off for Italy."

Mr Flockhart insisted that they stay at his home until the woman and her son were ready to fly to New York and then to Rome. She accepted the invitation, then looked at her son lovingly.

"Italy is where Tonio belongs," she told the group, "but I promise you all that his English will not be neglected. I plan to send him to a special school where children learn many languages and talented young artists get fine training from the masters."

"That's great," Nancy said. "Tony, I'm counting on you. Some day I hope to see many beautiful paintings by Antonio Rocco Bolardo."

He tried to speak English, but gave up, and finished in Italian. His mother translated, then told

Nancy the boy's smiling answer.

"I won't disappoint you, I promise. But in the meantime, please keep up your own interest in art, Nancy. It helped you solve the mystery of the parchment and gave me back my lovely mother!"